SHAKEN

ALSO BY ERIC WALTERS

SHAKEN

ERIC WALTERS

DOUBLEDAY CANADA

Doubleday Canada and colophon are registered trademarks.

Library and Archives Canada Cataloguing in Publication
Walters, Eric, 1957-
Shaken / Eric Walters.

ISBN 978-0-385-67081-4

1. Haiti Earthquake, Haiti, 2010--Juvenile fiction.
I. Title.

PS8595.A598S43 2011   jC813'.54   C2010-905128-9

This book is a work of fiction. Names, characters, places and incidents are
products of the author's imagination or are used fictitiously. Any resemblance to
actual events or locales or persons, living or dead, is entirely coincidental.

Printed and bound in the USA

Published in Canada by Doubleday Canada,
a division of Random House of Canada Limited

Visit Random House of Canada Limited's website: www.randomhouse.ca

10 9 8 7 6 5 4 3

SHAKEN

CHAPTER ONE

I looked up at the board behind the counter and then at the clock suspended from the ceiling. We'd be boarding in less than ten minutes if the flight was on time—were Air Canada flights *ever* on time? I took a sip from my Timmy's—the last good cup of tea I was going to have until we got back on Canadian soil in two weeks.

I guess I shouldn't have complained. It was a small price to pay, because it also meant leaving behind the winter weather of January in Canada for the tropical warmth of Haiti. Technically it was their winter, too, but that just meant that the temperature would be *down* in the *low* thirties. It was also their dry season, so not only would there be no snow, there'd probably be no rain, either. I'd been checking the weather reports on the Internet every day since Christmas. The coldest day had been thirty-one degrees, with the long-range forecast predicting two weeks of nearly perfect weather. Hot, dry, and not only away from winter weather but away from school. This extended Christmas holiday was more like an extended Christmas present!

If this had been the summer, with no school and good weather at home, I would have kicked up a lot more fuss about being dragged along in the first place. It probably wouldn't have done much good, but I'd have at least tried to make it so uncomfortable for my father that he would have found somebody to take care of me in Toronto while he went. After all, he wouldn't have wanted me to be an embarrassment.

And that, of course, was the biggest downside to all of this—my father was not only coming along, he was the leader of our little mission trip to Haiti. All of the other kids—with the exception of my sister, of course—got to leave their parents behind. But my father would be there, front and centre, all the time. And the worst of the worst was that there was some sort of bizarre expectation that I would be a good role model on this trip, a reflection of his *goodness*. Barely three months into his appointment at a new church, with a new congregation, I knew that everybody was still watching us closely, and this little trip would be 24/7 observation. I pulled my cap down lower on my head, slipped on my sunglasses, and went to reinsert my earbuds.

"Air Canada Flight 950 to Port-au-Prince will begin boarding shortly for executive class, business class, and those passengers requiring additional assistance or travelling with small children."

I always thought it was strange that those groups were put together—were businessmen like children? Did executives require physical assistance because their wallets were so big?

My father got to his feet. "Could I have everybody gather around, please?" he called out.

The rest of our group got up—some practically leaping to their feet in response to his request. If I'd put on my earbuds sooner I could have maybe faked not hearing, but that wasn't going to work now.

We all trailed after him into an open space away from the seating area.

"Could we all gather in a circle, please?" he called out in a loud voice.

Oh, goodness, now I *knew* what he was going to do. Maybe I could slip away or—my little sister, Sarah, took my hand. She knew what was going to happen next, too.

Kids started tentatively taking places and sort of shuffling and bumping until a rough circle of people formed, with my father on the far side, directly across from where I stood.

"Please join hands," he commanded.

Suddenly there was more significance to the person each one of us was standing beside. Some quickly grabbed hands while others hesitated or rubbed their hands against their pants to wipe away the sweat. Sarah was already holding my right hand and a girl named Naomi grabbed my left—she obviously wasn't worried about the sweat factor because I could feel the wetness of her palm. I had the urge to take away my hand to wipe it off but she held on with an iron grip that was well beyond what I'd have expected from somebody of her size.

"As we get ready to take the next step, I want to take a moment to ask for God's blessing. Please bow your heads in prayer," he ordered.

I lowered my head slightly but kept my eyes open.

"O God, you called Abraham your servant out of Ur and kept him safe and sound in his wanderings," he said.

His voice was much louder than it needed to be to reach our little circle. The looks on the faces of other passengers waiting and walking past were a combination of curious, amused, disgusted, and embarrassed. Take out the amused and curious and that was basically how I was feeling myself. I almost closed my eyes to hide, like a two-year-old who covers his eyes and figures because he can't see you, you can't see him. That made no sense, but still I lowered my gaze so I wasn't looking beyond the circle any more.

"Be for us a support when setting out, shade from the sun, a mantle against the rain," he called out, "and provide friendship along the way."

Friendship along the way? I raised my gaze to carefully, discreetly look around the circle. There was my father, a woman next to him named Iris, another much older woman from our church congregation named Michelle, and fifteen kids, including me and my sister. The oldest was only a year older than me at seventeen, but most were my age or a year younger. My sister, at twelve, was the youngest and had been allowed to come along only because my father was leading.

I could look at people with impunity. Every head was bowed, every set of eyes tightly closed, as ordered, so nobody could see me looking. And, if somebody did look up, who were they to tell on me since their eyes were open, too?

I looked from person to person. I knew most of these kids, by appearance if not by name, but there was nobody here who I'd have even remotely considered a friend, nobody I spent time with outside of the obligatory church events, and, quite frankly, nobody I wanted to spend time with. The few friends I'd been able to make since we'd moved were at school—a couple of guys from the basketball team, some people I ate lunch with—but nobody who went to our church, or, for that matter, any church.

Our little group had five boys and ten girls. That would have been good odds for the boys if the girls had been hot. But they really weren't. The style theme for this trip was a combination of Baptist bland and fashion faux pas. The dress code, apparently, was clothing your mom bought for you that you didn't have the good sense or the guts to refuse to wear. Naomi—the one holding my hand in a sweaty iron grip—was the best-looking of the bunch. If she'd dressed better she could have actually been good-looking, period.

I really didn't much care about the kids, though. I was more concerned about Iris. Okay, *concerned* wasn't the right word. I was more *annoyed* by Iris. There she stood, head down, eyes closed, standing at my father's side, holding one of his hands. No surprise there. I actually would have been shocked if she *hadn't* been standing there.

Iris was one of those women . . . those . . . those . . . *groupies* who seem to be drawn to ministers. They flirt and flit around ministers, volunteering for committees and fawning over the pastor as if every word from his mouth is gold. My mother had pointed them out to me. They'd been at every church we'd ever been assigned to. It was stupid and really rather insulting that they behaved that way even around my mother, and . . . I guess that wasn't a problem any more.

Iris was single, at least a few years younger than my father, and dressed in a style that was almost too revealing, almost too young, but not quite. I was positive that she was only coming on this trip because my father was leading it. But so far, in spite of her advances, my father wasn't biting. Not yet, at least. Maybe he was still too hurt. Maybe he was being respectful. Maybe he still couldn't get my mother out of his head. I knew I couldn't.

"Bear us up in fatigue and defend us under attack!" my father said, his voice rising, taking on that minister-like quality, a sort of Southern twang that evangelists pick up once they get going. I just wasn't sure what he thought was going to happen . . . defend us from attack? Were we going to Haiti or Afghanistan? Was this a mission trip or a military operation?

"If it is your will, protect us, Lord!"

If it was God's *will* to protect us? Talk about making up an excuse. So, if something did happen it wasn't because God didn't listen or didn't care, but because he'd decided to do something bad. Yeah, right, God sat up on his throne thinking, "Yep, I'm going to kill that girl Ashley because she didn't pray hard enough." What a cop-out: *It is God's will . . . God works in mysterious ways.* People use that quote like it was something that Jesus said, or as if it was a quote from the Bible when it's just a line from some old hymn—and not even a *good* hymn.

My father continued with his sermon . . . his prayer. I had to hand it to him, he did know the Bible, and he could throw out a good sermon, prayer, or service. If I hadn't heard this one so many times before, I would have been more impressed.

My father had an impressive repertoire of well-rehearsed ad libs, set pieces, and quotes that all sounded completely spontaneous. Didn't fool me, though. I'd heard them all a million times before. He was like a live remix tape, a "best of" compilation available only on TV from Time-Life, like music from the Seventies . . . no, that wasn't right, I *liked* music from the Seventies.

Strangely, that was one of the few things my father and I still had in common. He loved the music from the Sixties and Seventies. I'm not sure how his congregation would have felt about him grooving on Led Zeppelin, Pink Floyd, and the Stones, but it was at least something we could agree on, listen to, and talk about. He definitely didn't think that Eric Clapton was God, but he probably thought he was as close to God as a guitar player could get. Well, maybe Hendrix fit in there, too.

As my father continued to ramble on, I couldn't help but think what would have happened if a bunch of Muslims had gathered to praise Allah and say prayers before they got on a plane. Well, really, I didn't need to wonder. The whole bunch of them would have found themselves in a back room being stripped down and exposed to a cavity search. God may be great in all religions, but there was a definite advantage around here if your God was from the Bible and not the Koran.

"With your grace let us fulfill the purpose of our trip and return safe and sound to our homes." He paused. "Amen."

"Amen," we echoed.

Everybody looked up and released hands. Everybody except the girl holding my hand.

"I think you can let go now," I said.

"Oh, yeah, sorry!" Naomi started to blush.

Great. I hadn't meant to make her feel bad, I'd just wanted her to let go of my hand. I knew she had a little crush on me. I'd made the *mistake* of being nice to her after church one day and she'd taken that as a sign of interest instead of polite indifference.

I shuffled away, trying to wipe the sweat from my hand on my pants nonchalantly, without her noticing.

"This is very exciting," she said as she trailed after me.

"Yep. Exciting," I agreed.

"I'm sure we'll fulfill the purpose of our trip," she added enthusiastically.

"The purpose?" Did she mean making my father look like a good Christian leader, or making a bunch of rich, white teenagers from a rich suburb feel that they were somehow doing something for the world?

"You know, helping to build the addition to the orphanage and caring for the needy," she said.

"I'm sure we'll do something," I agreed, "although I'm not sure I'd want to live in any house that a bunch of kids helped to build . . . unless you're a trained bricklayer and didn't tell anybody?"

She looked confused. "No . . . I've never done any-thing like that before. Have you?"

I chuckled slightly. So much for subtle sarcasm.

"No. And I'm afraid I've never trained as a bricklayer, either," I said.

"General boarding will commence for all remaining passengers on Air Canada Flight 950 to Port-au-Prince," the P.A. announced.

"That's us," I said. "See you on board."

"That would be great . . . maybe we're seatmates."

"Maybe," I said. I didn't really care. I was going to put on some headphones, watch a movie, and try very hard to ignore whoever was sitting beside me. Especially if it was my father. No, I probably didn't have to worry about that. My guess was that Iris would somehow manage to snag that seat.

CHAPTER TWO

I threw my backpack into the overhead compartment and settled into my seat. I didn't know who was going to be my seatmate but I knew that our eighteen seats were all together, so it was going to be somebody from our group. Strangely, I actually hoped that it was going to be my little sister. She was annoying, but at least I could tell her to shut up or deliberately ignore her and nobody would be offended.

There was lots of giggling and twittering from the other kids. Was this their first time on a plane? Were they nervous? I knew that when people giggled it was sometimes just a nervous reaction. I'd seen that before. I understood. And I guess you could say I'd learned that fact the hard way.

We'd been at the funeral home, for my mother's visitation. The visitation is what happens before a funeral, when people come to see the family and pay their respects, and you all stand around making polite small talk . . . with the casket right there in the room with you. That part feels really weird. Some woman came over to talk to my father, and I couldn't hear what she was saying but she was actually giggling. I couldn't believe it! I was shocked, and then a rush of anger surged through me so strongly that I knew my whole body had flushed, and I thought I might actually start to yell at the woman. But I didn't, and my father pulled me over and explained. At first I didn't get it, but he was good at explaining things, and he kept talking until finally I did understand.

I knew in my head that nobody thought my mother dying was funny, it was just that they didn't know how to react or what to say. And after that I noticed how many people said the strangest things or giggled or smiled or even laughed. "Nervous laughter," my father called it. Awkward laughter was what it seemed like to me.

That wasn't even the worst thing that people did. What I really hated were the stupid platitudes. "She's in a better place"—yeah, right, a coffin six feet underground was a better place. "It was God's will"—did anybody really think that God decided to kill my mother? "At least she's found peace"—as opposed to the battle that was our life?

Maybe it was an advantage being a minister's son. My father had handled his share of death and funerals, and so I'd been around all that too. Not just at the church, but late-night phone calls and grieving people coming to the house. It wasn't that unusual to come home from school and find my father huddled around the kitchen table with three or four sobbing people between me and the Oreos. I'd found that the smartest thing to do was just look sad, nod my head solemnly, listen, say things like "I'm so sorry" or "We'll all miss her" . . . and then slip out with the bag of cookies and get to the TV room, shut the door, and turn up the volume loud enough that I couldn't hear anybody crying.

I couldn't imagine laughing at a funeral or visitation, but I knew that awkward-laughter feeling from being at church. Sometimes, sitting right up front in the first pew, I'd watch my father preaching and he'd say something that just struck me as peculiar and I'd have to choke back the laughter. Sometimes it was just his tone of voice, or the fact that I'd already heard him say the same thing a dozen times, practising his sermon, standing in front of a mirror wearing his sweat clothes or a pair of shorts, and I'd picture him still like that—talking about Noah and his ark while wearing an Alice Cooper concert T-shirt and a pair of cut-offs.

I could hear my father making his way up the aisle behind me now, stopping at every seat to make sure people were settling in nicely and reassuring the nervous fliers.

"How are you doing, Joshua?" he asked as he hovered overtop of me.

"Good . . . fine . . . hoping the movie is something I haven't seen already."

"You know, I really appreciate your being here."

"No problem," I answered, while I was thinking, *What choice did I really have?*

"It's great to have you along, but I'm especially glad to have an extra set of eyes to watch your little sister. In some ways, it might have been better to have left her with friends."

"Not better for her," I said. "Besides, she really doesn't have friends here."

"She's making new ones."

"She shouldn't have to be making new ones," I snapped.

He leaned in closer. "This isn't the time or the place," he said, his voice barely above a whisper.

This was probably the biggest issue between us right now. I knew that coming to the new church had been like a big promotion, but really, did we honestly need our lives turned upside-down when so much had already changed? Maybe it was too painful for my father to be around all those memories in our home—maybe it was too painful for us, too—but still, they were *our* memories, and he'd had no right to just arbitrarily take them away . . . along with our school, our friends, and the house we'd lived in for almost five years . . . the last five years of our mother's life. Those memories were all we had left now.

"Joshua, even if we were still back home . . . in our old home . . . taking Sarah with us would have been the right choice. She really needs to have us around right now."

"More you than me," I said.

"Both of us. We're like her security blankets. She's sitting with me . . . we're a few rows behind you. Sarah seems to be a little nervous about flying."

I nodded my head. She was a little nervous about everything now. She'd developed a whole new set of fears: fear of car accidents, fear of strangers, a fear that when she was feeling even just a little bit sick she was going to die . . . or my father was going to die. I understood that. We were only one parent away from being orphans. If Dad died, at least she'd have me to take care of her. But who would I have? I didn't need to be thinking about that.

"How long is this flight?" I asked.

"Under four hours."

Suddenly I heard some voices start to sing. I recognized the song—it was a hymn. Unbelievable, these kids were singing a hymn . . . no, wait . . . it was coming from the *front* of the plane and not from our group, who were mostly behind me.

"This plane is filled with missionaries," my father explained, "all going to do God's work."

I smirked but didn't say anything. According to the Bible, God had created the whole world in six days, so did he really need any of us to do his work for him? Couldn't he just think it, or use a magic wand, or wave his staff in the air?

"This should be reassuring to your sister," my father said.

"What should be reassuring?"

"The plane is filled with Christians, so I'm sure God will offer his protection to us."

That was so much like something my father would say. And what was I supposed to think? I guess my mother hadn't been a good enough Christian, or God would have protected her, too.

My father added his voice to the hymn at the chorus. It wasn't surprising that he knew the words, but it was just plain sad that *I* could have sung along as well. Growing up in church, the music and lyrics had just sunk into my subconscious. Those, plus Christmas carols and the jingle from every

McDonald's commercial ever made formed the foundation of my musical knowledge . . . along with Seventies rock.

My father's voice got louder—he did have a very good voice. He started walking up the aisle until he was almost at the rows occupied by the choir. I peered down the aisle as they cheered him on, his voice rising above all the others. He certainly knew how to impress people—although most of the people I knew from school would have been impressed in a whole different way.

I turned my head to the window and closed my eyes, thinking, hoping, that there might end up being an empty seat on this flight, and that it would be the one beside me.

CHAPTER THREE

"Could I join you?"

So much for an empty seat. I looked up to see Naomi. She looked nervous, which made me feel sad. I didn't want to make anybody nervous.

"Of course. Do you want the window or the aisle?"

"Either one is fine," she said.

"But which one do you want?" I asked.

"Whatever one you don't want," she replied, and shrugged.

"What I want is for you choose the seat you want. Please," I said.

"Well . . . I guess the window seat."

I stood up and she squeezed past me. We kind of squished together and I could almost feel her uncomfort-able-ness. She flopped into the seat and instantly put on her seatbelt. Not a bad idea. I fumbled around and found the two ends and snapped on mine as well. I could still here my father's baritone voice supporting the choir at the front of the plane.

"Your father has a good singing voice," Naomi said.

"Not bad," I said. I wondered if she'd have thought it was so good if he'd been singing a Led Zeppelin song in a fake falsetto to sound like Robert Plant.

"He's a good minister, too," she continued.

"That's what people tell me."

"Last week's sermon was really good," she said. "But you weren't there, were you?"

"Nope. I heard it a few times at home, though, as he was practising." What I didn't say was that I'd heard him give that one before at our last church. Another "best of" sermon.

"Our last minister, all his children came every Sunday to both services," she said.

"Poor kids. Maybe they were being punished," I joked.

"Your sister comes to all the services," Naomi pointed out.

"She needs to do that so she can be around . . . " I stopped myself. "She just likes church." I paused. "But how would you know that she's at both services unless *you're* at both services?"

"I guess I'm being punished, too. I'm in the junior choir so I have to be there."

"Another fine reason not to be in the choir."

She looked surprised and hurt by my response. I really wasn't trying to hurt her feelings.

"It *is* a very good choir," I said, hoping to make her feel better.

She smiled. "Thanks. We do practise a lot."

"It really shows . . . or, I guess, *sounds*."

She giggled at my little joke. Apparently nervous laughter wasn't just for funerals.

The flight attendants were coming down the aisle now, checking on seatbelts and the overhead luggage. They had herded my father back toward us to take his seat. As he passed by we made eye contact and he winked at me. Oh, good Lord, I was just sharing a seat with a girl and . . . was that why he winked?

"This is very exciting, to be part of this mission trip," Naomi said. "And it's wonderful that your father is leading it."

"This was planned long before he was appointed to your church," I said.

"But he did agree to take it on. Our church believes very strongly in mission, in service."

"Have you been on one of these before?" I asked.

"Last summer I went to northern Manitoba to volunteer at a summer camp for First Nations children."

"That must have been interesting," I said, trying to fake some interest.

"It was a good experience, but I think this is going to be even more rewarding. After all, Haiti has so many needs."

"I don't know much about Haiti," I admitted before I'd thought better.

"I guess that's because you didn't come to any of the orientation sessions at the church."

"Tuesdays don't work for me," I said. "Other commitments." Of course those "other commitments" were basically doing anything that didn't involve going to any orientation sessions.

"Really, you weren't even part of our church during the first four sessions," she said, making a polite excuse for my absence.

"No, I wasn't." In fact, I *still* didn't feel as though I was part of the church, even though sometimes I was physically in the building.

"I just wish I hadn't been part of getting the shots," I said. "My arm is still hurting."

"It did hurt," she agreed, "but I got mine a couple of months ago."

"I understood some of the shots," I said. "Yellow fever, hep A and B, and even typhoid made sense, but why rabies? Is somebody going to bite me?" I said, joking.

"Not some*body* . . . some*thing*. There are lots of stray cats and dogs, and we were told that rabies can be a problem."

Note to self: avoid using humour with Naomi.

"And, of course, there are the malaria pills we have to take very day, as well," she added.

"That was confusing to me, too," I admitted. "Why did we have to start taking them before we even got to Haiti?"

"They have to build up in your blood, and that takes time. Have you had any side effects?" Naomi asked.

"I didn't know there were side effects."

"The most common are disturbed sleep and sensitivity to light," she explained.

My sleep was already so messed up I wouldn't have noticed that one. "I guess I'll just have to make sure to wear my sunglasses when we go to the beach."

"The beach?"

"We'll get some downtime, so I'm figuring I'll hit the beach."

Naomi gave me a strange look.

"It is a tropical island . . . Caribbean Sea . . . warm water . . . hot sun . . . right?" I asked.

"And mountains. We're going to be up in the mountains, not even *close* to the ocean."

I think she realized that she'd been sharp with me, and she now looked apologetic.

"I guess we could get to the beach on one of the days in or out. At least we won't have to worry about hurricanes, because it isn't the season."

"Hurricanes . . . yeah . . . I heard about them on TV. They happen more in the summer, right?"

"Almost all of the major storms happen between June and November, with September being the very worst. And with the hurricanes and tropical storms come flooding and mudslides that kill a lot of people."

"I guess we don't have to worry about any of that."

"No, just the earthquakes."

"Earthquakes? Seriously?"

"In the past, earthquakes in Haiti have killed thousands of people and destroyed the whole capital."

"I didn't hear anything about any of that!" I exclaimed. "I didn't see anything on TV."

She laughed. "That's probably because the first one we know about happened in 1770 and the last big one was in 1842. I don't think they had even black-and-white TV back then."

Her joking around caught me a little off guard. Maybe she did have a sense of humour after all.

There was a "binging" sound, signalling that we were getting ready for takeoff. I was grateful for the excuse to stop talking—no need to show off any more of my ignorance. The engines started to roar and we were picking up speed and vibrations as we rolled more rapidly along the runway.

"I really, really don't like flying," Naomi said as she leaned over toward me.

"It'll be fine. It's safer than driving a car." Although, to be honest, I'd never heard of a car plunging from the sky.

She reached over and, to my shock and surprise, grabbed my hand. Was she going to say another prayer or—?

"I hope it's okay . . . it's embarrassing, but my mother or father always holds my hand when we're taking off."

"Am I your mother or your father?" I asked.

She burst into laughter, which probably surprised her even more than me. The plane lifted off—I could feel it in my stomach—and the ride became smoother, freed from the runway. We quickly rose into the air and I looked past Naomi—whose eyes were closed—and out the window. We banked to one side and the ground became much more visible. Mississauga and Toronto rushed by—houses and factories and roads and shopping malls—all becoming smaller and smaller as we quickly gained elevation.

Her grip on my hand became even tighter.

"It's okay," I said. "We're up. Takeoffs are the worst time."

"And landings, and everything that comes in between," she said. Her eyes were open but it was obvious that she was deliberately not looking out the window.

"Are you afraid of heights?" I asked.

"I'm not crazy about them."

"Then why did you take the window seat?"

"I thought you'd have more space for your legs in the aisle seat . . . that you'd be more comfortable. The window's okay for me as long as I don't look."

I reached over and pulled down the shade, blocking out the world below. "There you go. It's all gone . . . well, at least out of sight."

"But don't you want to look out the window?"

"There's nothing to see right now," I answered. Maybe what she really needed was to get her mind off things. "Could you tell me about Haiti so I'm more up to speed?"

"Sure, of course! What do you want to know?"

"Everything, just tell me everything," I said.

"You must already know some things."

"I've pretty well told you everything I know. Clearly, I have no idea about anything except that Haiti is an island and it's going to be hot because it's in the tropics . . . right?" I asked, and smiled.

She smiled back.

"Come on, teacher . . . go ahead and teach me."

CHAPTER FOUR

Naomi made a little whistling sound through her nose as she slept. Her mouth was open and there was a bit of drool coming out of the corner. Not the most attractive combination, but somehow it almost worked for her. She did have really clear skin, and nice hair, and her eyes—when they were open—were big and blue. If she'd had the right clothes, a bit of makeup, and maybe had her hair done differently, she might have been kind of pretty. And in this group she would have been nothing short of spectacular. It was sort of like the one-eyed man being king in the land of the blind.

She was definitely friendly. Maybe a little over-anxious, but friendly. And I thought, maybe it wouldn't be bad to have a friend on this trip. I'd lost a whole lot of friends because of the move, and I really hadn't made a lot of new ones. There were vacancies available . . . although part of me almost didn't want to make friends. What was the point? Sooner or later I was going to move or they were going to move or somebody was going to go off to university, or die . . . And what normal fifteen-year-old thought about people my age dying? It certainly hadn't been part of my thought process six months ago.

Naomi made a little snorting sound. It was funny and almost cute and probably something she had no control over. She had explained to me that just before takeoff she'd taken a couple of Gravols—both to settle her stomach against airsickness and to help her fall asleep. During our little lesson she'd gotten more and more groggy, until she'd started to slur her words a little and she'd had to force herself to keep her eyes open. More than once her head had dipped forward, and instantly popped back up, until finally it had stayed down and she was asleep.

I'd taken one of the little airline blankets and tucked her in. I knew it would be better for her to sleep, and it would give me an opportunity to check out the in-flight movie. Instead, though, I'd just kept thinking about the things she'd told me about Haiti.

It hadn't been a particularly encouraging lesson. Haiti was, far and away, the poorest country in the western world. It had more than nine million people in a country that was smaller than Lake Superior, and most of those people were crammed into the slums around the capital, Port-au-Prince, where we were going to be landing. People lived in rundown little shacks. There were lots of orphans, and because school wasn't free there were more kids who didn't go to school than kids who did.

She'd described a land of highs and lows—low annual income, low life expectancy, low resources, low levels of education and employment, combined with a high infant mortality rate, and high rates of crime, AIDS, disease, incarceration, and corruption. The country really didn't have a government, and if the United Nations hadn't been supplying aid and troops the whole place would have basically slid off the map and into the ocean. It sounded like a place awash in despair and hopelessness. If God was everywhere, this place sounded like proof that he wasn't everywhere all the time.

I sensed the airplane was slowing, heard it in the engines and felt the pressure change in my ears. I was anxious to get my first sight of the country. Carefully, I reached over Naomi and lifted up the window cover. The sun was incredibly bright and it took a few seconds for my eyes to adjust. My first view was of brilliant blue sky with not even a wisp of cloud. No danger of a hurricane, tropical storm, flood, or mudslide with this weather.

I wasn't wearing my seatbelt, so I was able to rise up in my seat and angle myself so I could look down. I caught my first glimpse of Haiti . . . or at least what I figured was Haiti. There certainly were mountains, rough and rocky and worn. As well there was lots of reddish-brown earth punctuated by little patches of green that stretched into the distance.

As we continued to descend I could start to pick out individual features—roads, and the occasional house. The roads were practically deserted. The odd truck appeared but there was no rush hour going on down there.

Then, more and more houses seemed to pop up out of nowhere until the sides of the roads, the entire sides of hills, were cluttered with hundreds, no, *thousands* of little houses. The light bounced off their metal roofs. We banked sharply and I got an even better look at the ground. The entire view was nothing but all these little houses, all crowded so close together it was impossible to tell where one stopped and the next started. It looked like one gigantic, glimmering, shimmering metal roof, catching the sun's rays and bouncing them up into the sky.

Naomi groaned and started to stir. I reached over and pulled the blind back down. Her eyes popped open as I was still basically on top of her, and she looked up at me. Her expression was confusion combined with a still semi-asleep stare.

"We're almost there," I explained. "We'll be landing in a few minutes."

"Oh . . . okay," she mumbled.

The flight attendant was walking down the aisle, checking to make sure trays were up and seats were in the upright position and everybody had on their . . . I grabbed the ends of my seatbelt and snapped it on.

"You'll have to put your seat up," she said to Naomi, who nodded her head groggily and complied.

"Thank you," the flight attendant said sweetly, and then she continued to move down the aisle.

I heard the wheels being lowered, and Naomi startled at the sound.

"It's okay," I said, trying to reassure her. "It's *really* good that they've lowered the wheels before we land."

"What?" she asked, sounding alarmed rather than amused by my little attempt at humour.

"Nothing, nothing. Everything is good."

She reached out from under the blanket and took my hand again. If that's what she needed to be reassured, that was fine with me. Besides, it wasn't like I knew the right thing to say. Maybe it was like being at a funeral—just keep your mouth shut and nod your head at the right times.

Once again that familiar "binging" sound signalled that we were about to land. Naomi reacted to it by gripping my hand even more tightly. I remembered reading something about how landings were the second most likely times for plane crashes. I looked over at Naomi and smiled reassuringly and kept my mouth shut about fatality statistics.

I peeked over the seats in front of us so that I could catch a glimpse out the window in the next row. I could see the world rushing by and then the brief outline of asphalt—a runway—before the wheels touched down. There was a slight bounce, and a corresponding tightening of Naomi's grip on my hand, as we rolled along the runway, the engines firing loudly to slow us down.

It had been a relatively soft touchdown but now a very *rumbly* roll along the runway, not as smooth as I'd come to expect. We decelerated quickly until we were just barely rolling.

"Would you mind if we opened the blind now?" I asked.

"No, not at all . . . of course!" Naomi said as she reached over and lifted it up.

I leaned over her to look out the window. There really wasn't much to see. Little patches of green and lots and lots of dirt, but I couldn't see any other planes or runways. And where was the terminal?

"Please remain seated until the plane has reached the terminal and has come to a complete stop," the flight attendant announced over the P.A.

That was reassuring—they *had* a terminal.

When the plane finally stopped there was an instant barrage of clicking as seatbelts were undone and people got to their feet. I stayed seated. Where exactly did they think they were going? We were all stuck in here until they opened the door, and even then it wasn't like row 52 was getting out before row 51 or 50 or . . . all the way to the front of the plane.

"It's good to be on the ground," Naomi said.

"It'll be good to *be* on the ground. We're still a few feet short of that."

I could see the front of the line start to move as the first passengers disembarked. I got to my feet. The overhead compartment was already open and I pulled out my backpack. People were bumping and shuffling down the aisle.

There was a lot of excited chatter all around me. I had to admit that even I was excited. This was, really, pretty cool. Instead of being knee-deep in snow and waist-deep in school work I was in another country in a different part of the world, and even if it was a *mission* trip it was still a change.

Bright sunlight and hot air streamed in the door and I hesitated for a split second before I stepped out. I pulled out my sunglasses and put them on before going out onto the

steps leading down from the plane. I held onto the railing—
my legs felt a little rubbery after the flight.

We were parked in front of a building. I assumed it
was the terminal, but it certainly didn't look very fancy or
very big. Black tarmac stretched out in both directions,
bordered by green grass and reddish dirt at the edges. There
was only one other plane bellied up to the building. Not
quite Pearson International Airport busy.

I followed behind the little line of passengers snaking
into the building. Overtop of the conversation and the sound
of a generator humming away I heard another sound . . .
music . . . live music. Approaching the door leading into the
terminal I heard, and then saw, a steel-drum band playing
a song. It sounded bright and friendly and familiar, but I
couldn't quite put my finger on what it was—and then it
came to me. They were playing "No Woman, No Cry," by
Bob Marley! I guess that made sense. This wasn't Jamaica,
but it *was* a Caribbean island.

I stepped out of the line to listen. They were pretty
good.

"*Bonjour!*" one of the players called out to me.
"*Bienvenue!*"

Right, French was the official language here, along
with Haitian Creole. I strained my brain to come up with
what I could remember from grade nine French—the last
grade I'd been forced to take it. He'd said hello—that was a
no-brainer—and welcome.

"Um . . . *merci*," I replied.

"Are you American?" he asked, in perfect English.

Obviously, the accent I'd used giving my one-word answer hadn't been good enough for him to even imagine that I was fluent in French.

"No, Canadian."

"Ah, Canadian!" he called out to me and the other members of the steel band.

They all burst into smiles—perfect white teeth—and called out greetings.

"Welcome to Haiti, my young friend!"

"Thanks."

There was a big hat on the floor in front of them and people passing by had been throwing in change. I dug into my pocket and dropped in some Canadian quarters and loonies.

"Thank you!"

I starting walking and then looked around, trying to find our group. The terminal wasn't big or crowded and it was easy to pick them out standing around a luggage carousel. It was the only carousel in the building and there was no luggage on it yet. I joined up at the back of the group. My father was in the centre of a tight knot of people. At one side, holding his hand, was Sarah, while on the other there was a stranger— although he wasn't acting like a stranger. Between the big smile and the white collar around his neck I figured he was our contact, the minister who ran the program down here. He was full of smiles and handshakes and greetings and—

"Joshua!" my father called out, and gestured for me to come over.

The little puddle of people parted to allow me through.

"Pastor David, this is my son, Joshua."

"Pleased to meet you, sir."

"I'm glad to meet you, Joshua," he said, shaking my hand. He had a firm grip.

"I get called Josh by most people."

"I always call him *Joshua*," my father said firmly.

The pastor looked at me, then at my father, and then back to me. "And what do you want me to call you?" he asked.

"Josh."

He reached out his hand again. "Josh, you can call me Pastor Dave, or Dave . . . that's what my friends call me."

We shook hands again. I liked this guy.

"Now that we're on a first-syllable basis, we'd better get going."

"What about our bags?" my father questioned.

"I've arranged for them to be picked up and put on the bus," Pastor Dave said. "And then we're driving across town so you can register at the embassy."

"That's right," my father said. "We need to notify the Canadian embassy of our arrival and where we will be staying while we're in Haiti."

"Why would they need to know that?" I asked.

"In case they need to get in touch with us in the event of an emergency," my father explained.

"Emergency?" Sarah asked.

Great, in the country for ten minutes and she was already getting upset and scared.

"There's nothing to be nervous about," my father said as he lowered his head and looked Sarah straight in the eyes. "Right, Pastor?"

"Nothing to worry about at all!" Pastor Dave said. "It's just in case—standard practice when anybody travels to any foreign country . . . better to be safe, that's all. This way they know where you are located and how to get in touch with you if people at home need to reach you for some reason. Besides, it's often reassuring for people to know that there is a little piece of Canada right here if they need it."

"Why would we need it?" Naomi asked.

I wished she'd just let it drop. Sarah didn't need any of this.

"Well, say you needed medical treatment, or to be evacuated out of the country because of a medical problem. It's highly unlikely . . . but they'd be here for you."

"That's good," I said to Pastor Dave, although I was really speaking to Sarah. "They're a backup if anything goes wrong. We know that Dad won't let anything go wrong, though."

Sarah gave me a nervous smile. That promise probably would have had more weight before Mom died. After all, if he really could take care of everything, then she wouldn't have died, right?

"I'll give you another example of how the embassy can be helpful," Pastor Dave said. "We had another group down here a few years ago, and two of the young people got separated from everybody else."

"Something that isn't going to happen with us, right?" my father said loudly.

"Of course not," Pastor Dave said. "But they knew that the best place to go was the embassy. If anybody got separated they could simply ask a police officer or soldier to take them there and they'd be safe, secure, and taken care of until they were reunited."

"That is good to know," my father agreed. "Not that it's going to happen, but I want all of you to remember that the embassy is a place where we can go if anything goes wrong."

He sounded calm and reassuring—the way a good minister should—and that was what Sarah needed. If a minister had the right collar, the right words, and the right tone he could convince people of almost anything. I wasn't most people, though.

"Come on, my children, you will be the flock and I will be the shepherd!" Pastor Dave called out. "I will lead you to the promised bus!"

CHAPTER FIVE

We stayed clumped tightly together. No fear of anybody in this group getting separated. Pastor Dave led us out the doors of the terminal to an old, yellow bus that didn't look as though it would meet the safety standards of any school bus I'd ever been on. There were three men loading luggage—our luggage—onto the top, tossing it up and tying it in place. I looked for my luggage and was quickly able to spot the big blue backpack with the bright red Canadian flag on the front.

"Come, everybody, climb aboard," Pastor Dave said. "I'm afraid there isn't much time. We need to get to the embassy, register, and get on the road as soon as possible. We don't want to be travelling after dark."

I wanted to know why travelling after dark was bad, but I didn't really want Sarah to hear any answer that might be troubling to her. It probably was best to drive in daylight because the roads might not be too good.

We piled on and I grabbed a seat right up at the front. That way I could look out the front windshield instead of just the side window. I could hear the men above us, the roof groaning under their weight and movement.

Then I started to think, why had he hustled us onto this hot bus when we couldn't leave before the luggage was tied on anyway? Was it because he wanted to leave the second we could, or because he didn't want us standing outside the vehicle? I looked all around. It looked fine. It looked safe.

"Let's open up all the windows!" Pastor Dave yelled out. "We'll get a little breeze blowing through."

Instantly kids got up and started opening the windows. If you wanted to be listened to, the best group in the world was a bunch of eager-to-please church kids. Windows thumped open all over and I could feel a difference almost immediately as air started to stream in. It went from unbearably hot and stuffy *still* air, to unbearably hot and stuffy *moving* air. But that was better, and it would probably be much better when we were driving.

The men climbed down from the roof and one of them got in behind the wheel of the vehicle. He started it up. The engine roared and then settled into a low rumble. I recognized both the sound and the smell—it was a diesel-fuelled bus. We started driving. He raced away and a strong breeze came blowing in. This was probably the closest thing to air conditioning we were going to experience on the trip.

The brakes of the bus squealed and I held tight to the rail in front of me as we came to a complete and sudden stop. In front of us the street was packed with vehicles.

There were hundreds and hundreds of cars and trucks and buses. The vehicles were an odd assortment of new and old, really old, and practically falling apart old, while the buses were bizarrely, brilliantly painted, with slogans on the side, and people practically hanging out of the doors. Mixed in with the vehicles were donkey-drawn carts plodding along the road. Then, just to add to the confusion, there were hundreds and hundreds of little motorbikes and regular bikes weaving around the vehicles, which were just bumping along.

We edged into traffic and inched forward. So much for the breeze. So much for getting anywhere fast.

I sat on the bus—the stifling hot bus—and watched out the window as people on foot passed us. We were making less progress—far less progress—than the people who were walking. We'd been on the bus for almost two hours and I was getting sick of it. There was even grumbling from the church kids, who hardly ever grumbled about anything. I could have quieted them down by telling them that this traffic jam was "God's will," but I was enjoying them being at least somewhat annoyed.

"Is it always this busy?" my father asked Pastor Dave.

"Not always this busy, but it is a lot busier than it used to be. This city just wasn't built for this much traffic or this many people. Every day, thousands more people move in, but there are never any more roads built."

I couldn't believe how many people there were. They were walking, standing, sitting on the curb, and sitting behind little stalls, small sidewalk stores. And they weren't limited to the side of the road. We were continually approached by people walking along the road, passing between the vehicles and calling out to us, holding out bracelets and necklaces and souvenirs—and, strangely, world maps, brushes, dishpans, and kitchen strainers—for sale. Some of them were friendly and polite, and others were very persistent, almost aggressive, and a little bit frightening to some of the kids on the bus.

Pastor Dave had finally closed some of the windows, which added to the heat but seemed to make them feel safer. As well, he'd warned everybody to keep their valuables—cameras and bags and purses—on the floor and not on their laps.

"How much farther is it?" my father asked.

"It's only a few more blocks."

"It would be quicker if we walked," I chipped in.

My father looked at Pastor Dave. "It would be. We could walk, couldn't we?"

He looked uneasy and he didn't answer right away, as though he was thinking it over. "I guess we could."

He said something in French to the driver, who nodded and then edged the vehicle over to the side and brought it to a stop. The door popped open.

Pastor Dave stood up. "We're going to walk the last little bit," he said.

A cheer went up.

"As we walk, I want everybody to stay together, *close* together."

Did he want us to hold hands or hold onto a piece of rope? Come on, we weren't little kids.

"This is a very crowded section of the city," he continued. "Things are very . . . very . . . *busy.*"

That much was pretty obvious to everybody . . . maybe he was trying to say something else.

"Please, everybody, follow behind. Stay close," Pastor Dave reiterated.

He got off the bus and I was the first off behind him. The heat and the fumes and the smells that had been with us during the bus ride became stronger. I felt as if I'd been hit by a wave of heat, sunlight, and a strange combination of smells that included diesel fumes, sewage, and cooking.

Inside the bus, looking at the crush of people through the window, had been almost like watching everything on high-def TV. Now, as the people flowed around us, it was very different. I felt hemmed in by the crowd, the smells, and the chaos that pressed on us. Maybe it would have been better to have stayed on the bus after all.

Sarah came off, holding my father's hand. That was good. One by one the other kids clambered off the vehicle. They all looked like such wide-eyed innocents.

I waited while they formed a line behind Pastor Dave. I wanted to be the last in line. Somebody had to watch the back, and it shouldn't have been any of these kids. I didn't know much about them, but I did know that nobody on this trip was in any way street smart . . . heck, they weren't even *sidewalk* smart, and there wasn't really any sidewalk that I could see other than the little sliver that wasn't taken up by those little stalls.

I let them pass, two by two, and—

"Are you waiting for me?" Naomi asked as she stopped beside me.

"Sure . . . why not?"

The last two passed us and we fell in at the end of the line.

"This is really different, isn't it?" she said.

"*Really different* pretty well describes it."

"Is this . . . is this okay, us being here?" she asked.

I wanted to give her some reassuring platitudes but I had to admit that I wasn't feeling very comfortable myself. Our little line of white faces stood out, and it seemed as if every eye was on us as we passed. I started to think that in a country where so many people were so poor, they must have been assuming we were all really rich. Rich targets.

I reached over and took Naomi's purse and shifted it off her outside shoulder so it was hanging between us. She didn't stop me but a very confused, questioning look came to her face.

"It's always better to have your things in the middle rather than on the outside. Harder for somebody to rip it off."

"Oh, that makes sense . . . I really need to keep this safe."

"You should have your money in a moneybelt," I said, involuntarily tapping my hand against mine, tucked against my hip.

"My money *is* in a moneybelt. I have my insulin in here."

"Insulin . . . why would you . . . you're diabetic?"

"I was diagnosed three years ago," she said.

"Should you be—?" I was smart enough not to finish the sentence, even though I was stupid enough to have started it. "So, there's enough insulin in that little bag for the whole trip?"

"I only brought enough for the first few days. Arrangements were made so that there's some waiting for me here. There's refrigeration at the orphanage, and they arranged for a supply to be delivered. I'll be fine."

"That's good thinking, because—"

There was a scream—my sister's scream—and then a man raced by us, almost bumping into Naomi. In his hand was my sister's backpack!

CHAPTER SIX

The thief raced through the crowd, bumping into people as he ran. I froze in place for a split second, and then, without thinking, I turned and charged after him.

"Stop! Stop him!" I screamed.

Faces turned toward me—toward him—but nobody did anything to stop him. It seemed as though the crowd was actually parting to move out of his way. I ran behind in the path he'd ploughed for me.

"Stop . . . thief!"

He looked back over his shoulder at me chasing, and I saw his eyes open wider in shock. Instead of stopping he started to run faster. I tried to pick up my pace but I didn't have much more left in me.

He cut to the side, through a couple of stalls and down a side street. I bumped into a woman and staggered a bit as she screamed at me—I'm pretty sure she was swearing in

French—but I kept running. If I let him get out of sight he'd be gone. I shot through the stalls and dodged between the stalls and there it was . . . my sister's backpack lying in the dirt halfway down the alley!

I ran up and skidded to a stop, looking all around. The thief was nowhere to be seen. I bent down and picked up the backpack. It was still zipped up and it was still heavy. He hadn't had the time to take anything out of it.

I was drenched in sweat and I felt flushed and light-headed. The running, the excitement, and the heat had all combined to make me feel as though I was on the verge of passing out. I bent over slightly and took a deep breath. When I looked up again I realized that everybody was looking at me, and everybody else was black. I was a white face in a sea of unfamiliar faces. I suddenly felt very alone and vulnerable and a little bit afraid. That fear, the anxiety, made it even worse, and my breath seemed to catch in my throat.

The faces looking back at me looked curious, surprised, even a bit shocked. But they also seemed friendly and concerned. I straightened up and tried my best to smile, and a couple of them smiled back at me. Slowly I started to walk.

"Excuse me . . . *excusez-moi* . . . *s'il vous plaît!*" I said, falling back on my high school French once more.

Two of the women smiled even more broadly, said some things in French that I couldn't hope to understand, and parted to let me through. It felt better to get out of the alley, past the stalls, and onto the main street. But still, there wasn't anybody who I recognized or who even had the same skin pigment as me. I hurried along, firmly clutching Sarah's backpack to my chest. It wasn't going to go away again. The others couldn't be that much farther ahead. It hadn't been that long a chase, although it had all happened so fast that maybe I had travelled farther than I'd thought.

"Joshua!"

It was my father, with my sister still clutching his hand. And with them was Pastor Dave and two police officers.

"You got it!" Sarah screamed out, and I handed her the backpack.

My father threw his arms around me, catching me off guard.

"I'm so glad you're all right."

"Why wouldn't I be all right?"

"You could have gotten hurt. You shouldn't have done that!" he said.

"I couldn't just let him get away."

"You should have let him have it," Pastor Dave said. His smile was gone, his tone very serious.

"He is right," one of the officers said in stilted English. "That man . . . that man could have . . . " He drew his finger across his neck like a knife and made a cutting sound.

"You mean he could have had a weapon?" my father asked.

One of the policemen nodded his head. "Everybody here has a weapon of one sort or another."

It had all happened so suddenly and I'd reacted so instantly that I hadn't even thought about that possibility.

"If not a knife then a machete, or worse still, perhaps a gun," the officer said.

"It was not . . . how do you say . . . *wise*," the second officer said. "Not wise for you all to be down in this area."

"It's not that dangerous," Pastor Dave said. "I'm here by myself all the time and nothing has ever happened to me."

"Being lucky does not make one wise," the officer said. "Port-au-Prince is a dangerous place."

"Many, many bad men," the other officer added. "Many robberies . . . many murders."

"We need to get out of here," my father said. "Your life is worth more than a backpack."

"It wasn't the backpack that was important," I said. "It was what was inside of it."

I gestured to Sarah with my eyes. She was standing, holding the backpack with its zipper open, and she was hugging a faded blue sweater—my mother's faded blue sweater—the sweater that she always slept with since my mother's death.

My father looked at the sweater, looked over at me, back to Sarah, and then burst into tears.

CHAPTER SEVEN

The bus hit another pothole and I bounced way up into the air. If I hadn't been holding on I think I might have gone flying up to the roof of the vehicle.

"It's quite the rough road," Pastor Dave said.

"This is a road?"

He laughed. "More like a goat path, but it qualifies as a road around here. Speaking of which, what are your impressions of this country so far?"

"It's bigger than I'd thought it would be."

He laughed again. I got the feeling that laughter came easily to him.

"People see Haiti on the map and think this little end of the island can't be that big, but it does take a long time to get from one side to the other."

"It would be a lot quicker if they had real roads." I paused. "We're not actually driving to the other side of the island, are we?"

"It just feels like that," he said. "We'll be where we're headed in less than an hour."

We'd already been on the road for close to four hours. It had taken the first hour just to leave the city behind. Port-au-Prince was an unbelievable clutter, a chaotic collection of roadside stores, houses and shacks, cars and trucks and donkey carts and people . . . people everywhere . . . millions and millions of people all crammed together in such a tiny space that it was beyond anything I'd ever known.

And it wasn't like I'd never been in a city before. My family had lived in Toronto for five years—but that was a *real* city, with roads and lights, traffic that at least pretended to follow rules, and houses with yards and lawns. Port-au-Prince wasn't a city as much as something slapped together by a bunch of hyperactive toddlers. There seemed to be no order or organization—at least none that I'd seen.

Leaving the city behind had been like a weight coming off my shoulders. There was something unnerving about being around that much chaos and that many people. Of course we hadn't left people behind completely. All along the road—all along this *goat* path—there had been people, walking, riding in carts or on donkeys, working in the fields, sitting by their tiny houses, or just standing in groups, mostly men. Pastor Dave had called it "being idle."

There were increasingly fewer vehicles as we travelled farther away from the city. Aside from the occasional private car we saw mostly beat-up old working trucks hauling cargo, and even more dilapidated old buses, brightly painted, covered in slogans proclaiming Jesus or Bob Marley, or named after Hollywood movies. They were crammed full of people and drove as if they owned the road—which, in a way, if you didn't count the carts, they did. Pastor Dave had said that they always gave the other traffic a wide berth. He'd said his motto was *"Trust God only so far, and then get out of the way of the buses."* He said that despite having been in the country for almost twenty years, the traffic and driving patterns still unnerved him. And worse than being unnerved, he said that the only fatalities suffered by missionaries in his order had been from traffic accidents.

We'd been on a fairly steady climb since we'd left the city. The country was pretty, but not what I'd expected. There was a *rawness* to the landscape . . . too few trees or bushes, too few crops growing in the fields, and way too much mud or bare dirt or dust. I'd expected more tropical jungle and less open, bare ground.

Pastor Dave leaned in close. "Your sister . . . is she going to be all right?"

I looked back. She was snuggled in close to my father, wearing our mother's sweater now.

"She'll be okay. She just needs more reassurance after . . . after . . . " I let the sentence trail off.

"Your mother's death must be hard on all of you . . . even your father."

I knew he was referring to my father's tears. They had caught even me off guard. I knew he still cried, but to do it in public like that had shocked me. He was always trying to put on a brave face, not just for me and Sarah but for his congregation. Churchgoers liked their pastor to dry their tears, not shed tears of his own.

I figured his outburst had to be a combination of relief that I was okay, tiredness from the flight, compassion for my sister, and surprise at seeing that little remnant of my mother. Still, it had been unexpected. Thank goodness it was only a few tears, and the rest of the group hadn't been there to see it.

"You know that this isn't a country where reassurance abounds," Pastor Dave said.

"Sarah will be okay, as long as one of us is around, either me or my father."

"Good. And now that we're outside of the city it will be safe . . . well, safer."

Now *I* didn't feel so reassured.

"That wasn't a very good part of the city, was it?" I asked.

"There are few parts that we would consider good by our standards. It's unfortunate that the embassy is right smack in the middle of a less desirable area, but it was important to register."

Registering at the embassy had been sort of reassuring. It was good to know that somebody knew where we were, especially as we continued to drive into the middle of nowhere. I got the feeling that if we didn't actually get to the end of the world, we'd at least be able to see it from where we were going.

"Don't worry," Pastor Dave said, obviously reading the look of worry on my face. "Where you have poverty, you have crime. But up here everybody knows us, respects the work we're doing, and treats us well. You won't have to be chasing down any more thieves." He paused. "By the way, that was pretty brave of you back there."

"Thanks."

"I guess it's true, though, that fools rush in where angels fear to tread," he said.

I chuckled. "So you're saying that wasn't the brightest thing to do?"

"Not the wisest, no. At least it happened on a main street. Things could have been much worse if you'd followed him down a side street."

I startled ever so slightly. Right, they didn't know about the whole chase because I really hadn't told them.

"There are places in Port-au-Prince, in the slums, where even the soldiers don't go unless there are at least a half dozen of them."

"Yeah, right." He was trying to scare me and—

"Yeah, *right*," he insisted. "There are slums that are about the most dangerous places in the world. And that's not just my opinion, the United Nations says so, too. It once deemed the slum of Cité Soleil the most dangerous place on the planet. There's always violence, but remember that extreme poverty and extreme desperation create the climate for desperate actions. I also try to remind myself that things are getting better."

"That's good . . . I guess."

"Haiti is a country born in violence. Columbus landed here in 1492, and it only took the Spanish a quarter of a century to completely annihilate the original inhabitants.

Eventually Haiti was given to the French, and it became home to more than half a million slaves. They revolted and overthrew their masters, becoming the first black republic to declare independence, in 1804."

"That's more than sixty years before Canada became independent."

"But Canada has been blessed with stable government. Haiti has suffered under one form of oppression or dictatorship or corrupt government since then. In some ways it exists as a country in name only. Without the ongoing support of the United Nations peacekeepers and policing forces and outside aid it would not be possible."

"Those two men . . . after I came back . . . the police that were with you . . ."

"Those were United Nations soldiers. You can tell by the blue helmets they wore. Those are the police forces you can trust in this country. The United Nations soldiers and police have worked to gain the trust of the people. They are trying to help create a better Haiti . . . sort of the reason you're here."

I almost said something but didn't. That *wasn't* the reason I was here.

"Some have given up on Haiti. All the corruption, all of the violence, and all of the poverty—it almost seems hopeless even to try."

"It is the poorest country in the western hemisphere," I added, repeating what Naomi had said to me.

"And one of the poorest in the entire world. Too many people in too small an area, with limited and degraded natural resources, no significant manufacturing base, in a country with dysfunctional infrastructure and a history of corruption. Not the most hopeful scenario." He paused and then turned directly toward me in the seat. "I don't want to paint too dark a picture, but this is a country of desperation . . . which is why that man stole your sister's backpack."

"We have people who do that in Canada."

"There are thieves everywhere. The United States, where I'm from, certainly has its share of poverty and crime. Here, people are driven to violent acts by the situation in which they find themselves. You know they say that God is everywhere. There are times even I struggle to find him here . . . but then he appears."

The bus came to a stop in front of a metal gate leading into a walled compound.

"We have arrived!"

Above the gate in painted letters it read "Home of the Angels." I guess if there were angels then there had to be God, as well—although I'd never seen much proof of either.

CHAPTER EIGHT

The driver beeped his horn and almost instantly two little boys appeared. They worked to unlock the gate and then swung it open. The bus started up and inched forward, through the gate and into the compound. There were four or five bright, white buildings and out of them streamed a whole lot of children. There were dozens and dozens of kids of all ages, all smiling and laughing and bouncing and skipping as they came. They were dressed in white shirts or blouses, the girls in blue skirts and the boys in matching pants. For a bunch of orphans, they were dressed as if they attended a private school.

"As I said, God is everywhere," Pastor Dave said, gesturing to the children.

He got to his feet, and almost before the bus had even stopped he was down the stairs and out through the open door. He was mobbed by the children, who greeted him as though he'd been gone for a month—he had said he'd just come to town for the day, hadn't he?

The rest of us on the bus started to get up. I think we were all a little anxious to get off and be outside. It had been a long, bumpy, dusty trip. I made my way along the narrow aisle and down the steps, ducking to get through the doorway and then to the ground.

The mob that had been surrounding Dave had now become two orderly lines of children practically standing at attention like little soldiers. Dave shepherded us to two rows of chairs placed directly in front of the waiting rows of children. I went to settle into one of the seats in the second row, but he grabbed me by the arm and positioned me up front with my father, my sister, and Iris and Michelle. Iris, of course, grabbed one of the seats beside my father. Ugh . . . how eighth grade! Quickly everybody settled into the rest of the seats.

"What a beautiful morning!" Pastor Dave sang out. "And how *blessed* we are to be here under *God's* care!"

I recognized that tone of voice: the drawn-out emphasis for the important words so that "God" almost had an extra syllable, the way his voice started to rise and fall, and how he was almost developing a Southern accent. He was becoming a minister, and this was going to be a little sermon welcoming us here.

He suddenly switched into French, and although I couldn't understand more than the occasional word, the *minister* voice remained the same in both languages.

"And to welcome our guests," he said, once again in English, "we would like to offer a song."

Some of the children broke free from the military ranks and came forward until there were twenty of them standing together directly across from where I sat. The others, who weren't part of the song, stayed in line, standing perfectly still. A woman—I imagined she was one of the people who ran the place—took her place in front as choirmaster. She blew a note on a little pitch pipe and their voices picked it up—a perfect note—in reply.

She signalled and they started singing. The words were in French, but since I was a good little preacher's kid I not only recognized the song, I knew most of the English words . . . although strangely I couldn't remember the title. I assumed it was something about God or Jesus or the Bible. They were very good singers and they were adding little touches to the song that I hadn't heard before. They seemed to be really enjoying it. Lots of smiles, lots of enthusiasm.

The song stopped and we all applauded—me included. They'd done a good job, and it was only polite, and besides, they were orphans. They needed all the applause they could get. They filed back into their places in the rows.

"That was just a small sample of one of our choirs," Pastor Dave said. "Tomorrow, at our Sunday service, you will receive a *full* serving of singing, as well as dance, and, of course, the sermon."

I suddenly remembered something my father had mentioned. I had teased him about how his last service had run long—almost an hour and fifteen minutes—and he had told me that down here I should expect a three- or four-*hour* service. I'd thought he was joking, but he had insisted he wasn't. He'd said that, one way or another, church was going to take up most of Sunday morning and a chunk of the afternoon. I didn't think I could fake interest for any longer than an hour and a half, at best. Maybe I could fake being sick.

"But for now," Pastor Dave continued, "I know that you are all tired and need to settle in and rest. You will each be assigned one of our older children to be your guide, to assist and offer help in any way they can." He turned to my father. "Pastor Roberts, would you grace us with a closing prayer?"

"Certainly."

My father rose and came forward.

"Please, I'd like us all to stand."

We all got up from our seats and joined the orphans already on their feet.

"Now bow your heads in prayer," he began.

I lowered my head and closed my eyes.

"Lord, I stand before you offering my thanks. Dear Father, I have so much to be thankful for, both seen and unseen, all of which you have provided."

I had a gut feeling that he was going to make this one a really, really long prayer. This was his chance to strut his stuff as a minister for another minister and a bunch of new people, so he'd have to show them what he had. It was sort of like a religious *throw down*, a polite duel. I listened in— what choice did I have, unless I was going to walk away?— as he kept going on and on. He threw in the appropriate biblical references, a little homily, all the time adding extra syllables and dramatic tone to all the right words—*Jesus, God, Lord, salvation*, etc., etc., etc.

I felt sweat dripping down my side. Standing there in the sun, still dressed in a long-sleeved shirt and long pants, it was getting really hot. I opened my eyes and glanced up, slowly scanning the row of orphans facing me. They had their heads down, dutifully, in prayer, taking in the Word, even if they couldn't really understand the words he was saying in English. Everybody, of course, had their heads down like obedient little soldiers. I wanted to look into their faces, into their eyes, to see who they were, to try to figure out how they'd handled what had happened in their lives that had brought them to this place.

I wondered if I'd be able to see the hurt in their eyes, the way I could see it in my father's eyes, or my sister's, or even mine when I looked in the mirror. I wondered what it was like to lose both parents. But I couldn't see anything except bowed heads hiding closed eyes and—wait, there was one boy at the far side who was scanning our line the way I was looking at his.

Before I could think to look down our eyes locked. He nodded his head slightly and I nodded back, and then he smiled and I couldn't help but smile back. We were sharing a little joke that nobody else knew about. He was bigger, older than the other kids, pretty well the oldest one there.

"For your *mighty* power, dear *Lord*, is at work in me!" my father sang out, his voice getting louder as he was bringing it home, selling the final words. "You, Lord, are transforming me, renewing my mind and body!"

My new friend and I still had our eyes open, connected, listening, or at least pretending to listen.

"To you, *Lord*, belong thanks eternal . . . In *Jesus'* name, *Amen!*"

"Amen!" we all echoed back, and eyes popped open and heads were raised. Everybody did seem thankful—perhaps if only that this extended prayer had finally ended and we could at last go inside, get out of the sun, and settle in.

I walked directly toward my new friend as he walked toward me.

"Hi, I'm Josh."

"'ello, I am Philippe."

"I see you two have already connected," Pastor Dave said. "Philippe is my head boy here, and he'll be your guide. Now, let me get everybody else joined up."

"Come," Philippe said, gesturing for me to come with him.

I followed him to behind the bus, where our bags had been unloaded and were lined up on the ground. I saw mine and started to pick it up.

"*Non*, let me 'elp."

He went to take the bag from me and I resisted. I didn't need any help carrying my own backpack. He pulled harder, and I realized it wasn't worth a fight. Maybe he'd even be in trouble if he didn't carry it. Besides, I was tired.

"It is 'eavy, but not too 'eavy," he said.

I fell in beside him as he started to walk away with the bag.

"Your English is pretty good," I told him.

"Thank you. You speak French?"

"*Bonjour, comment ça va?*"

"*Très bien!*" he said.

I was feeling encouraged, so I thought I'd try something a bit more challenging. I could tell him that I spoke only a little French. "*Parlez-vous une petite français,*" I said. I had a feeling it wasn't right, but at least he didn't laugh.

"Then better we speak English," he said. "Better for me to prac . . . practise."

He opened the wooden door to a small, grey, concrete building and I followed him in. There were four metal bunk beds. On each was a thin, uncomfortable-looking mattress, and on top of that was a blanket, a sheet, and an equally uncomfortable-looking pillow.

"Which one?" Philippe asked.

There didn't seem to be one that looked any better than the others, but I decided I would rather be by the window, so I chose that one.

"This one . . . bottom bunk."

He nodded his head and then placed my bag on the floor beside the bed. He started to make the bed.

"That's okay, I can do it."

I tried to take the sheet from him but he wouldn't let go.

"How about if we do it together?" I suggested.

He nodded his head, smiled slightly, and released one end of the sheet.

As I tucked in the first corner I quickly realized that it wasn't much of a mattress—just hard foam, covered in heavy plastic. Probably for the best. No telling who or what had been in this bed before me, so plastic was a bonus.

Awkwardly we worked as a pair, bumping into each other, getting in each other's way. It would have been better if I'd just done it myself, or easier if I'd just stood back and let him do it alone. And once we were finished, we stood staring at each other. That was as awkward as making the bed together.

"Your eyes," he said, placing his index finger beside his eyes.

"Yeah, they're blue," I replied. I'd been told to expect that people here would be interested in my white skin and blue eyes.

He shook his head. "No . . . they were open."

"Of course they were . . . " Then I realized what he meant. "Oh . . . during prayers."

"Yes."

"So were *yours*."

He shrugged. "Pastor says that God is always watching . . . but sometimes I think it is also good that Philippe is also watching."

"Philippe *and* Josh."

"Maybe both, *oui*."

We were interrupted as other kids from my group—led in by enthusiastic helpers—noisily, cheerfully entered the room.

There'd be time to talk with Philippe later. I was looking forward to that.

CHAPTER NINE

I moved slowly. The ground was unfamiliar and uneven and I wanted to be as quiet as possible. The whole compound had gone to bed—me included—hours ago. The difference was that they seemed to be able to go to sleep.

Despite the darkness I could see fairly well. It was amazing just how much light was being thrown down by the stars and the moon, because it was a certainty that none was coming from the buildings on the ground. The generator had been turned off hours before. I missed the light—well, what passed for light, coming from those yellowy little bulbs—but I certainly didn't miss the noise. It was more a roar than a hum. Or the smell. During the day, the diesel fumes from the generator "perfumed" the air all around. Now that was gone, but there was still the smell of fire.

All around us, hidden in the darkness on the other side of the walls of the compound, were houses. I couldn't see them but I could occasionally pick out a human voice, a laugh, and once a baby crying. Mixed in with that were the sounds of barking dogs and crowing roosters. Obviously, since it was the middle of the night, those roosters were rather confused.

I walked along the wall, one hand against it to guide me. It was made of concrete blocks and it was rough against my skin. It reached way above my head, so high that I couldn't have jumped up to see over it, or even easily climbed over it. Of course the climbing part would have been hindered by the three strands of barbed wire that topped it. I could see those against the night sky. What I couldn't see, though I'd seen them in the daylight, were the shards of broken glass embedded in the top of the wall. You'd really have to work very hard to get out of here.

Of course, I was pretty sure the glass and barbed wire weren't there to keep people in. I remembered Pastor Dave's words—safer, not safe, here. I came up to the gate, which was held firm with a big chain and locked, and I peered out through the iron pickets. It was amazing how dark it could be without electrical lights, but how bright it could be from just the twinkling stars above. I could see the outlines of little houses, really not much more than shacks and shanties, not far from the compound. They made a darker shadow in the night. There were dozens and dozens of these shacks scattered along the road and down the hillside, beyond the light necessary for me to see, invisible in the distant darkness. Funny, the smell of smoke was thick in the air, so there had to be fires somewhere, but they didn't seem to be casting any light.

Then I heard something. It was a human voice . . . no, many voices . . . but not talking . . . they were singing, or . . . I turned my head. It sounded like music. Whatever it was, it was getting louder. And then I saw a shadow moving along the road, and there was a little bluish light moving along with it.

I watched and listened and it soon became clear. It was a person, walking along the road, and he was carrying a radio. That was the light. That was the sound—it was a song playing on the radio. I couldn't make out the words, although I was pretty sure it wasn't in English. And then a human voice, off key, was added to the radio. Whoever was carrying the radio was singing along. Again, I couldn't understand his words any more than I could follow the singer on the radio. There was one big difference, though. I was pretty sure the singer on the radio was sober, and equally sure the singer on the road wasn't. His words were slurred, and he had that drunken tone that was the same in any language.

"That's Louidor."

I practically jumped out of my shoes and spun around. It was Pastor Dave.

"Sorry, I didn't mean to startle you," he said.

"I wasn't startled," I lied.

"Really? I'd hate to see how you'd react if you ever *were* startled, then. That is our neighbour. Louidor is his name."

Louidor was getting much closer—and much louder.

"He lives in one of these houses?" I asked.

"Calling it a house would be a little more than simple Christian charity. He lives in a shelter just beyond our front gate," Pastor Dave explained.

"*Bon soir,* Louidor! *Comment ça va?*"

The dark figure stopped, the singing stopped, but the accompanying music kept playing.

"Louidor!" Pastor Dave called out, and he waved an arm through the bars of the gate.

"*Bon soir!*" Louidor replied, in a loud, slurred accent.

He walked—no, staggered—toward us, and as he came forward the two of them began speaking in French. I could only pick out a word or two at best, and my lack of comprehension wasn't helped by the blaring radio. The song had stopped and now there was an announcer, or a commercial, or somebody saying something in loud, jarring tones.

The two men shook hands, and close up it was even more obvious that Louidor's stagger and slur were by-products of alcohol. It wasn't just that he smelled like he'd been drinking—he smelled as though he'd been using the stuff for cologne, or even bathing in it. It was overpowering.

Even in the dim light I could see that his clothing was a mashup of assorted items, right down to the two different shoes he was wearing and a layering of clothes at least two deep. His face was dirty, and there was a wild-eyed look to him.

"Louidor, this is Josh."

"*Bon soir!*" he yelled. He grabbed my hand through the bars before I could react and began shaking it vigorously while jabbering out words at a pace so fast I couldn't even find the gaps between the words I didn't understand.

"Louidor, *il faut parler anglais,*" Pastor Dave yelled out.

The words and the hand-shaking stopped, but he still held my hand firmly.

"American?" he asked.

"Canadian," Pastor Dave said.

"Ah, Canadian! Ice hockey, Mounties, maple syrup . . . *O Canada . . . my home and native land!*" he sang out.

At least he'd let go of my hand finally as he burst into the national anthem.

"Relatives . . . I 'ave relatives in Quebec!" he shouted. "Maybe you know of them!"

"I'm not from Quebec. I'm from far away in Ontario."

He started to speak to me in French but stopped mid-sentence. He looked confused.

"You are . . . you are Canadian but you don't speak French. But you . . . you are Canadian . . . Canadians speak French . . . no?" he asked, sounding puzzled.

"Some Canadians do."

"It is not so . . . so 'ard to learn . . . 'ere, even little babies speak it."

He broke into loud laughter that quickly degenerated into an awful-sounding coughing fit, as though he were drowning.

"Here, Louidor, I have something for you," Pastor Dave said. He held something in his hand but I couldn't quite make out what it was.

"*Merci, mon ami!*"

"You are most welcome. Now go to sleep, get some rest."

"I will try, but you know . . . sleep . . . it is 'ard. I 'ope you may sleep well too," Louidor said.

"From your mouth to God's ears," Pastor Dave said.

Louidor turned on his heels and started away. He didn't go very far. He made a quick turn and then ducked down, disappearing behind a little pile of wood. I couldn't see him any longer but I could still hear the radio, and then there was a sound, like a door slamming, and the radio faded away to almost nothing.

"Where did he go?"

"He went into his home," Pastor Dave said. "Or at least what he calls his home."

"I don't see anything."

"It's right there . . . not big. He built it out of a packing crate that came for the centre. He's added a door and some other touches of things he's found. It has a mattress, a place to put his things, and a lock on the door so that he and his things are safe."

I moved my head to try to make it out. I could see a little structure, partially hidden behind a small, stunted tree. Now that I knew what I was looking for I could pick it out.

"It's not much, but it does keep out the rain and the wind," Pastor Dave said.

"What did you just give him?" I asked.

"Batteries for his radio."

"Batteries?" That seemed so strange, but he did seem to like his radio. I could still hear it faintly playing.

"He goes through quite a few batteries," Pastor Dave said. "He has his radio on 24/7."

"I guess he likes music," I said. What I wanted to say was that maybe he should shut it off, save a little money, and add a couple more two-by-fours to his home.

"Music, commercials, talking. He needs to have something playing all the time. The voices on the *outside* help to drown out the voices on the *inside*."

I gave him a questioning look.

"Louidor has, shall we say, some mental health concerns."

I burst into laughter before I realized how wrong that was and stopped myself. "Sorry, I know it isn't funny."

"It's all right. Sometimes you laugh to avoid crying. I know you don't find his situation amusing or humorous."

"It's nice of you to give him the batteries," I said, trying to redirect the conversation away from me.

"Nice for him and nice for me. When he doesn't have his radio he can be very distressed . . . and distressing. He has very loud arguments with himself and the voices. Mental illness is such a terrible thing."

"And I guess the alcohol doesn't help either," I commented.

"Actually, it does help. He seems to use the alcohol as a form of self-medication. It helps him sleep, calms him down. I've seen mean drunks. He is a nice drunk," Pastor Dave explained. "Of course, I would never give him alcohol, or even money for batteries because he would drink it away. So . . . I give him batteries. And when we have extra food, a meal or two appears on his doorstep."

"That's nice of you."

"Jesus said something about loving your neighbours, not just loving those who were good, or sober, or only heard voices from the outside of their head. I'm sure you'd be doing the same."

I nodded my head because that was the expected response, not because I was certain of the answer. I couldn't even imagine living in this place to begin with.

"You couldn't get to sleep?" he asked.

"No. I just wasn't tired."

"Often after a trip people will have trouble adjusting to sleep the first night or two."

"I always have trouble sleeping," I replied, before I'd thought through my words.

"Always?" he asked.

"Sometimes . . . most of the time . . . but only the past few months."

"Since the death of your mother?"

I felt myself step back emotionally, and I suddenly felt a rush of anger. Why did everybody with a collar think they could ask you about—?

"I'm sorry," he said. "I shouldn't be prying. It wasn't my place to ask that. Please accept my apology."

"It's . . . it's all right," I sputtered.

"It just seems like you strap a collar around somebody's neck and he thinks he has the right and the need to ask questions about everybody's personal life. And worse still, he actually thinks he's an expert!"

It was unnerving to hear him say what I'd been thinking. Maybe just as unnerving to hear a minister actually admit it.

"It's okay . . . really." All the anger was gone. "It started before my mother died."

"See? There you go. Me thinking I was an expert."

"It was since she got sick and we knew she was going to die."

"How long between the diagnosis and her death?" he asked. "If you don't mind my asking . . . if you're okay talking about this."

I wasn't sure whether I did mind and I wasn't sure if I was okay, but still, there was something about being out there in the dark, both of us looking away into the distance, that seemed to make it better, safer . . . something. Besides, it wasn't like what I was going to say to him was going to follow me back to Canada. Somehow, talking to him seemed safe.

"She had been unwell for a while . . . not herself. But after they found out what she had it was only seven weeks."

"That's too short and too long." He paused. "I'd better explain that. You want life to go on, so obviously it was too short, but if I knew I was going to die I'd want a few days to get my affairs in order, say my goodbyes, and then leave. I'm no good at sitting around waiting."

"It was too long," I said, my voice barely a whisper.

"At the end it must have been almost a relief."

That was what it had felt like—as if she was free and I was free.

"The worst part is that sometimes people start wishing on some level that the person would hurry up and die," he said.

I looked over at him. He was still looking off into the distance. That was how I'd felt at the end. I couldn't tell anybody. Because they'd think I didn't love her, or wanted her to die, or—

"And then they feel so much guilt," he said. "They

can't tell anybody about their feelings because somebody will misunderstand them, maybe judge them for feeling what they feel."

My whole body shuddered—not from the chill in the air, but from relief, and because it was so eerie to have him voice my thoughts again. Now, somehow hearing him say those words allowed those thoughts, those feelings, to escape from my body in a rush.

"Is that how you felt?" he asked. His voice so soft now that I almost couldn't tell whether he had said the words or I had thought them.

I looked over. Now he *was* looking at me. I nodded my head ever so slightly.

"It's okay to think that way . . . to *feel* that way. I know you loved your mother. I know you all loved her. It's been hard on all of you. Your father . . . those tears today . . . does he cry about it often?"

"Never . . . hardly ever . . . even then."

"Members of the clergy can be the hardest on themselves. They don't think they should show weakness, they have to be strong, for their family, for their congregation. Stupid idiots often just mutter banalities like 'It was God's will,' or, 'She's with her Maker,' or the one I personally hate the most, 'God works in mysterious ways.'"

I burst into laughter again, and that shocked me.

"I've known a couple of idiots who actually acted as if they were happy. Spouting witty little Bible school sayings about how the person was 'in a better place,' or was 'sitting by God's side.'"

"Were you there at the funeral service?" I asked jokingly.

"Human nature is human nature. We might all be individuals but there aren't that many variables in the way we act and react. How long has it been since her death?"

"Almost six months since she died, and three months since we moved."

"That's right, your father just recently took charge of this congregation. That must have been difficult for you, to leave behind your church family."

"Not as hard as it was to leave behind our friends and schools and our home."

He now looked serious and confused. "You mean, it wasn't just your father changing churches but that you actually, physically moved?"

"Same city, but the other side."

"Your father seems far too intelligent a man to do such a *stupid* thing!" he snapped. "And please accept my apologies for calling your father stupid."

"No apologies necessary."

"But he should have known better. Especially for the kids, especially for your little sister, it's a basic rule of grief, and your father would know that with his training, that you try to keep everything else constant when you've already lost so much. That at least explains why your sister is so needy, so clingy."

That did explain it. I'd never really thought about it that way, but he was right.

"And, of course, that also explains why you're so angry at him."

"What makes you think I'm angry?"

"The whole 'Joshua' or 'Josh' business. Why does your father insist on calling you Joshua when you don't like it?"

This guy certainly didn't waste words, or time.

"It's not a big deal."

"It must be something, or it wouldn't be such an issue between you two."

Again, very direct. Normally I would have really liked that, if it wasn't aimed directly at me. But I'd opened up about a lot of things already, so why not this?

"It's just . . . this is going to sound stupid . . . but I'm named Joshua after Joshua from the Bible."

"I sort of know something about this whole Bible thing . . . I am a pastor, remember?" He chuckled. "My parents named me David after King David."

"It's just that my father thinks I should be proud of my *real* name because of who Joshua was."

"He was a great person. He was a major figure in the Exodus, even accompanying Moses for part of the journey up Mount Sinai, where he received the Ten Commandments."

He wasn't telling me anything I didn't already know. I knew the Bible too. I knew lots of stories—that didn't make them true.

"After the death of Moses, Joshua led the Israelite tribes. He is revered by the Jewish faith as a wise, faithful, and humble man. In Islam he is held up as the imam who followed after Moses. You are named after a great man, so I understand your father's point."

"And you're named after David, another leader, but you still go by Dave."

He smiled. "Maybe I understand better than anybody why you go by Josh. It's pretty hard to live up to that reputation, to follow in either of their footsteps."

"I wouldn't *want* to follow *all* of his footsteps," I snapped. The words came out so quickly they caught me by surprise.

"I guess I understand that myself. King David was a great man and a faithful servant of God, but he was caught by temptation."

"And Joshua thought that God was talking to him. Maybe if he'd had a radio, like Louidor, he wouldn't have listened to the voice inside his head that said he should kill everybody in Jericho!"

"Every man, woman, child, and ass, as I recall," Pastor Dave said.

Of course he'd have known the story. Joshua had told his people, the tribes of Israel, to surround the walled city of Jericho and circle it for seven days until finally the horns sounded and the walls came tumbling down. The victorious Israelites then slaughtered every man, woman, child, and donkey because Joshua said that God had instructed him to do that. Some God. Some leader.

"Some people would be greatly offended that you're comparing one of the great men of three major faiths to the mentally ill man passed out in a hovel outside my gates," Pastor Dave said.

"Are you?"

"What do you think?" he asked.

I wanted to say that I didn't care, but I did. I shook my head.

"Some people talk about how every word in the Bible is sacred. That it's all God's word. Those people are idiots." He paused. "I appear to have a lot of strong words today. Your father isn't one of those idiots, is he?"

"Of course not!" It was one thing for me to criticize my father, but I was beginning to feel that he might be stepping over a line in coming down so hard on a guy he barely knew. I guess that was a bit of loyalty kicking in.

"Good. I can excuse him making a bad decision based on his grief, but I have no time or tolerance for fanatics. The Bible is a series of sermons, stories, psalms, parables, and lessons. Some are so contradictory that they couldn't all be true. Others seem to be advocating such wondrous concepts as incest, infanticide, and genocide . . . as you've so aptly pointed out."

"Exactly!"

"I wouldn't want to say these things too loudly, and I know as a pastor I'm not even supposed to consider such things, but I think that my God is more of a New Testament sort of God . . . of course without Revelation . . . what a terrible book . . . Old Testament sort of fire and brimstone and vengeful God . . . so *pre*-Jesus."

I had to laugh—again.

"Jesus was a kind and gentle man who was loved, not feared." Pastor Dave paused a moment and looked me in the eye. "You know, Josh, I'm really happy you're here. Even if you're not."

"Is it that obvious?"

"It couldn't be more obvious if you were wearing a sign. But look, this is just one of many things that have happened over the past months that you didn't want to happen, and this is probably the *least* of them."

He was right about that. This at least had some upside . . . like this conversation.

"I'm not going to bore you with little bromides, but sometimes God does place us where we need to be. Maybe this is where *you* need to be. But for now, let's both get to bed. You'll need your rest. There's a lot of work to be done tomorrow. Not to mention the church service. Wouldn't want you to have an excuse to fall asleep during my sermon."

"Don't worry, if I fall asleep it'll have more to do with your sermon itself," I said.

He looked surprised, then burst into laughter. "It really is a pleasure to have you here."

CHAPTER TEN

Philippe trudged forward, a bag of cement on his shoulder. He was bent under its weight, but he still moved faster than I thought he had any right to. He was reed-thin and that bag was incredibly heavy. I knew how heavy it was because I'd heaved a few of them myself, and I was a lot bigger than him. Not just taller, but bigger. I had to have outweighed him by thirty pounds, and the weight of that bag had staggered my legs.

At the start I'd been moving pretty fast—certainly faster than Philippe—but now, four hours into our work, I'd slowed down, while he'd kept working at exactly the same pace. I guess in part that was because of the heat—which I wasn't used to—or the jet lag, or the fact that I'd hardly slept the night before. Or maybe it was just because he was strong in ways I couldn't see.

Philippe dropped the bag to the ground and then took

a machete and cut open the top. In one quick, fluid motion he picked the bag up, turned it over, and dumped the contents into the growing mound of concrete powder in front of me. There was a swirl of dust and I turned away so I wouldn't have to breathe in any more of it. The air was filled, and another thin layer was added to my clothes and skin and hair. I certainly wouldn't have to worry about applying any more sunscreen because I already had a protective layer of cement dust on every exposed bit of skin, and probably lots of places that weren't exposed as well.

If it had rained—and judging from the brilliant blue sky that wasn't going to happen—I wondered if the water would set the cement and I'd become a concrete statue. Sort of like the Tin Man in *The Wizard of Oz*, frozen in place by the rain, but instead of rust it would have been concrete that locked me in.

Philippe picked up a shovel, and now my time to daydream and lean on my shovel was officially over. We worked to create a hole in the middle of the pile of concrete and sand, sort of the cone in the middle of a volcano, and then other kids, including Naomi, started to pour water into the hole we'd excavated. That was the process, how concrete was mixed, by shovel and muscle. There were no cement mixers here other than us.

I worked hard to mix the cement and sand with the water. It had to be a certain consistency—not too thick and not too thin. It was kind of like making a gigantic cake mix—that was the closest experience I could compare it to. And none of these kids with me had any experience, either. I couldn't imagine any of us even being allowed near a building site back in Canada—that probably would have violated a dozen or so safety laws back home. Here, I didn't think there were so many rules.

Thank goodness we had the locals—men who did this sort of thing for a living—telling us what to do and helping us along. We were certainly "helping" to build, but the real builders were those men. Them and, of course, some of the kids from the orphanage itself, like Philippe.

Philippe did seem to know everything. He was definitely helping to run the show, and since he spoke more English than any of the men who were working he was also translating directions. It wasn't that they couldn't speak *any* English—everybody had some basic words. It seemed as though they understood more than they spoke, though. That only made sense. My years of French—forty minutes a day up until the end of grade nine—certainly hadn't made me bilingual, but I did understand more than I spoke, and I was often surprised by how much I could understand when I read French. Not that I read much more than the back of the cereal box when I was bored and eating breakfast, but still, I could read it . . . a bit, sort of. I'd be in great shape if somebody wanted to talk about the ingredients in a box of Cheerios.

Philippe yelled for more water and Naomi trundled over with a big bucket, water slopping over the edges.

"Where should I pour it?" she asked.

Philippe tapped his shovel against the pile to indicate the exact spot. She started to pour until the bucket got away from her and she dropped it into the pile.

"Here, let me," I said as I picked up the bucket.

"Thanks . . . it's hard work."

"And you've been working hard," I said.

Different kids were helping with different levels of enthusiasm. A number of them were now spending more time standing in the shade holding shovels and buckets than actually using them. Naomi hadn't been one of those kids, and neither had I. It wasn't that I felt some sort of obligation as the "preacher's kid" to set an example. I just didn't like standing around. If you had a job to do, I always thought you should just do it and get on with it.

Slowly I poured the water into my damp concrete cake mix—all I needed now was to crack in a couple of eggs. My mother had this knack of doing it with one hand, cracking the egg on the side of the bowl, opening it up and letting the insides ooze out and then tossing away the shells. We'd made cakes and baked all the time when I was little, but we hadn't done that in years. And never would again. I felt a wave of sadness wash over me. No time for sadness. I pushed it back down where it belonged.

I drained the bucket and handed it back to Naomi.

"Thanks," she said. She looked very pale. I guess we all looked pale from the concrete dust.

"My pleasure." I reached over and brushed away some hair from in front of her eyes before I realized that I shouldn't have done that.

"Sorry . . . it just looked like it was getting in your way."

"That's okay . . . it was getting in my eyes . . . thanks."

Philippe tapped me on the shoulder. "Time for work, not for play."

"Oh, yeah, of course," I mumbled, grateful to be rescued from the awkwardness of the situation. Why had I done that?

I took the shovel in both hands and started to fold the cement into itself. We'd mixed enough already that I had a pretty good idea how it should look—and it was looking pretty good now—but that call was Philippe's to make. Luckily, he agreed.

He started shovelling the cement into the wheelbarrow and I instantly followed suit. It was much heavier now, water and sand and concrete, all mixed together. I tossed in a shovel of cement and it almost tipped the wheelbarrow sideways. Soon it was filled to the top. Philippe worked to scrape up the last vestiges of cement, and I went and stood between the arms of the wheelbarrow, ready to move it. He plopped down that last shovelful.

I bent slightly at the knees and then, using my legs and arms, muscled it up. It now weighed probably as much as I did, and the little homemade wheelbarrow sagged under the load. I pushed forward, and once I'd set it in motion I almost felt as if I was being pulled along with it instead of having to push it. I followed down the little path to the site of the construction.

My father—along with Pastor Dave, some of our kids, a couple of the older residents of the home, and the hired men from the community—was working on the actual construction. As I looked up I was impressed with how much we'd done today. With each wheelbarrow full of cement I could see part of another row of cinder blocks set in place.

There were now almost five complete rows of blocks, so the whole structure was almost waist-high already. It was going up fast, although it wasn't like they were putting together a skyscraper, or, for that matter, even a complicated jigsaw puzzle. It was cinder blocks cemented into place against a concrete pad and then each row cemented into the next. The whole thing wasn't that big, with two gigantic rooms— one would be a girls' dormitory and the one on the other side would be for boys—and between that an eating area and a bedroom for the matron.

The blocks formed not only the outside wall but the inside wall, and you could now see where the doors were going to be, leading into the building and then into the three bedrooms. As the blocks got higher there would be spots left open for windows. Off to the side I could see timbers that would become the roof supports and then gigantic pieces of sheet metal that would form the roof.

The rooms weren't that big, maybe three times as big as my bedroom at home, but they told us that each room would hold six bunk beds. Simple math meant that each room would hold twelve people, so the whole building would be for twenty-four orphans. That's where simple math broke down because they figured that there would be two children per bed so this little building would actually hold forty-eight kids. Unbelievable. This little space would be home to forty-eight human beings, forty-eight kids, forty-eight orphans. Just thinking that through made me realize that maybe we were doing something important. Maybe we weren't changing the world, but we were going to change the world for forty-eight kids. Maybe this wasn't quite as lame as I'd thought.

My father nodded at me as I let the wheelbarrow down. He gave me a big smile. He'd been smiling all morning. He really looked as though he was enjoying all of this. I guess it was so different from his usual job. Here you could see, row by row, the progress. In his line of work, progress was usually a little bit harder to judge or gauge or count. As well, there was no harm in putting your head into new places to replace old thoughts. And memories.

A dozen shovels dipped into the wheelbarrow, taking away a scoop of cement. This was the "glue" that would be placed along the top row of cinder blocks, and then the next blocks would be placed on top of those.

Technically my job was to stand and wait for the wheelbarrow to be emptied, but I hated to just stand there and watch. Besides, Philippe didn't stop, and I had an unofficial competition going with him to see who could do the most work. I was so glad it was unofficial because after I'd sprinted out to an early lead he'd passed me . . . actually, he'd almost lapped me.

I walked over and took a cinder block from the pile. It seemed a lot heavier than it had earlier in the day, but— wow, Philippe was carrying two blocks, one in each hand! For a split second I contemplated grabbing a second, but I thought better of it. It was time to call off the unofficial contest—the best man had won.

I dropped the brick to the ground in front of the rising wall and it landed with a loud thud.

"How about putting it right here?" my father said. He patted the wall where he wanted the block. In his other hand he was holding a trowel.

I had the urge to tell him if he really wanted it there he could lift it himself, but of course I couldn't say that. I bent down and picked it up. Unbelievably, it had gained weight in the few seconds since I'd dropped it.

"Just set it down right here," he said. He had already laid down a thin layer of cement.

I put it, carefully, in place, and streams of concrete flowed out from the edges of the block. It reminded me of toothpaste coming out of the tube. My father took his trowel and skilfully skimmed away the excess and plopped it onto the top of the block, waiting for the next layer to begin.

"You're pretty good at that," I said.

"Not bad. There's something very satisfying about this job. You can see what you're doing. No shades of grey or fine distinctions. Each layer, one after the other, is rising up to the heavens."

"I don't think we're going to go quite that high," I suggested.

"Merely a metaphor."

"I thought we were building an orphanage, not a metaphor," I joked. "But either way, it certainly is happening fast."

"I guess that's what happens when you don't have to go through committees, zoning bylaws, local government, or getting building permits," he said.

"There are none of those here?"

"Apparently you're basically free in Haiti to build whatever you want, wherever you want, without asking for permission. Dave told me there aren't even building codes in Haiti."

"None?"

"None at all. It makes you question the quality of any building here."

"The one we're building is pretty solid," I said.

"I think it is," he said, smiling.

I went back for another cinder block, and instead of dropping it this time I waited till my father showed me where he wanted it and set it in place. After he'd cleaned up the cement with his trowel, he asked me, over his shoulder, "I was wondering, what did you think of Pastor Dave's service today?"

Was he feeling a bit insecure, up against a fellow pastor? "I'm not sure it was the best I've ever been to, but I'm completely sure it was the longest," I said.

He leaned in closer. "I have to admit that three hours is a little bit beyond my attention span, but it was interesting . . . and different."

"*Different* pretty well sums it up," I agreed.

The actual service had taken place in the chapel on the grounds of the orphanage. Along with the residents of the children's home, the staff, and us visitors, there'd been lots of people from the community. Along with the sermon—which had been pretty good—there had been lots and lots of dancing and singing. The dancing was strange but the singing was great. So great, in fact, that for the first hour or so of the building this afternoon many of the kids had continued to sing or hum some of the songs.

Even stranger, I'd actually caught myself softly singing along. I felt grateful that nobody I knew or cared about was within a few thousand miles of here. Here, I wasn't trying to impress anybody. What did I care what a bunch of church kids thought of me?

I wouldn't have said anything to my father, but what I really thought was that Pastor Dave had delivered a very good sermon today . . . funny, the words "good" and "sermon" didn't usually come out of my mouth together in the same sentence.

While the service had been long, the sermon itself had been simple and short. He'd basically said that there are two types of lakes in the world—those where water flows in and flows out, and those where it flows in and never flows out. He'd described the first type of lake as being healthy and alive, and then explained how the second type gets more and more salty until it can't support life any more. Sort of like the Great Salt Lake and the Dead Sea. Then he'd said that people were like that.

Some people get things and give, and others just get and never give. Those people that never give become dead inside, while those who get and also give stay alive. Of course he was talking about us there doing our mission trip to help build the extension to the orphanage, which made us all feel good inside. "Onward Christian Soldiers," and all that. But really, it did make sense. I knew that lots of people—actually, *most* of the people I knew—were always getting things, or taking

things, but weren't necessarily so good at giving back. They
never did seem that happy, just angry or resentful or jealous.
No matter how much they were given it never seemed good
enough, or just plain *enough*. Goodness . . . I was thinking
like a preacher's kid, or worse, like a *preacher*!

There'd been a time, years and years ago, when I used
to actually think that I might follow in my father's footsteps
and become a minister. Now that was probably the last
thing in the world I could see myself doing. I was thinking
more and more about becoming an engineer—an environ-
mental engineer. My father could try to save the world his
way and I'd try to save it my way.

"I'm impressed with how hard everybody is working," my father said. "Although it looks like there are lots
of scraped knuckles, bruises, and sore backs among the
group. I have sore muscles in places where I didn't even
know I had muscles!"

"You have muscles?" I questioned.

"You're lucky I'm too tired to fight you," he joked.

"Just tired? I was thinking tired and old."

"Hey, hey, a little respect for age."

"Maybe a lot of respect for a lot of age might be even
better."

He broke out laughing. It was a deep, real, hearty
laugh. It sounded like my father. At least, my father from
before. Seeing this little sliver of him almost shocked me.
I'd almost forgotten that was in there. It had been locked
behind a role, a mask, of being serious, or stoic, or sad, or
brave. I'd lost track of there being anything else there.

I smiled back and then realized that that was different for me as well. Smiling used to come naturally. Now a different look—all of those same ones that occupied my father's face—had become my default expressions. The smile quickly dissipated. What right did I have to be happy?

"How much longer do we have to work?" I asked.

A loud, clanging bell interrupted. I looked toward the source. Pastor Dave was standing by the dining hall, ringing the bell to call us for dinner.

"Is that soon enough?" my father asked.

"Just barely . . . do you think you can carry me up the hill?"

"I was hoping you'd carry *me* . . . you know, because I'm so old and have so little muscle."

He put down his trowel, walked through the "door" of the building, and came to my side of the cinder wall.

"I think coming here was a good idea," he said.

I nodded my head ever so slightly. Maybe it wasn't as bad an idea as I'd thought. It was probably good for my father.

"So, am I carrying you up?" I asked.

Instead of climbing on my back he put an arm around my shoulders, and we started to walk away. Somehow having the weight of his arm around my shoulders seemed to make things lighter.

CHAPTER ELEVEN

I looked around the room, trying to figure out where to sit. My options weren't the best. I could sit with the orphans—most of whom spoke pretty fractured English—or with the kids from the church—most of whom spoke in English about things I didn't want to hear about. The only other choice was sitting with my father, sister, and Pastor Dave—and, of course, Iris. That was probably the best. I wanted to check to see how Sarah was doing, anyway. She'd spent a good chunk of the day playing dolls with the littlest orphan girls, so I really hadn't had much of a chance to see or talk to her.

"Mind if I join you?" I asked.

"Pull up a seat and take a load off," Pastor Dave said as he pushed out a chair with his foot.

I sat down beside him and opposite my father and sister.

"Well, I think, as our guest, you should do the honours," Pastor Dave said to my father.

"No, I do believe that this is your house, and you should be the one to say grace," my father replied.

As long as the two of them were discussing who should say a prayer before we ate, nobody could start eating. All our plates were untouched, utensils clean.

"No, I insist that it be you," Pastor Dave said. "You've already heard me spout off through a sermon today, so I'm not going to inflict myself on you poor people any further."

If I hadn't been so hungry this might have been cute . . . well, cute in a pathetic sort of stupid way. But I didn't want to be part of any of this. I just wanted to eat.

"I would be delighted to have you say—"

"How about if I say the grace?" I asked, cutting off my father.

"You?" My sister sounded shocked.

"That would be wonderful!" my father exclaimed. He didn't look any less shocked than my sister.

"What an excellent idea and a generous offer!" Pastor Dave answered. "It is most appropriate that one of the young people provide the blessing. It's wonderful that the spirit has moved you!"

It had nothing to do with any spirit moving me. It had to do with my stomach moving me. Even if they'd eventually sorted out their little argument, whoever won would have to say a grace to impress the other, and that would be one long, long prayer. I wanted to eat. I could say a little prayer in less than thirty seconds and we could all get on with dinner. Now that would be something to be grateful for.

"Then it's settled, Joshua will say grace," my father said.

He looked so happy he was practically beaming, and I suddenly felt at least a little guilty about my selfish motives. But still, if it made him happy, that wasn't the worst thing in the world. He deserved a little happiness. It had been so nice to hear him laugh out there—not a forced, trying to be brave, put-on laugh but a real from-the-gut laugh. He used to do that all the time. So did my mother. One I couldn't do anything about.

Pastor Dave suddenly stood up and took a few steps to a little elevated platform. What was he doing?

"I would like everybody to please rise to their feet so that we can say grace before we share our meal!" he called out to the room.

Everybody . . . the room erupted with the sound of scraping chairs, which replaced the loud conversations, as the entire room rose. I staggered to my feet as well, in a state of semi-shock.

"Tonight's blessing will be given by Josh," Pastor Dave called out to the crowd.

The "Josh" part made me happy for a split second before the reality of the situation resurfaced.

"Josh, come on up here," he said, and there was a burst of applause. Great. Just great.

My feet suddenly felt incredibly heavy, a heaviness that had nothing to do with the amount of work I'd done today. I stumbled forward until I was standing beside Pastor Dave.

What was I going to say now? I fumbled around in my mind. My plan had been to say the shortest prayer imaginable, just a few words, but now, here, in front of everybody, that wasn't going to be possible. Not only was I the preacher's kid, but I was representing all of us "young people," with every eye now cast expectantly on me.

It didn't help that both my father and Pastor Dave were pretty good at this prayer stuff. Two big collars to fill. But being the preacher's kid did have some advantages. I'd heard enough prayers in my time that they'd been absorbed into my head through osmosis.

"Would everybody please bow their heads," I said, to begin.

A general genuflection took place around the room. It felt good to have their eyes off of me. I glanced around the room quickly, trying to pick out Philippe. There he was, off to the side, and even his head was down. I'd better get started.

"Dear Lord, we thank you from grateful hearts for your love . . . for this meal and for those who prepared it . . . for your *fellowship*."

I knew how much my father *loved* that word. Sometimes I felt like I was going to scream the next time he used the word "fellowship" and it wasn't followed by "of the rings." I almost chuckled to myself, thinking about throwing in a further reference to *Lord of the Rings* in my prayer, but thought better of it. Prayers weren't a time to try for humour or topical references. Better get moving again.

"Help us to remember that you are with us around this table, and may our hearts and words be a blessing to you."

That was a good line. I could almost imagine my

father nodding along in agreement. Was that enough? Should I throw in an "Amen" and call it quits? Probably a little more was still needed.

"Thank you for food in a world where many walk in hunger. For faith in a world where many walk in fear. For friends in a world where many walk alone. We give thanks, O Lord."

I'd heard my father say this one before. I was even using his inflections and tone of voice—oh, great, I was doing a minister impersonation. Probably I should say "God" as a two-syllable word at the end . . . the end . . . I still needed something else.

"Um . . . um . . . Thank you for the food we eat. Thank you for the friends we meet. Thank you for the birds that sing. Thank you God for everything . . . Amen."

"Amen!" came a chorus of responses from across the room.

Heads came up, smiles on their faces. Either I'd done really well or they were just grateful that it was over and they could eat. I couldn't believe I'd thrown in the birds singing part. When in doubt I subconsciously went back to Sunday school lessons. At least I hadn't actually *sung* about the singing birds.

"That was very nice," my father said as I returned to the table.

"Very impressive," Pastor Dave added.

"Singing birds?" Sarah asked.

"I thought it was very sweet," Iris chipped in, with a smarmy kind of smile on her face.

"They *are* God's creatures, you know," I said to my sister, trying to sound offended. "Either way, it's time to eat."

I slumped into my seat, picked up my spoon, and plunged it into the bowl of . . . of . . . what was this, anyway? I wasn't the most adventurous eater, but I was really hungry, and what other choice did I have? It wasn't like I was going to go out to Wendy's for a Number 1 Classic Combo. My sister was shovelling it in and my father did look as though he was enjoying it. But still, it wasn't wise to put anything in your mouth that you couldn't readily identify.

"So, what is this?" I asked, gesturing to my spoon.

"*Mayi moulen*," Pastor Dave answered.

"Okay . . . and what exactly is *mayi . . . moul . . . moul. . .?*"

"*Mayi moulen* is made up of cornmeal, with kidney beans, coconuts, and peppers," Iris explained. How did she know so much about Haitian food?

"It's good," Sarah added.

"It's a staple food of Haiti. All those carbohydrates are good when you're doing physical work," my father said.

Tentatively, with all four of them looking at me, I put the spoonful in my mouth. It actually wasn't bad. Then again, I was so hungry that dirt would have tasted good. My mother always said the best time to try something new was when you were hungry. I wondered what she'd think when I told her . . .

It was like getting slapped in the face. I hadn't done that in a long time. It had been months since I'd heard the phone ring and wondered if it was her. And since we'd moved to the new house I hadn't walked in and had to stop myself from calling out, "Mom, I'm home!" . . . because it wasn't really our home.

Still, there were times I thought I saw her, in a crowd or passing by in a car. My father said that she was "with us in spirit" or was "looking down on us." But if she was a spirit, or looking down from Heaven, I wouldn't be seeing her reflection in the window of a store on a busy street. I was so tired of all that crap about her still being with us. She was gone.

"Don't you like it?" Pastor Dave asked.

"No, no, it's good . . . I was just lost in thought."

The looks aimed at me by everybody at the table were asking, "What thought?" But there was no way I was going to be offering that up. It almost felt as if the only place she was still real was in my head, and by talking about it I'd let some of her escape.

"I was just wondering what sort of day you had, Sarah," I said. That wasn't the truth, but it wasn't a lie. I did want to know.

"It was great!" She beamed. "I was helping out in the nursery with some of the really little kids. Mostly we played with their dolls, and then at lunchtime I helped get their meal ready and helped clean up. Hardly like working at all! After supper I'm going to go back and play with them again, then help with bedtime."

"Your sister is very good with the younger children," Pastor Dave said, and Sarah looked delighted.

"She's always been a very social child," my father added. "Joshua has been more of an independent soul."

"But I've seen you connect with Philippe," Pastor Dave noted. "You spent the day with him."

It wasn't exactly as though we'd been hanging around the mall, playing video games, or playing road hockey, but we had been together the whole time. I nodded my head in agreement, but again, I didn't want this conversation aimed in my direction. Maybe that was because I was such an *independent* soul.

"The kids here at the orphanage, can you tell me how they got here?" I asked.

"Each child is a different story," Pastor Dave said.

That was good. One hundred children would be one hundred different stories, none of which had to do with me.

"Can I join you?"

I looked up. It was Naomi, standing, plate in hand, beside our table.

"Of course, we'd be delighted to have you join us!" my father exclaimed.

Both he and Pastor Dave got to their feet. I knew I had to do the same and rose slightly out of my seat. My father moved his chair a little to the side to allow Naomi to slide into the seat beside his. I couldn't help but notice that he moved in the direction of Iris. She seemed to notice too, judging from that smug little smile.

"I didn't mean to interrupt your conversation," Naomi apologized.

"We were just talking about how the kids got here," I said. "Would you like to hear some of the stories?"

"Definitely . . . if that's okay."

"Certainly," Pastor Dave said. "There are few secrets here. To start, you have to know that each of the children here is a *true* orphan," he said.

"What does that mean?" Sarah asked.

"It means that they have neither a father nor a mother. For example, you and your brother are without a mother, but you still have a father, so you are not orphans."

So much for steering the talk away from me. That comment had been aimed straight at me—and at Sarah—and it hit us right between the eyes. Was that an accident or was it deliberate?

"Is AIDS the major factor?" I asked, remembering something I'd read—no, something that Naomi had told me. I looked over at her and gave her a little smile, which she returned.

"It is a factor, but only one of many. Car accidents, childbirth where the baby lives and the mother dies, misadventure, and other illnesses all leave children parentless. So many people here die unnecessarily. In a country with no health care system, and almost no proper medical treatment for the poor or adequate provision of medications, the life expectancy is notoriously low. Combine that with poor diet, near starvation or being deprived of healthy food, and then add in the violent deaths."

"Is violence a major problem?" my father asked.

"It's much, much better with the United Nations soldiers being in charge now, but there are literally hundreds and hundreds of murders in the slums of Port-au-Prince every year."

"That's hard to even comprehend," my father said, shaking his head slowly in that minister-like manner of his. "This country is so full of tragedy."

"I try not to look at the whole picture but at the individual stories," Pastor Dave said, gesturing around the room. "Each child is one little success. We also try to make sure that if there is somebody—a parent somewhere—that they be given the support they need to care for their child themselves."

"That must be appreciated," my father said. "I know I've been so grateful for the support that I've been given by people through the difficult days."

He reached out and took my sister's hand. I tucked my hands in under the table to make sure there was no chance of him doing the same with me. This conversation kept coming back around to where I didn't want it.

"Some people appreciate it and some don't," Pastor Dave explained. "There are some parents who are not connected to their children, possibly have hardly known them. The most difficult for me are those parents who know and care for their children but still try to give them away."

"Give them away? Why would a parent do that?" Sarah asked, sounding distressed. I could almost see her tightening her grip on my father's hand as she wondered if that could happen to her.

"They try to give them away because they love them so much."

"I don't understand," Sarah said. Now she sounded confused *and* distressed.

"They do it because they love them so much that they

want the best for them, they want them to have the things they cannot provide," he explained.

"But the best thing for children is to be with their parent or parents," my father said. I was pretty sure he was saying it to Sarah to reassure her.

"It *is* best to be with a parent. At least, when there is a roof over their head and food in their stomachs and they can go to school. So many parents are so destitute that they cannot provide those most basic needs. That's when we find the children, alone, at the gate of our building . . . some are just babies, left in baskets. Others are toddlers, with a rope tied to the gate and looped around their ankle so they don't wander off."

"And the parent is gone?" my father asked.

"Gone. Sometimes they leave a note, and other times nothing."

"And what do you do then?" Iris asked. She had a horrified look on her face.

"Of course we bring them in, and if possible we try to locate the parent, or at least the person who dropped them off. Thank goodness for Louidor."

"Who is Louidor?" my father asked.

"He's a neighbour," I answered. "He lives just outside the gate."

"Yes," said Pastor Dave. "He knows most everybody, or at least knows somebody who knows somebody. He's almost our unofficial night watchman, and nothing happens without him noticing. He gives us information or helps us track down a relative."

"You're lucky to have such a fine and helpful neighbour," my father added.

It was obvious that he'd never seen Louidor or he wouldn't have used either "fine" or "lucky" as adjectives to describe him.

"We are lucky. He is a good neighbour," Pastor Dave said. "It is the youngest that are the most difficult to track down," he continued, "but in many ways they are the best to have. We can do more with the younger children . . . more potential . . . fewer issues and problems to overcome or undo."

"So the older children have been with you a long time," my father said.

"Some for more than a decade. Twelve, or fourteen years in some cases."

"And is adoption a possibility?"

"In a country overwhelmed with poverty and orphans, there are few in a position to adopt," Pastor Dave explained.

"What about families from other countries?" my father questioned.

"There are occasions when overseas adoption is done, but it's not really something we believe in here."

"Why not?" my father asked. "If they could have a better life, wouldn't that be a better alternative?"

"They could certainly have a more material life, but 'better' is another question. We really try to keep the children of Haiti in Haiti. Though the children in our residence are true orphans, almost all of them have some family connections somewhere in the country. Perhaps it's an auntie or uncle or a grandparent. We try to encourage ongoing contact, even though that relative is not in a position to provide care. It's hard enough to lose your parents, harder again to lose everybody and everything, including your culture and your homeland."

Or your house and school and friends, I could have added.

"Does that make sense?" Pastor Dave asked.

"I guess it does," my father agreed. "I just hadn't thought it through from that perspective."

"It's something that took me quite a while to understand. I truly appreciate how people in the developed world want to help, and they see adoption as a route to helping. It's just that it's not necessarily the best way to help."

"So the kids here are going to be here until they grow up," I said.

"For the most part, and since we most often get them when they're very young, they're here for a long, long time," Pastor Dave explained.

"So I guess Philippe, because he's the oldest, has been here for a long time," I said.

"Less than a year."

"But . . . but . . . he is one of the oldest here, right?" I asked.

"He'll be sixteen soon."

"Like you," my father added.

"So you're right, he is amongst the oldest, and I do think he could run the place if I weren't here, so I can see why you'd think that he's even older than that," Pastor Dave explained.

"Did his parents only recently pass on?" my father questioned.

"I don't know exactly when they died, but Philippe says he hardly has any memories of them."

I wondered if he had memories but just didn't want to share them. I remembered my mother, but that didn't mean I was going to talk about her.

"Was he living with other relatives or at another orphanage?" my father asked.

"Philippe was what we call a street boy. He lived on his own, living from hand to mouth, scrounging on the street to try to survive. That's why he's only in grade six."

"Grade six? But how can that be if he's almost sixteen?" I asked.

"He didn't have money for food so he certainly didn't have money for school tuition. It's only since he's come here that he's been able to go to school again. He's such a bright boy, and he works harder than anybody I've ever met. We're so proud of him. He has come leaps and bounds forward from that first day we met."

"How did you meet?" my father asked.

"It was in Port-au-Prince. I was walking down one of the alleyways and he just came up to me," Pastor Dave explained.

"Because he knew you ran the orphanage?" my father asked.

"No, more likely because he thought I had money . . . at least, I assume that's why he pulled that knife on me."

"He pulled a knife on you?" both my father and I exclaimed together.

"Yes, he pulled a knife on me . . . a *big* knife."

"And he robbed you?" my father asked.

"Like I said, he had a big knife. Wouldn't you give somebody your money if he pulled a big knife on you?" Pastor Dave asked.

"Yes, but how did you get from him robbing you to him living here?" my father questioned.

"I gave him my money. Then I told him he had to take my address, because if he needed a good meal he should come and see me."

"Heavens! What did he say when you told him that?" Iris asked.

"He didn't say anything. He just took my money and ran off."

"And the police caught him?" I asked.

Pastor Dave shook his head. "Police do little here for minor crimes."

"And pulling a knife and robbing somebody is a minor crime?" I questioned.

"Here it is. Regardless, I don't think Philippe believed me at first, but then again, why would he believe me?"

"Wouldn't the collar have convinced him you could be trusted?" my father asked.

"There has been as much wrong as right done here in the name of religion. I didn't see him again for over a month. Then, he just showed up at the gate. He wasn't well . . . he hadn't eaten for days . . . he was sick . . . he had been beaten up by some older boys."

"That's awful," Naomi said.

"We took him in, gave him a bed, a meal, and some medical treatment. He said he was only going to stay for a few days. That was over a year ago."

"You acted as a good Christian," Iris said.

"I acted as a good person," Pastor Dave said. "And I know that Philippe wouldn't mind me telling you any of this. He has told his story, he's given testimony to help inspire others."

"It is inspirational," my father said. "Don't you agree, Joshua?"

"Yeah, of course."

"Naomi?"

She didn't answer. It was as though she hadn't heard him.

"Naomi?"

She looked sort of glassy-eyed and she was shaking slightly.

"Naomi, are you all right?" my father asked as he reached out and touched her arm.

She started slightly and then looked at him. Her expression was vacant, as though she hadn't realized he was even there.

"Naomi, are you feeling okay?"

She tilted her head to the side and then vomited onto the table.

CHAPTER TWELVE

I sat bolt upright in bed, and for a few seconds I wasn't sure where I was. It came back quickly. I was in the bottom bunk of a bed in an orphanage in Haiti. Not where I wanted to be, but certainly better than where I'd been in my dreams. It had been months since this had happened, months since I'd even thought about the funeral, and now it was popping into my head while I was asleep. That wasn't fair, because I couldn't defend myself when I wasn't conscious.

I threw my legs over the side and went to slip my feet into my shoes when I remembered: I was supposed to pick up each shoe and shake it out in case there was a little scorpion or spider in there. Nothing dropped out, so I went ahead and slipped them on.

There was an assortment of sleeping sounds coming from the other bunks—breathing, soft snores, springs sagging under shifting weight. As far as I could tell I was the only one awake. That wasn't surprising. There was probably no one in this dorm room who had ever worked harder in his life than he'd worked today. I'd certainly gotten to sleep easily enough, but staying asleep had been more challenging.

I got up and slowly shuffled through the darkened room, heading for the door. I opened it and stepped outside. I was disappointed that it was no less warm or sticky or humid than inside. Somehow I'd just expected outside to be cooler. I was tempted to check up on Naomi, but I knew that wasn't really possible. The girls' dormitory was, obviously, off limits to the boys. But really, I was sure she was fine. A little too much sun, combined with too much physical exertion and not enough liquids, had left her dehydrated. And since she was diabetic, getting dehydrated caused her blood sugar levels to rise, which apparently wasn't good. At least that was what Pastor Dave had said. She'd started to feel better as soon he'd got some tea into her and a cold compress on her forehead. Tomorrow she'd take it easier, and I was sure she'd be okay.

I was really more concerned about Sarah. She seemed so disturbed by what had happened. I guess it had brought back bad memories of how my mother was during treatment. Some people weren't badly affected by chemotherapy, but most were. My mother got violently ill sometimes, so suddenly that she couldn't get away and she threw up right in front of us . . . in front of Sarah. I was sure that was what had triggered my dreams tonight, what had invaded our reality and then my sleep.

I strolled toward the gate and caught sight of Pastor Dave and Philippe just as they caught sight of me. They waved and I waved back and changed course toward them.

"Don't you ever sleep?" Pastor Dave asked.

"I get the feeling that I probably get more sleep than you do."

"That's not saying much, but there always seems to be one more thing that needs to be done before I rest my head on my pillow," he answered.

"What are you doing now?" I asked.

"We're just bringing a meal, some leftovers from supper, down to Louidor."

"I could go instead . . . with Philippe," I suggested.

"That would be very helpful."

He turned to Philippe, who was carrying the meal. "*Soyez attentif au danger*," he said.

"What danger do you think there could be within thirty feet of the gate?" I asked.

"I thought you didn't understand French," Pastor Dave said.

"I don't speak it, but I do understand a word or two. I'll stay out of trouble."

He bowed from the waist. "Then try to get to sleep, okay?"

"I'll try, but there are no guarantees."

Pastor Dave said something else to Philippe in quick, quiet French that I didn't understand and then walked away.

"Come," Philippe said.

I followed him to the gate. He handed me the plate of food. He then took out a key and undid the lock holding the chain in place and the gate closed. He pulled the chain free and swung the gate open and we stepped out of the compound. It was dark, but there was enough light to see, and it wasn't as though we were going far.

Within a few steps I could hear Louidor . . . well, at least I could hear his radio playing. Then I could see a few thin lines of light escaping out of his little home, his shack, his packing case.

Philippe knocked on the top of the box and the music was turned down a notch. The front of the crate opened and Louidor popped his head out.

"Hey, *mon ami*!" Louidor called out.

The two shook hands and engaged in excited conversation, speaking so quickly that it defied my limited French and I couldn't pick out any of the words.

Philippe grabbed me by the arm. "He has invited us in."

"In where?"

He pointed at the little crate.

"You're joking, right?"

He wasn't. Philippe bent down and crawled into the little crate. I didn't want to go in with him, but I didn't want to stand out there alone. I got down low enough to peer into the box. It was like a little treehouse without the tree, about the size of a kid's play fort. There was a little propane lantern hanging from the ceiling that lit the entire crate brightly. There were magazine pictures plastering the walls inside— bright, colourful pictures of smiling faces. Louidor and

Philippe sat on the floor, which appeared to be one gigantic mattress. There were half a dozen neatly folded blankets, and the radio sat on the only piece of furniture, a little table in the corner. Louidor was already eating the meal Philippe had brought for him.

Between bites he and Philippe continued to talk. Again, I couldn't pick out more than an occasional word. Philippe gestured for me to come in. Reluctantly I dropped to my knees and climbed in.

"*Fermez la porte*," Louidor said.

I was so shocked. I actually understood what he'd said. He wanted me to close the door. Great, I understood, but I really didn't want to do it. I had no desire to be shut into the same tiny space with a crazy guy and a kid who might be carrying a weapon.

"He wants you to close it," Philippe said, not realizing that I already understood.

"Yeah, sure," I said. It was better that he thought I couldn't understand than think I didn't want to be in there with them. Hesitantly I pulled the door closed. It sealed up very snugly.

"This is very . . . very nice," I said, gesturing around the room.

Louidor's smile broadened. "*Merci*."

"It is very cozy."

"Yes, yes . . . it is cozy. It is my home. It is . . . it is . . . enough for me."

It certainly wasn't much, but I guess it was better than the alternatives. I'd seen people like him in Toronto, living on the street or in cardboard boxes. This was certainly better than that.

"I build with my own . . . my own . . . " He held up his hands.

"Your own hands. You built it yourself," I said.

"Yes, by myself. Maybe someday I add a little bit more."

"That would be nice," I agreed. Maybe he'd put in a guest room or a pool or a basement . . . or a bathroom. Where did he go to the washroom? I really didn't want to ask and I certainly didn't want to know.

Suddenly Louidor got a serious look and he was staring at me. I had to fight not to look away from his stare. Slowly, on his hands and knees, he came forward, toward me, his eyes still locked onto mine. Now the urge I had to fight was to jump up and run out of the box. Then again, I felt almost frozen in place.

He didn't stop coming until his face was directly in front of mine, our noses no more than a few inches apart. I felt a rush of fear, but neither fight nor flight came to me. I stayed stone still.

"I see it," Louidor said softly. "In your eyes."

He was so close that he couldn't help but look into my eyes, and I into his. His eyes weren't what I'd expected. They were soft and gentle and . . . and not crazy.

"You have been 'urt," he said. "Badly . . . very badly."

I was more than a little stunned by his words.

"You are a little, *un peu*, better, but still . . . you miss her very much, and she misses you too," he said.

I felt a shiver go down my spine. "Who . . . who misses me?" I gasped, my voice so quiet I could barely hear my words.

"Your mother . . . she misses you and your *soeur* and your *papa*."

I felt as if I couldn't even gather in my breath to answer him, even if I'd known what to say.

"She is 'appy and wants you to be not so sad."

"I have . . . I have to go," I stammered. I broke off eye contact and quickly, almost desperately, scrambled out of the little box.

Awkwardly I got to my feet, practically falling over, regaining my balance and stumbling toward the gate.

"Josh! Wait!" Philippe called out.

I didn't want to wait. I didn't even want to turn, but I knew the gate was locked and he had the key. I wasn't getting inside without him. My whole body felt weak and my legs became rubbery. I leaned against the gate, using it to prop me up.

Philippe pulled out the key and unlocked it, removing the chain so the gate swung open.

"Was he right?" Philippe asked. "Your *mère* . . . she is . . . she is gone?"

"Pastor Dave must have told him about her," I snapped. That wasn't fair. He had no right to talk about my family to some crazy guy living in a box!

Philippe shook his head. "Some people think he can see things that other people cannot see because he has special powers."

"He doesn't have any special powers, he's just crazy!"

"He could be both," Philippe said. "Maybe it is those things he sees and hears that make him act crazy."

We stepped through the gate, and Philippe looped the chain through the bars of the gate and then put the lock through the links to secure it. We were now inside, behind a locked gate, surrounded by a high wall topped with barbed wire. We were safe from whatever was out there in the darkness. Was there anything out there to fear?

"What would happen if you left the gate unlocked?" I asked.

He shrugged. "Maybe nothing. Maybe something. Do you want to find out?"

"No, of course not!"

He chuckled. "A little joke . . . funny, yes?"

"Funny, no."

I looked back out through the bars of the gate. I couldn't see anything except the vague, darkened outlines of little houses, really little huts, down the road, and the only sound was from Louidor's radio. It sounded as though he'd turned it up. Did that mean the voices in his head had suddenly gotten louder, or just that he liked that song?

"Your mother . . . you knew her?" Philippe asked.

"Of course I . . . " I stopped myself. I realized that I wasn't the only one whose mother had died. "It was only six months ago."

He nodded his head. "My mother was . . . was . . . I did not know her."

"I'm sorry," I said.

He shrugged. "Maybe it is easier to not know."

"Neither way is easier."

"Time for bed," Philippe said.

"Definitely. Good night, Philippe. See you tomorrow."

"Yes, tomorrow."

I quietly opened the door to the dormitory and silently, slowly, moved through the darkness and slumped down on the bed. I was now feeling very tired, so tired that my body was almost hurting. But while my body was tired, my mind was racing.

I couldn't stop thinking about Louidor and what he'd said. Stupid, stupid, stupid. But what did it matter what a crazy person thought or said? He didn't have any special powers. Pastor Dave must have told him, or he'd just made a wild guess. Or maybe he'd just looked into my eyes. I knew I saw the hurt there when I looked in the mirror. I closed my eyes so the hurt would stay inside.

CHAPTER THIRTEEN

"Time to get up, sleepyhead."

"Just a few more minutes, okay, Dad?" I mumbled. I went to pull the covers over my head to block out the light when I suddenly realized that I wasn't in my bed . . . that I wasn't even in my *country*.

My eyes popped open and I sat bolt upright. My father was sitting at the end of my bed with a bowl in his hand. Quickly I scanned the room. All the other beds were empty. Everybody else was already gone.

"What time is it?"

"It's still early. It's almost eight o'clock."

"But everybody else . . . they're up and—"

"And eating breakfast in the dining hall. They got up quietly so that they wouldn't wake you. Wasn't that nice of them?"

"Yeah, nice, really nice. I'd better get dressed and eat and—"

He gestured to the bowl. "Breakfast in bed. Still hot."

"Thanks."

I stretched, threw off the covers, and spun around so I was sitting on the edge. Then I took the bowl and the spoon he offered.

"I did a bed check at ten and all the kids were sound asleep, snoring in their beds," he said. "Not that that was surprising. We all worked hard yesterday . . . although not hard enough to knock you out. What time did you get to bed?"

"Not that late." I left the answer deliberately vague and he didn't push me for more details.

"And were you able to sleep when you got to bed?" he asked.

"Yeah, I was sleeping very well . . . until *somebody* woke me up," I joked.

"I was tempted to just leave you in peace. I know sleep hasn't come easily to you lately," he said.

I'd had about enough of that subject. "How did you sleep?" I asked.

"Not badly at all. Once they turn the generator off it's pretty quiet here."

"Dead would be another word. No lights, no video games, no TV, no Internet, and even the radio is gone once the generator is turned off . . . why do they turn it off so early?"

"The generator uses gas and gas costs money. Besides, everybody except you was ready to pass out long before that."

"Not everybody. I was talking to Pastor Dave and Philippe last night. Philippe and I even went to deliver something."

"Deliver something . . . out there?" he asked, sounding alarmed.

I wasn't trying to alarm him . . . well, maybe just a little, but he looked more than a little worried.

"It's really not that safe to be out there by yourself," he said.

"I wasn't by myself. I was with Philippe. Besides, we didn't go far. We just brought a meal to a neighbour. Louidor . . . he lives just outside the front gate."

"I guess that's okay."

"Pastor Dave knew about it. He was the one who said I could go."

"Then I'm sure it's fine. I know he wouldn't put any of us in danger. Now, you'd better dig into that breakfast before it gets cold."

I knew what my father would have liked me to do next, to bow my head and say a little prayer before I started my meal. When you're raised in a minister's family you learn that prayer is just a part of your day . . . before meals, at bedtime, obviously at church, and for special *performances* when in public. I knew I didn't have to say a prayer, but I also knew he expected it.

I put my hands together, closed my eyes, bowed my head, tried to put a thoughtful expression on my face, and then ended with an audible "Amen."

"Amen," my father said. "I'll leave you to get dressed. See you out front in a few minutes."

"I'll be there."

I looked down at my breakfast meal. It was still steaming. Rice and beans. I was starting to think that everything in this country had rice or beans in it, or both. I took a big spoonful. It was tasty, which probably said more about how hungry I was than the quality of the food.

I had seriously thought about not saying a prayer, but that would only have made my father unhappy or sad. He didn't need any more unhappiness or sadness. Besides, it wasn't like saying a prayer, or not saying a prayer, was going to make any difference. Did anybody with a double-digit age or a triple-digit IQ really think that God was up there somewhere listening to our prayers? If that was the case, they should have been pretty worried about him reading their thoughts, because I was willing to bet they were a lot less innocent than the words they said out loud or in their prayers. In fact, I figured if God could read people's thoughts he'd be so disappointed he'd never answer any prayers at all.

When my mother got sick my father started to pray even more. Every time I looked over, his head was down, in silent prayer. He did more than that, though. He organized the entire church to pray for her, and then other churches, and finally there were literally thousands of people in a whole prayer chain that spanned the planet, so that twenty-four hours a day there was somebody praying for her health, for her recovery. Thousands of prayers being said silently, and not so silently, sent up into the ether, trying to bend God's will. Quite impressive. Then she died.

There were lots of rationalizations for what happened. The usual stories about God's will, and God having another plan for her. If he had another plan and he wasn't going to listen to us anyway, what was the point in saying prayers about anything? Let him do what he was going to do and stop pretending that we had some control over it.

The strangest thing was that after my mother died, when it was obvious to anyone that all of this prayer stuff hadn't worked, my father kept up his ritual of intense prayer. It was as though he hadn't made the connection. You know, like, wake up—more prayer had not resulted in her life being saved. Maybe it had even *caused* her to die. Maybe God was so impressed that so many people cared for her that he thought he'd just bring her up to meet her . . . I shook my head. Would anybody really believe that? Possibly, maybe, who knew?

I just knew that the definition of insanity is doing the same thing over and over and expecting a different result. Prayer hadn't worked; my father kept praying. I'd almost stopped completely, praying only when I had to in order to keep people happy. After all, it wasn't making God happy— or, for that matter, making him sad—if I didn't pray. Maybe there was a God. Maybe there wasn't. But if he did exist, did an all-knowing, all-powerful God who made the heavens and earth in six days really care what I wanted or desired or requested or needed? Really . . . people needed to get a life, or at least get on with their lives and stop bothering or begging or blaming God for what went wrong.

I scraped the last spoonful of mush from the bowl and

into my mouth. Now I needed something to drink. I climbed out of bed. I was already dressed. I hadn't wanted to risk waking anybody last night so I'd just stayed in my clothing. I grabbed the shoes—again holding them upside down and shaking them first. Nothing came out but some sand, but better safe than sorry, better sand than something that stung. I slipped them on, leaving the laces untied.

I went through the dining room. It was deserted except for two women who were starting to wash the dishes. It was later than I'd thought. I wasn't really in a rush to work, but I wasn't going to let anybody think that I couldn't do my fair share. I hurried out the front door and . . . the orphans were all standing in a straight line, wearing uniforms, all with little matching book bags at their feet. They were arranged in some sort of order, from oldest and biggest to smallest and youngest. It wasn't an exact order, though, because Philippe was in the middle.

Pastor Dave was giving them some sort of speech.

Off to the side stood my father, Michelle, and Iris, and all of the kids from our mission. I sidled over until I stood right beside my father.

"What's happening?" I asked.

"They're just getting a little talk from Dave before they head off to school."

"They're going to school?" I asked. Of course, that was why they were in uniforms.

"It's Monday, so they have to go to school."

Pastor Dave continued to talk. It was, of course, in French, and while I couldn't really pick out many words I could understand the tone. It was some sort of little sermon-like pep talk. He stopped talking and the kids began clapping and cheering. All the kids beside me started clapping as well— as if any of them understood what he was saying. Monkey see, monkey do.

The kids all started moving toward the gate. Philippe looked over, caught my eye, and gave me a little wave. I waved back. My father noticed.

"You two are becoming quite the friends, aren't you?"

"Friends might be a bit too strong a word. For sure, though, we're going to miss him here today. Who's going to supervise the cement mixing?"

"That would be you," Pastor Dave said as he walked up behind us.

"I'm not sure I'm qualified to do that."

"Philippe said you can handle it, and I have complete faith in him, so I have complete faith in you," Pastor Dave said.

"I'd have more faith in him doing it. Couldn't he miss a day at school?" I asked.

"I'm afraid he's already missed *years* at school. Besides, he's needed out there more than he's needed in here," Pastor Dave said.

I wasn't sure what that meant.

"Philippe takes his role as big brother very seriously," Pastor Dave explained. "He walks the kids to and from school every day. If somebody falls down he picks them up and brushes them off. If they're having trouble with their homework he tries to help, and if anybody, and I mean anybody, bothers our kids they have to go *through* Philippe."

That I understood.

"He wouldn't tell you, but he's just been named the head boy at his school."

I shook my head. "I don't know what that means."

"He is a student but he's given extra responsibilities, almost like a teacher in training, to assist the teachers, to monitor proper behaviour, and to be a role model for the other students."

"I guess being a role model doesn't involve robbing ministers," I joked.

"No, but they all know about his past. He's not proud of it, but he wants them to know the road he's walked so they won't walk down the same path. Now, enough talk, the rest of us should get down to work."

Pastor Dave walked away. My father turned to our assembled group.

"Is everybody ready to work?" my father asked our kids.

There was grumbled agreement from some and enthusiastic shouts from others. I was somewhere in the middle.

"I'm sorry," he said, holding a hand to his ear. "I can't hear you all. Are you ready to work?" he yelled.

This time everybody cheered and clapped and screamed out a big "Yes!"

My father climbed up on a little hill of sand so that he stood above the group. Okay, I knew what he was doing. Not that I was pleased or impressed, but at least he was predictable. This was going to be his pulpit to do for us what Pastor Dave had done for his kids. This was going to be his little Sermon on the Mount . . . of sand.

I didn't need a pep talk and I certainly didn't need a sermon. I walked off to get my shovel and my gloves. Forget about talking about work . . . what was that quote? . . . *Work while you pray.* Too many people spent too much time praying and not enough time working. I'd have liked to see cement that could be mixed by a few words or Bible verses. Now that would be a miracle that even I could believe in.

I slumped down, resting my back against the rough wall, capturing a little slice of shade cast by the building. I took off my gloves and opened and closed my fingers, trying to work out the kinks. My knuckles felt swollen . . . they looked swollen. I had worked as hard as I could all day. Thank goodness they hadn't left me by myself. I'd worked along with a local man, Emmanuel, mixing the cement and wheeling it over to the building. He had just taken another load over and I was taking a short break before he returned.

Emmanuel stood less than five feet tall and couldn't have weighed more than a hundred and ten pounds. He was paper-thin and looked as if a strong wind could blow him away. Instead, he blew me away. He worked with more intensity than any human being I'd ever worked with . . . heck, any human being I'd ever met. I remembered reading something about how an ant could lift ten times its own body weight. I didn't think Emmanuel was much behind that.

He brought over the bags of cement, on his back, two at a time, all bowed over, looking as if he was going to be snapped in two or crushed under the weight—which was more than *his* weight—but he never wavered, never stopped. He'd drop the bags down, slit them open, dump them, and then start to mix. When the concrete was all mixed, he was ready to wheel it over to be applied as the glue holding the blocks in place.

And those blocks were rising up. We'd almost reached the final height. When I say "we," it really wasn't us but the local people who had been hired to do the building. We were working, in most cases harder than we'd ever worked before, but this building was going to go up with or without us. For me, I just wanted to let the locals know that we weren't a bunch of spoiled kids from North America playing at building. I was trying to work my hardest.

A couple of times I felt tired . . . actually, a couple of times I felt as though I was going to keel over. The hard work, the hot sun, the heat, the lack of sleep all combined to make me feel a little bit queasy. I wanted to stop. Actually, I wanted to sit down or lie down or take a little nap in the shade. But each time I saw how hard they all worked—how hard Emmanuel worked—and I kept going.

It wasn't just that I didn't want to look like a wimp. There was more. Watching Emmanuel work was strangely inspiring. All the time he had a smile on his face, and he was singing or humming or whistling to himself. He really did whistle while he worked. He was also unfailingly friendly with everybody. It was hard not to try, not to want to give your all, around a guy like that.

Naomi came walking toward me. She tripped over a rock and almost fell forward on her face before recovering. She looked annoyed, then giggled to herself.

"Mind if I join you?" she asked.

"It looks like you'd better sit down before you fall down."

"Rock . . . didn't see it," she said. "Tired . . . I'm really tired."

"Me too. You feeling better today?"

"I feel fine, good, great," she replied.

There was something about how she was talking. She was slurring her words a bit. I looked over at her questioningly. She had a silly grin on her face and her eyes were a bit glazed. If I didn't know better I would have sworn that she was drunk. That was ridiculous.

"Are you sure you're feeling okay?" I asked.

"What?" she asked.

"How . . . are you . . . *feeling?*"

"Feeling . . . I feel fine," Naomi said slowly, hesitantly.

"You're shaking," I said.

"I am?"

"Yes, you are." It was noticeable—her hands were quivering. "Are you cold?" I asked, although that was impossible in this heat.

"Not cold . . . I'm sweating . . . a lot," she said. "But my fingers, they're . . . they're tingling." She held her hands up and rubbed her fingers together.

She tumbled over, falling right on top of me!

"Are you all right?" I asked as I untangled her from me and set her down on the ground.

"Just lost my balance. I'll go and get—"

"You're not going anywhere. Sit, stay!" I ordered, and instantly felt bad. She wasn't a dog. "I mean, please just sit . . . I'm a little worried. Let me go and get Pastor Dave."

CHAPTER FOURTEEN

"Drink this down," Pastor Dave ordered as he handed her a glass.

She hesitated.

"It's just water with lots of sugar. You need to drink it all to get your sugar levels up."

She nodded and then tipped the glass and drank until it was all gone, the last little bit of liquid dribbling down her chin. This was the second glass of sugary water she'd been given.

"How long before she's better?" my father asked Pastor Dave.

Naomi answered, "Soon. Fast. No more than a few minutes. I'm already feeling better." She paused. "It just came on so fast that I didn't even notice my blood sugar levels were off."

"I guess the important thing is that you're feeling better."

"I am . . . really. I'm just so sorry that I've caused everybody so much trouble."

"It's no trouble," Pastor Dave said.

"And it's not like I didn't test my blood this morning or take my shot, the way I was supposed to. I did, believe me."

"We believe you," my father said reassuringly. He placed a hand on her shoulder. He was very good at reassuring people. I guess that was part of the job.

"It's just that this doesn't usually happen."

"It's probably all the hard work, and the heat, and everything being different," my father said. "And how has your sleep been?"

"My sleep's been a little off, but I've been taking my insulin exactly the way I'm supposed to take it. I'm usually very good at regulating myself. I'm so sorry about worrying everybody."

"You don't have to worry about worrying us," my father said. "We're just lucky that Joshua noticed."

Everybody turned to me, and I felt embarrassed.

"I didn't do anything. I just saw she was a little different . . . and then she fell over . . . would have been hard not to notice."

"I'm glad you were there," Naomi said. She smiled at me, and her eyes seemed to smile as well. Her eyes were different than they'd been twenty minutes ago—bright instead of sort of hazy.

"It's been a long time since I've had any problems with my blood sugar," she said. "Yesterday the levels were too high, and now they're too low. Exactly how low?" she asked.

"Very, very, low. You were below one," Pastor Dave said.

"That's just . . . just terrible . . ."

I didn't understand any of what they were talking about. I'd just seen them—with her offering some assistance—prick her finger and then test the blood, but I really didn't know anything more.

"Can you explain it to me, what all of this means?" I asked.

"With a non-diabetic, the body self-regulates, releasing insulin to keep the blood sugar levels in a normal range between four and six," Pastor Dave explained. "And she was much lower. It means, technically, she was hypoglycemic—that she had too little sugar in her blood."

"And that's bad?"

"It's as bad as when I had too much sugar in my system before," Naomi said. "That's called *hyper*glycemic. Yesterday I was at almost twenty-five."

"Being at either extreme is dangerous," Pastor Dave explained.

"How dangerous?"

"As in people *die*," Naomi said. "Especially with low blood sugar levels. If they fall below a certain point a person can lose consciousness. If nobody notices, they can go into a coma and die."

"But people would notice if you were unconscious," I said.

"Not in the middle of the night," Pastor Dave said. "Even if somebody was checking on her, they'd probably just assume she was sleeping."

"We'll have somebody wake you up tonight, just to make sure," my father said.

"I'm fine now," Naomi said.

Again, she was both looking and sounding like she was okay.

"I understand what happened yesterday," she said. "I guess I wasn't careful enough. I didn't test my blood but just assumed everything would be normal. But today I was *really* careful. That's what worries me a bit. I did my blood levels this morning. I took my insulin exactly the way I was supposed to. I was eating right." She paused. "I don't know what I did wrong."

"Maybe you didn't do anything wrong," Pastor Dave said.

"I must have done something," Naomi said.

"Maybe you took a shot but it wasn't what you thought it was. Have you been using the insulin you brought down or the insulin that we're providing?"

"I only brought down enough for the first two days, so I used it all up. I started using your insulin this morning," she said.

"I should have known," he said, shaking his head. "Come with me and we'll have a look."

Naomi got to her feet. She still seemed a little wobbly.

"Here, let me help you," I said as I offered her my hand.

She hesitated for a split second and. I felt awkward holding my hand out like that, but she took it.

"Thanks."

Now, hand in hand, I felt awkward for another reason.

Pastor Dave led, my father followed, and we trailed behind them as we left the dining hall and went into the little room that served as the infirmary. The shelves were basically empty except for a few bottles of pills, some syringes, and some gauze and bandages.

Pastor Dave picked up a small bottle from one of the shelves. "This is the insulin you've been using, right?"

"Yes, that's the bottle you gave me," she said. She sounded guilty, as though she'd done something wrong.

He looked closely at the bottle, reading the label. "The expiry date says April 2010, so it *should* still be good for the next few months."

"Then it can't be the insulin," my father said.

"It could be," Pastor Dave said. "This is the Third World. There's no telling how this insulin was stored before it came to us."

"I don't understand," my father said.

"Insulin has to be stored and transported in a certain way or it could be damaged."

"He's right," Naomi said. "If it freezes it goes bad."

"Not much of a worry down here," I said, jokingly.

"Not down here, but on the way down here," he said. "If it was transported in the cargo hold of a plane it gets close to freezing. But it's also sensitive to light and heat, both of which we have here."

"But if it wasn't any good, then why did taking the shot this morning get Naomi's blood sugar levels to fall so low?" I asked. "If it wasn't working, wouldn't they be too high?"

The two men looked at each other and then at me.

"That's a good point," Pastor Dave said. "But wrong could be wrong in different ways. It's hard to keep your blood sugar levels where they should be if you can't trust the grade of the insulin."

"Do you have any more insulin that she can use?" my father asked.

Pastor Dave shook his head. "That is our only bottle."

"We have to get some more," my father said. "That is possible, right?"

"Yes, of course, but only in Port-au-Prince."

"You don't have to do that!" Naomi protested. "I'll just use what you have and be more careful around food and exercise, and I'll test more often and just be more aware. I don't want to put you to that much trouble."

"I appreciate the offer," Pastor Dave said, "but we can't have you using tainted insulin. Besides, it's not much trouble."

"But it's so far," she said.

"Not that far, and I have to go to Port-au-Prince tomorrow anyway."

"And I'm going with him," my father added.

That was the first I'd heard of this. I looked at my father.

"It's to meet with people from the church office to get final approval on some additional funding for Pastor Dave and the orphanage."

"I really appreciate you being there with me to help argue my case. It's different having somebody other than me telling them that we're doing a good job here."

"But what about Sarah?" I asked. "Is she going with you?"

"I thought she'd stay here . . . if that's okay with you," my father said.

"It's not whether it's okay with me or not. It's how *she* feels. Is she okay with that?"

He looked sheepish. "I haven't told her yet."

"Don't you think you'd better?" I scolded him.

"There was no point in telling her too far in advance because she'd just worry."

He did have a point, but that still didn't make it right. "How about if we let her decide," I suggested.

My father looked uncertain. "It's a long drive, and she'd be bored just sitting there watching a bunch of people sit around and talk."

"It's not that long a drive, and she could bring a book. It should be her choice."

My father nodded in agreement. "I guess you're right." He paused. "I'm just beginning to think that we're doing her no favours by not pushing her to become a little more independent."

"I agree, but this isn't the time or the place for that. If she needs to be with you then she should be with you."

"I guess you're right. I'll go and tell her right now. Do you want to come along?"

I knew this wasn't really a question. I turned to Naomi. "You take it easy, okay?"

"Don't worry. I'm fine, really, there's nothing to worry about."

"Yeah, I guess that's why we're standing in the infirmary

talking about your insulin and blood sugar, because you're *just* fine."

"I'm fine *now*," she said. "But thanks for caring . . . I do appreciate that."

I felt myself start to blush. I turned away and followed after my father, catching him quickly.

"Don't you think that maybe somebody should stay up here to keep an eye on Naomi?" I asked.

"We'll be back just after nightfall," he said. "We won't be long. Besides, there's the matron and the other women, and of course Michelle and Iris will stay here to watch over things."

"I'm sure Iris will be thrilled with that," I said, before I could stop myself.

My father gave me a questioning look. "Why wouldn't Iris be happy?"

We both knew the answer to that question, but neither of us had ever verbalized it.

"She's just here as part of a mission trip, a commitment to God," he said. "You know that, right?"

I knew lots of things, some of which I wasn't going to talk about.

"I'm just not sure why you don't like her," he said.

"I didn't say I didn't like her," I protested.

"You didn't need to say anything. You don't like her, do you?"

Now I was caught. I didn't want to say yes, but I couldn't really say no. "I don't really know her," I answered. A good dishonestly truthful comment.

"Then staying here with you will be a good thing, because it might offer an opportunity for you and Iris to get to know each other better."

"And why exactly would I want to do that?" I questioned.

"It's just that if you got to know her I think you'd really learn to like her."

"I know lots of people who I don't like, so that's no guarantee," I argued. "Maybe I'd like her even less once I got to know her."

My father stopped and placed a hand on my shoulder. "You have to know that she's just a friend, a member of our new congregation."

"*Your* new congregation," I said.

"The church belongs to all its members. She's here as part of the mission trip, as a way to serve God."

Was he so dense that he didn't see what was happening, or did he just figure that I was so dense that I couldn't see?

"And how many other mission trips has she been on in her efforts to *serve* God?" I asked.

He didn't answer right away. Either he was thinking through my answer, totalling up the trips in his head, or he didn't want to give the answer.

"Well, I believe this is her first trip."

Obviously it was the second part of that equation.

"And she wasn't originally scheduled to be on this trip at all, was she?"

"She volunteered later on. I guess we all get the calling at different times," he said, defending her.

"So you think it's just coincidence, that she's just interested in God's good grace and not yours?" I snapped. I was tired of this game.

"Please . . . keep your voice down," he said.

"Sure, I'll keep my voice down. I'm not stupid, though. I've seen the way she acts around you, and also the way you act around her."

He now looked embarrassed. "I know she likes me," he said quietly. "And I have thought about it. I'll admit that. But you have to know that she isn't trying to take your mother's place."

"That's good, because nobody *could* take her place . . . *nobody* . . . and at least one of us knows that."

"That's not fair," he said

"I stopped believing in fair a while ago."

I turned and walked away.

CHAPTER FIFTEEN

I dumped the basin of water over my head to rinse out the last of the soap and hopefully most of the sand and concrete dust. This wasn't exactly my idea of a shower, but it was the closest I was going to get until we got back home again in seven days—seven sleeps. Now I sounded like a seven-year-old. It would be great to be home and . . . but it wasn't my home I was going back to. That place belonged to somebody else now. But at least I'd be going back to a place that had running water and electricity, and where I had my own bedroom. My sleep was too uncertain not to be disturbed by the sounds of the other people in the room. A couple of the kids—particularly a guy named Ryan—snored.

It had been another hard day's work. We'd finished up the blocks, installed the windows, and started to get the crossbeams up for the roof. Three days of work had built almost an entire building. The men had said that within a week they'd be finished, have moved in the beds and furniture, and kids would be sleeping there. Pretty amazing to think that I'd played even a small part in making this all happen! Prior to this the only thing I'd ever built was a birdhouse in shop class in grade eight.

I heard giggling and turned around in time to see three little faces disappearing behind a corner of the curtain. The washing area was outdoors, and what constituted privacy was dictated by the limited protection of those ragged and worn pieces of plastic sheeting. I wasn't used to having an audience—even a secret audience—while I bathed. I was just glad I'd decided against a full shower and instead had only washed my hair and the upper part of my body.

From what I could tell, we white kids seemed to gather a crowd of watchers, whether it was the kids at the orphanage or other kids and adults standing at the gate, peering in through the bars. A couple of times I'd been standing there and felt somebody touch my arm, and there'd be a little kid, just making contact, feeling my skin as if he was seeing if it was real. Pastor Dave had said that while there were lots of white people down in Port-au-Prince we were still a bit of a rarity up here in the country.

I was finding out that lots of things were rarities up here. Things like electricity, toilets that weren't just a hole in the ground, roads that were paved, stores, education, TVs. . . actually, most of those things weren't rarities, they simply didn't exist.

I wondered how my father and Pastor Dave had done in town. And Sarah—I was right about Sarah, she had insisted on going along with them. I hoped my father had been able to help convince the church to give more money to this orphanage. It was better to spend it here than on a newer and fancier church back home. Here it really meant something.

As I left the shower area I slipped my watch out of my pocket and looked at the time before I slipped it on my wrist. It was four twenty-three. It was still going to be hours before they got back. I'd feel better when they got home. I didn't like to admit it, but I really did understand how insecure Sarah felt, because I felt some of that myself. Maybe being here with all these orphans made me think more than I would have liked to about how we were only one parent away from being orphans ourselves. That thought had come to me often over the past months. One parent away.

Of course we'd still have my Uncle Jack and Aunt Cora—my mother's sister and her husband—and my father's brother, George. And even if we didn't have any of them, we still wouldn't be facing the same problems as the kids here. Kids back home weren't abandoned to live on the streets. Kids back home didn't starve to death or live in shacks or—

"You worked very hard today!"

I turned to find Iris smiling at me. It was amazing how her smiling made me feel even less friendly toward her.

"We all worked hard today."

What I didn't mention was that she seemed to be working hard to try to get on my good side. I wondered if my father had said something to her about getting to know me better. I wasn't going to let that happen. I was keeping my answers short and my interaction polite. Nobody could accuse me of being unfriendly—just not too friendly.

"It would be nice if they were back before it got dark," she said.

"They said they'd be much later than that," I reported, without saying I wished the same thing. No point in wishing—or praying—if it wasn't going to happen. "They're not going to be back for hours, and the sun will be down by five-thirty," I said. "It'll be dark by six."

"It does get really dark up here. Thank goodness for the generator. I just wish we had a TV. I miss TV . . . do you?"

An obvious attempt to start a conversation. I shrugged, providing no obvious entry point.

"Do you have a favourite show?"

She was persistent, but I was stubborn. "Nope," I answered.

She looked disappointed, which made me feel a little bit guilty. I was tempted to throw her a few words as a sort of peace offering, but not tempted enough to actually do it.

"I missed not having your sister around today. She's such a little sweetie."

I wasn't quite sure how I was supposed to respond to that, but I had been watching what she'd been doing. She'd been trying to get close to my sister in order to get closer to my father. That was her entry point. Poor little girl who needed a mother, and she could be that mother.

"You don't have any kids, do you?" I asked.

She shook her head. "I was never blessed, although I guess it was for the best since my marriage didn't last."

"You were married before?" I asked.

"For almost three years. I've been divorced for five years."

"Some people think that divorce is wrong," I said. "You know, until death do us part, let no man put asunder what God has joined, and all that."

She looked shocked, and genuinely hurt and distressed. I felt instantly guilty.

"Not that *I* believe that," I said. "I think a good divorce is a lot better than a bad marriage."

Her expression lifted. "Thank you for saying that . . . for understanding."

"No problem. I'd better put on a clean shirt before dinner," I said. "So . . . I have to excuse myself."

"Of course. Maybe we can sit together at dinner," she suggested.

"Maybe," I said as I turned away. *Or maybe not.*

I felt bad. I knew she wasn't trying to do anything wrong, and I guess I could have tried to be friendlier. Ironically, it would have been my mother who would have been very friendly to Iris. She was friendly with everybody. She went out of her way to talk, and she just seemed to remember every little detail about everybody's life, and she always asked questions. And it wasn't just that she was acting nice because she had to since she was the minister's wife. She really did want to know about people, she really did care. She would have been friends with Iris. But that didn't mean that I had to be.

It wasn't like I was treating Iris *that* badly. Really, I wasn't treating her any differently from the way I treated everybody else. I didn't want to get to know her any more than I wanted to get to know anybody else in the new congregation, or, for that matter, anybody who was on this trip or living at this orphanage. Really, what was the point in getting to know any of these kids when we'd be gone in seven days? And the people back home, well, people did just disappear, no matter how hard you prayed that they wouldn't.

Other than Pastor Dave and Philippe and Louidor, I hadn't had any real conversation with anybody. I chuckled to myself. Other than Pastor Dave, the two people I'd talked to were the street kid who'd pulled a knife on the pastor and the crazy man who lived outside the gate of the orphanage who people thought had special powers because he heard voices in his head.

By the time I got to the dormitory it was empty. Everybody else had headed into the dining hall. I grabbed a clean shirt out of my knapsack and pulled it over my head. I was hungry—so hungry, in fact, that even rice and beans would taste good.

I hurried over to the dining hall and then hesitated at the door. They all had their heads down, saying grace. Being late obviously had a few advantages. I looked around and my eyes locked on Philippe. Naomi was sitting beside him. Her head was down in prayer. His, of course, wasn't. He gave me a slight smile—really a smirk—and then we exchanged a silent nod. We were co-conspirators sharing a moment that nobody else knew about. Well, nobody but God, assuming he was all-seeing. Then again, if he was all-seeing he'd have a lot more interesting and important things to look at than the two of us not closing our eyes.

I entered the room and started over to the counter to get food and—

"Josh!" Naomi called out.

I turned. She was standing, holding a bowl of food in one hand and gesturing me over with the other.

"I got you some food already," she called out.

I caught sight of Iris out of the corner of my eye. *Sorry, won't be sharing a seat with you tonight . . . or any night.*

I sat down between Naomi and Philippe. "Thanks."

"It's the least I could do after you babysat me all day," Naomi said.

"I wasn't babysitting. Just keeping an eye on you."

"I was careful. Only my fingers are sore," she said, holding up her hands. "I tested myself five times today."

"And?"

"The sugars went up and then down. I ate extra to get them higher and then they went too high so I took a shot and it didn't have any effect so I took another, smaller shot and it went too low. But right now . . . " she rapped her knuckles on the table, "knock on wood, I'm all fine right now."

"Don't worry, they'll be back tonight with the new insulin."

"That will be good," she said.

I'd be happy when they got back too, but obviously for other reasons.

"It's okay for them to be travelling at night, right?" I asked Philippe.

"Night is not as good as day, but it is . . . it is . . . not so bad . . . good to leave Port-au-Prince before dark."

I tried to think through the timeline of the drive. It was about a three-hour drive and they were going to be here around nine-thirty, so they'd be leaving Port-au-Prince around six-thirty. But if they were driving in the dark the ride would be longer, maybe a lot longer. It wasn't like they had street lights to show them the road, or much of a road to drive on, for that matter. They might be much, much later than nine-thirty.

"The building, it is almost *fini*," Philippe said.

"That's because we were working hard all day while you were sitting around in school," I joked.

"I am sitting, but it is still very much work . . . for me."

I thought about what it would be like to be fifteen and in grade six. I guess it would have been hard, especially after having been out of school so long. There were so many things like that that we just took for granted. School, health care, a place to live . . . food.

All around us kids were bringing their plates over to the kitchen area and starting to head outside. I knew what they were rushing to do—spend some time playing games before the sun went down. There was still almost an hour of light before it got completely dark. After that they'd come back into the dining hall to work on their homework, the generator powering the few fluorescent light bulbs from the ceiling that dimly lit the room.

I didn't have any schoolwork to do but I'd come in and listen to the radio. It wasn't like there was much else to do after dark. It was hard to believe that I'd be remotely interested in hearing bad music punctuated by commentary from French-speaking DJs, but I guess I was going through multimedia withdrawal, and it was the closest thing I could get to MTV, or a stereo, or a telephone, or the Internet. Thank goodness I still had some power left in my iPod, but I was trying to save that for bedtime. Clipping on those headphones and listening to my music made it easier to get to sleep.

In the meantime it *would* be fun to go out and kick around a soccer ball. It was even more fun just watching the kids skipping and playing together. You couldn't help but smile when you watched them.

It was almost impossible to believe how happy these kids were. They had basically nothing, or at least nothing but the basics. And I didn't even want to *know* about all the terrible circumstances that had brought them to live here. But they were still, somehow, against all odds, happy. They smiled and laughed, and giggled and skipped and sang.

I felt a little sad that Sarah wouldn't be here for that this evening. When she was playing with these kids I saw something in her that I hadn't seen in a long time. It was like being here had brought back an innocence, something from before, that allowed her to smile and laugh without thinking or worrying. And her being that way brought something back to me as well.

I shovelled in the last few spoonfuls of rice, scraping the bottom of the bowl. I was still a bit hungry but I didn't feel right asking for extra. It was like I was taking food away from orphans.

"Shall we go out and play with the kids?" I asked.

"Are you asking me out on a date?" Naomi joked.

"A *play* date. Do you want to come and be our chaperone?" I asked Philippe.

He looked confused.

"Come outside and we'll kick around a soccer ball."

"Yes, yes, football."

We all got up and brought over our dishes, handing them to the two women behind the counter in the kitchen. The room was emptying out quickly. Iris and Michelle sat in the corner, finishing up a cup of coffee. Iris gave me a smile and a little wave—I waved back. It would have been rude if I hadn't. I wasn't going for rude or unfriendly, just indifferent.

The sun was low on the horizon but still bright and warm. All around the courtyard kids were in little groups, skipping or throwing or kicking a ball or playing tag. A couple of boys were wrestling, and over by the wall, sitting in the shade it cast, three little girls were playing dolls. That's where Sarah would have been, those were the three that had become her friends.

It was all so peaceful, so gentle, so playful, that I wasn't sure if I wanted to join in or just sit and watch and—there was a rumbling sound, and I suddenly felt uneasy on my feet, like I was going to fall or—

"It's an earthquake!" Naomi screamed.

CHAPTER SIXTEEN

Earthquake . . . how stupid was it for her to even think that . . . the rumbling became louder and the ground began to shake! All around me kids stopped doing what they were doing, as if they were frozen in place. Fear and confusion replaced the cheerfulness and smiles; silence overwhelmed and swallowed up any laughter or cries of joy.

Then, the whole ground seemed to heave upward, and as if in slow motion part of the wall shifted inward. Heavy cinder blocks came tumbling down. The three little girls, still holding their dolls, scrambled away, miraculously getting clear of the falling blocks, but they became engulfed in the cloud of dust and dirt that exploded outward.

I stumbled a few steps forward toward them, almost falling over, and then, out of the corner of my eye, I caught sight of the building—the dining hall—collapsing! Bricks and blocks fell inward and outward and the entire roof sagged and then collapsed on top of the debris. I could hear wood splintering and the blocks smashing against each other and onto the ground, releasing a gigantic puff of wind and dust so strong it blew me right off my feet, so that I landed in a heap in the dirt.

Instinctively my mind raced, looking for an escape, someplace to run or crawl or hide or—Naomi was on the ground beside me, caught up in the same cloud of dust, knocked off her feet as well. I reached over and grabbed her by the shirt and dragged her to her feet as I staggered up, only to be knocked over again, dragging her back down with me, as the ground continued to shake violently.

"Stay down!" I yelled, as if it had been her idea to get up in the first place. I held onto her, the only solid thing within my grasp, and clung to her for dear life.

All around me I could hear the sounds of splintering wood, crashing blocks, and screams—voices, crying out in terror. I didn't have any voice to add—I was too scared, too confused to even try to form words. I just lay there, desperately trying to steady myself, unable to believe what was happening and . . . had it stopped?

I pressed my body against the ground, spreading myself out as if I were going to steady the earth. There was swirling dust, and my heart was pounding, and my head felt as though it was spinning, and I was shaking . . . but was the earth moving?

"Has it stopped?" Naomi asked, voicing my question.

"I think so . . . I think so."

I released her hand and used both my hands to push myself to my feet, taking a wide stance as if I were on a ship that might shift with the waves. My legs were trembling so badly, my knees practically knocking together, that it was hard to tell. But there was no sound, no rumbling. It felt steady.

I took her hand again and helped her up.

"That was . . . that was . . . unbelievable," she said.

The haze of dust that hung in the air made it all seem like a dream, but the way the dust stung my eyes was very real. The cloud started to dissipate, settling back down to the ground, and was being blown away by the winds. All around us were little groups of kids, sitting or standing, hugging or holding hands or just huddled together in little clusters like animals seeking protection or shelter. The air was thick and silent—and then the tears started. Kids began crying, sobbing, calling out for somebody or something. And as if a spell had been broken by the voices, everybody seemed to start moving all at once, jumping up and down, or throwing themselves to the ground, or running back and forth, around and around in circles, racing but not going anywhere.

Philippe jumped to his feet. He climbed up onto an overturned wheelbarrow so he was head and shoulders above everybody. Was he trying to see or—? He started yelling, but he wasn't just screaming, he was giving orders. His voice was loud, but calm, in control.

All around us kids stopped screaming, stopped whatever

they were doing and came toward him until he was in the centre of a circle of children. And then I realized what he was doing. He was gathering everybody together to see if they were all right. He was counting, calling out names, checking on them.

Somebody had to do the same for the mission kids. That's what my father would have done—but instead it was going to be up to me.

"Everybody!" I called out. "All of the mission kids! Come here . . . now!"

I looked around. A couple came toward me while a few of the others just stood there, staring at me, or even ignoring me completely, blank expressions on their faces.

"Hey, look at me!" I screamed, my voice cutting through the remaining haze in the air and shocking some of them back to reality.

A couple more stumbled forward toward me while others still didn't react.

"Ryan . . . Amy!" Naomi called, and they started at the mention of their names. "Come here!"

I did a quick count in my head. There were fifteen kids. I counted thirteen white faces, plus me, that made fourteen. And Sarah . . . but of course she wasn't here. What about Sarah, and my father? Where were they when the quake hit? Were they all right, or—?

"Everybody is here," Naomi said. "We're all here. Thank goodness we all got out of the dining hall in time!"

I turned to the collapsed building and then looked around for Iris and Michelle. I couldn't see them. They'd been in the building when I walked out. Anxiously I scanned the grounds, hoping that they'd gotten out and I just couldn't see them, but no, they were nowhere to be seen . . . nowhere.

Oh, my goodness . . . they were still in the building . . . underneath the bricks and blocks and beams.

I staggered forward, almost toppling over, terrified that the earth was shifting again underneath my feet before I realized that it was my legs that were wobbly and weak. I stopped at the dining room entrance. The wooden door was shattered and splintered, the blocks all collapsed and compressed and cracked around it. Parts of the wall had collapsed inward and above that, above the cinder blocks that remained standing, the roof was sticking up at sharp angles, some beams pointing straight up, some of the metal roof panels still attached, and others missing.

"Are there people still inside?" Naomi gasped.

"I don't see Iris or Michelle."

"Or Marie-Claire, or Josephine . . . they are in there, in there!" Philippe cried out.

"Maybe they are in another building or—"

"No, no! In there!" Philippe yelled, gesturing to the collapsed dining hall.

He grabbed the door, trying to open it. The handle and a slice of the door came free and he tumbled backwards as pieces of masonry and blocks crashed down, narrowly missing Philippe as they fell to the ground around him. Other pieces of the wall fell inward, landing inside the crushed shell of the building.

Philippe jumped to his feet and rushed toward the door again. I reached out and grabbed him, wrapping my arms around him.

"No, just stop! Wait!"

He struggled to get away but I held firm.

"We'll get them out," I whispered in his ear. "We just have to figure out the right way . . . you can't do it with your bare hands. We have to think."

He stopped struggling and I let go.

"We have to be certain that they're in there," I said.

I looked around. We were surrounded by all of the kids, orphans and mission kids, forming a semicircle around us. They were all standing perfectly still. Some looked on with stunned, blank eyes, while others were sobbing and shaking, almost held up by those standing next to them. I couldn't stop the staring or shaking but I needed them to stop sobbing. Or at least move away.

"Naomi, get the children, all of the children, and take them away."

She nodded her head. "I'll take them to the girls' dormitory and—"

"No!" Philippe yelled. "Not indoors . . . no one can go indoors!"

"He's right," I agreed. "We have to check to make sure it hasn't been damaged before we go inside anywhere."

"No, no!" he exclaimed. "Not inside. There could be more . . . more shaking."

"Another earthquake?" I questioned.

"Yes. Yes."

"That's right," Naomi said. "There are often aftershocks after an earthquake. There could be aftershocks, smaller earthquakes could hit."

"Okay, I understand," I said. "Everybody stays outside," I announced, and then realized that it sounded as if I was giving an order. I had no right to give orders. That would be up to Pastor Dave or my father or one of the staff. But my father and Pastor Dave weren't here, and everybody else . . . well . . . they were in the dining hall. Maybe I was in charge.

"Take them into the middle of the compound," I ordered Naomi. "And you three stay here with us," I said, pointing to Ryan and Jonathan and a third kid whose name I couldn't remember. "Okay, we have to figure out what to do, how to get in, move some of the debris away. Follow me."

I started walking around the outside of the building. The wall on one side was almost completely standing except for a few rows of blocks at the top. The glass in the two windows was shattered, glass shards littering the ground, but the metal frames and bars were intact, only slightly bent. Turning the corner I was shocked to see that an entire wall had collapsed outward, and the roof had fallen down with it, so low to the ground that the beams would have crushed anything, or anybody, who was at that end. That was the end where Iris and Michelle had been sitting.

There was a loud yell and I turned in time to see two little girls, covered in dust and dirt, come running toward the crowd gathered in the centre of the compound.

"Is that them?"

Philippe wasn't there to answer. He was running across the courtyard and grabbed the two girls, scooping them up in his arms. I guessed that was an answer. The two little girls weren't in the building, they were fine. Maybe nobody was in the building. I looked all around. There was no sign of Iris or Michelle, but the matron and the ladies from the kitchen had reappeared. They were now standing in the middle of the huddle of children, being mobbed by them. Maybe I just had to wait and then the two women from our group would appear too . . . no, I just knew that wasn't the case. They'd been in the wrong part of the building. They were still inside.

There was a hole, a gap, between the last row of standing cinder blocks and the edge of the roof. I moved around the blocks lying on the ground, some of them whole, others splintered into hunks of rock, dropped to my knees and peered in. My view was blocked just a few feet in by more wreckage, but I could see far enough to confirm that the roof would have trapped or killed anybody standing beneath.

"Hello!" I called into the hole. "Is anybody in there?"

I knew there were people in there. I guess the real question was whether they were alive and conscious and could hear me and respond. There was no answer. I got back to my feet and continued around the corner and around to the back of the building. The wall at this corner was still standing tall, but as it ran down the length of the building it got lower and lower until it wasn't more than three or four blocks on top of each other, the blocks having fallen inward, the roof caved in.

I placed my hand against the blocks. They were cracked and fractured and there were little gaps between some of the blocks that remained standing. I tried to visualize what was on the other side of the wall. I placed my hand against the blocks, as if that would somehow help. That was where Iris and Michelle had been sitting at the table . . . a table that was about as high as the roof was off the ground.

I thought I heard something and cocked my head to aim one ear at the hole.

"Do you hear it?" I asked.

"I heard something," Ryan said. "I think."

I got down on my knees and placed my head against the wall—right by the largest fracture in the blocks. I listened and—there it was. There was something. A voice, a faint voice calling for help. They were in there, and they were alive.

CHAPTER SEVENTEEN

"Hello, can you hear me?" I yelled into one of the cracks in the wall.

"Help . . . help," a faint female voice called back.

"It's me. It's Josh!" I yelled. "Is that you, Iris?"

I waited for an answer but there was no response. Couldn't they hear me, or had the person passed out, or. . . ? I didn't even want to think about that.

"Yes, it's me," came the reply, so soft and muffled that I almost felt as though I'd thought it rather than heard it.

"We'll get you out!" I yelled. I turned to Philippe. "Get me a hammer, and a shovel, and a pickaxe. Ryan, you go with him!" I ordered.

They turned and ran off.

"What are you going to do?" Jonathan asked.

"I'm putting in a garden!" I snapped. "What do you

think I'm. . . ? Sorry . . . I'm going to try to take out a couple of the blocks so I can make a way in."

"Are you sure you should do that?" he asked. "What if you cause the rest of the wall to cave in?"

I hadn't really thought of that. What if trying to get them out killed them?

"Do you have another suggestion?" I asked, hoping he did.

"We should call somebody. The police or the fire department or—"

"Do you see a phone? Do you really think there's somebody around here to help? Look around," I snapped.

"Or we could just wait until your father and Pastor Dave get back."

That *was* an option. We could just wait until they got back, but how long would that be, and could the women wait that long?

"If that was you in there, would you want us to wait for somebody to come help?" I finally asked.

"No, but I wouldn't want you to bring the roof down on me, either," he said.

Again, a valid point.

"We'll just have to be careful. We'll try to open up a gap so we can see and talk to them," I said. "Besides, the roof might be just hanging there, and it could come down on its own if we don't get them out."

Ryan nodded his head in agreement. I'd convinced him, although I wasn't even that sure I'd convinced myself it was the right thing to do.

"You're right," Jonathan said. "If we don't get them out and there are aftershocks the whole thing could collapse."

I started thinking about the aftershocks. I'd seen reports of earthquakes on TV before and remembered that people would sleep outside for days and days afterwards because of fears of another quake.

"Earthquakes most often come in waves . . . we were taught about them in geography," he explained.

"So there might be more earthquakes, right?" I questioned.

"Not quakes, not like that, just little rumblings," he said. "Not after-quakes, but aftershocks. They're not as big . . . well, at least not usually."

Very reassuring, very.

"Here," Philippe said as he reappeared, offering me the pickaxe he was carrying. Ryan was beside him carrying a shovel and a small hammer.

"Let me start with the hammer," I said.

I took it from Ryan and then dropped to my knees. I ran my fingers along the crack that had opened up between the blocks. It ran the full height of the wall. This was probably the place to start. I turned the hammer over and, using the claw, started to dig into the concrete holding the blocks in place. It was reassuring—and frightening—how easily the mortar was coming away. Rather than giving resistance it was crumbling like sand.

"We need to remove three or four of the blocks," I said. "That way we can let in some air and light . . . and if we have to, we can go in to get them."

I said those last words with such deliberateness. Opening up the wall was one thing; going in there, especially now that I thought about these aftershock things, was another completely.

Philippe took the shovel and started sawing and chipping and scraping away at another seam of the block I was working on. Soon it was free on three sides, and the space where the mortar had sat was now open. It was reassuring that the blocks above hadn't caved into the vacant spot. That meant that removing that block wouldn't cause the structure to collapse. At least, that was the theory and the hope.

I dropped the hammer and inserted my fingers, pushing and pulling, causing the whole block to wiggle back and forth, but I couldn't get it to move out of the way.

"Look out," Philippe said.

I turned around in time to see him pull back the pick-axe and raise it above his head. I spun out of the way just in time as he brought it down against the block, and a large chunk of cement shot out as he cracked the surface! He brought the axe back up and another blow split the block into three or four pieces.

"Hang on," I said. I moved back over and pulled out one piece and then a second piece of the shattered block. I was now able to wrap my hands around the remaining chunk and I pulled the entire block free, leaving in its place a hole in the wall.

I leaned down and looked inside. The gap let in more light and I could see a short distance into the collapsed building. The light didn't penetrate far enough to see where they were, but what I could see showed that there was enough space, a gap of almost three feet between the floor and fallen roof. That was enough room for somebody to crawl through the building if need be. Somebody . . . I had a pretty good idea who that somebody was going to have to be.

"We need to take out this one and this one," I said, tapping the two blocks with my hand.

Ryan started hollowing out one seam with the shovel and I went at another with the claw of the hammer. Again the cement crumbled against the metal surfaces. Not quite a hot knife through butter but certainly not what I'd have expected from cement. Was that why this building had collapsed in the first place, because the cement wasn't good enough?

The second block dropped down and I wrapped both hands around it and dragged it out, doubling the size of the hole.

I looked into the hole. A little bit of light extended into the building but still not enough to illuminate anybody inside.

"Iris . . . we're getting closer," I called out.

"I can see the light," she answered, her voice clearer but still fragile.

"We're going to need flashlights, for us and for everybody else," I said.

Each of us had brought a flashlight in our backpacks.

"Sure, I'll go and get them," Jonathan said.

We started to chip away the mortar holding the third block in place. Again it gave way quickly, crumbling to the ground, until the block dropped free with a thud. Philippe pulled it out. The hole was now pretty big.

I stuck in my head and then twisted my shoulders so I could fit inside. Neither Iris nor Michelle was especially big, so I figured that was enough room for them to crawl out.

"Iris, can you see where the light is coming from?" I asked.

"Yes . . . I can see it," she replied.

"We've made a hole big enough for you to get out. Just crawl this way, toward the light, toward the hole."

"I can't," she said. "I can't move . . . I'm pinned down."

Not good. Really not good. "How about Michelle, can she crawl out?"

"She's . . . she's . . . *unconscious.*"

There was something about the way she said "unconscious" that just seemed wrong, different.

"Can you come and help me . . . help us . . . please?" Iris begged.

If the hole was big enough for her to come out through, then it was big enough for me to crawl in through—not that that was what I had wanted. However, I'd learned that what I wanted in life and what I ended up getting weren't always the same.

"I'm coming," I said reluctantly. "I'm coming in."

I pulled my shoulders out and turned to Philippe. Jonathan was back with a couple of flashlights. He flicked one on and handed it to me.

"Maybe somebody should come with me," I suggested.

"I could go," Ryan offered.

"No, I was thinking Philippe."

Philippe nodded in agreement and took the second flashlight from Jonathan.

Ryan looked relieved. "Just be careful," he said.

"If I was going to be careful I wouldn't be going in there to begin with. Come on."

I aimed the flashlight into the hole. It blazed a path. I should have been relieved, but what I saw only disturbed me more. There were beams shattered and splintered, smashed tables and chairs. The whole roof had fallen down to the floor in some places, and in others it was no more than a foot or so above, suspended, as if waiting to plummet the remaining distance. What would have happened if I'd been in there when it collapsed? I would have been crushed or killed or trapped . . . the way Iris was trapped now. If that had been me, I would have hoped that somebody would come in for me. I was that somebody.

I took a deep breath and then popped the flashlight into my mouth. I plunged my head in and then twisted my shoulders. Next, using my elbows to propel me, I dragged my body and legs and then feet behind me. The cement floor was cold, but despite everything it was still a solid slab.

I took the flashlight back into my hand and played it around, looking, unsuccessfully, for Iris.

"Iris, I need you to start talking to me so I know where you are," I said.

"What do you want me to say?" she asked.

I thought I already knew what direction she was in judging from her answer, but I really wasn't completely sure.

"Say anything, just keep talking, even start counting. Loud."

She began counting.

Philippe tapped me on the shoulder. He'd climbed in. He pointed in the direction I thought the voice was coming from. There was a problem, though. She was on the other side of a section that had collapsed almost to the floor. There was no way we could get under that. Maybe we'd have to try to open up a hole in the wall on the other side, or—

"This way," Philippe said.

He started dragging himself along the floor, headed across the building, aiming for the far side. I could see in the glare of his light the reasoning behind that. Over at the far side the ceiling was well above the floor, supported by the wall. That was the way around the collapsed centre beam.

I followed behind. It was reassuring to have him in there with me. Not that he could protect me from a beam that fell, but somehow I just had more faith in him than I did in Ryan or Jonathan, or, really, in me.

Iris continued to count. Her voice faded as we crawled along, away from her. Philippe pulled himself around the corner of the fallen beam and—

"I can see you!" Iris called. "I can see the light!"

Philippe's legs disappeared and I hurried to get him back in sight. I crawled around the corner in time to see Philippe and Iris, caught in the beam of his flashlight. We crawled over.

"Thank goodness you're here," she gasped. "Are all the kids safe, are they okay?"

"Yes, everybody on our mission trip, all the orphanage kids are fine. They were all outside when it happened. It would have been different if it happened a few minutes earlier."

"Thank goodness that God was looking out for them."

It crossed my mind that if God had really been looking out he wouldn't have let this happen in the first place, or he would have told her and Michelle to get out. Would it have been too much trouble to warn somebody?

"Where are you caught?" I asked.

"My leg, it's pinned."

I let the light lead down. Her right leg was free but the left was trapped beneath the remains of a table, pressed against the concrete floor.

"It hurts, but I can wiggle my toes. I just can't get it free."

I turned myself around and ran my hands down her leg to the point where it was trapped. The table was holding her in place but probably had stopped the ceiling from falling any farther. If I was able to remove the pieces of table, would the ceiling fall to the floor?

"I see where it's trapped, but I just don't know how to get it free. Maybe if I got a saw we could cut through the wood or—"

"Please don't leave me!" she said, and she reached out and grabbed me by the shirt, pulling me toward her with such power that I was shocked.

"One of us will stay with you," I reassured her.

"Wait . . . first try something," Philippe said.

He pulled something out of his sock. There was a glint of light against metal and I saw that he was holding a large knife! What was he going to do with that? He couldn't cut through the wood with it, and he certainly didn't mean he was going to cut through her—

"Put some light there," he said, aiming his flashlight at a spot at the top of the shattered table leg.

I focused my light there and he put down his flashlight.

With the edge of the knife blade he began to try to turn the screws that held the table leg in place. At first the knife just slipped out, but then it caught and the screw began to come out. He did the same with the second and third screw, and with his other hand he began wiggling the leg, freeing it from the table.

"Pull, pull your leg," he said to Iris.

"I can move it a little. Just a little more—"

All at once the leg of the table came free and the roof groaned and sagged down and—it stopped, just a few inches lower. My heart raced and I was hit with a rush of adrenalin.

"I'm free! It's out!" Iris cried out. She began sobbing uncontrollably.

I flashed the light on her. She had pulled herself away and was sitting up, rubbing her freed leg. It looked fine. Thank goodness we could get out of there.

"Can you move?" I asked.

"It still hurts, but I can move. But what about Michelle?"

In the rush of everything I'd almost forgotten about her.

"She's over there," Iris said, pointing to the other side of the sagging wall, the place where her leg had been. "Right after the quake I could hear her. She was sort of groaning . . . before . . . at the beginning. She was sitting right beside me when it happened. She's just on the other side of the beam . . . I'm sure of that."

"Okay, I'll get her. You have to get out. Philippe can show you the way. Philippe, I'll call if I need you to come back in."

Philippe nodded his head. He started crawling back the way we'd come.

Iris didn't immediately follow. "Will you be okay?"

"I'll be okay when we're all out of here. You go."

She reached out and squeezed my shoulder. "Thank you for coming in and freeing me."

"You would have done the same for me. Now just go, please."

Philippe had stopped at the turn, waiting for Iris. I watched her go, dragging her bad leg behind her. It was obvious that it was hurt and she was in pain. He turned around the corner and she followed. I could see a trace of light, underneath the collapsed beam, inching its way toward the opening, toward the outside, toward where I wanted to be. But there was only one way for me to get there.

"Michelle, can you hear me?" I called out.

No answer. I didn't figure there would be one. She probably wasn't able to answer. Did that mean she had been knocked out? Or did it mean something worse?

I played the beam of light around, looking for a way past the second fallen beam. There didn't seem to be a spot. It was either right down to the floor or only a few inches above it, held in place by smashed furniture. There was definitely no gap large enough for me to wedge myself through. I might have to go out and smash a way in through the wall on the other side. But still, there was enough room for me to see underneath, to at least know where she was.

I spun onto my belly and dropped down even lower, my head right against the cold, rough concrete of the floor. I poked the flashlight underneath the beam and with one eye tried to follow the light. There was a tangled mess of smashed furniture, shattered beams, crumpled bricks and blocks and—there she was!

I let my beam of light play over her. Her body was pinned beneath a beam, hidden from view. What I could see was her upper body and head—all twisted, and there was a large gash on the side of her head, and her eyes—they were open and staring, but unseeing, not even reacting to the light that was aimed directly at them. I felt shocked, scared, and my stomach did a little flip. She was dead . . . right? There wasn't much doubt, but if there was any I couldn't just leave her.

"Michelle!" I called out.

No answer.

I pushed myself forward, sliding along the beam to get closer, my face scraping against the concrete so I could keep my eyes on her, bizarrely afraid to lose sight of her. I got to a place where I was directly across from her, separated by the beam but no more than a couple of feet of open space.

I spun around so I could no longer see her but I could reach out a hand, an arm, through the gap and toward her—and I touched her arm. A shudder went through my whole body. Slowly I moved my hand down along her arm until I came to her hand. I worked my fingers so that they were pressed against her wrist. I took a deep breath and tried to slow down my own racing heart as I searched for hers.

Her skin was cool, almost clammy. I pressed, trying to find a beat. All I felt was a soft echo of my heart beating in my fingertips. But from her, there was nothing. The little doubt that had remained was gone. As was she.

Slowly I withdrew my hand, rolled over, and softly began to cry.

CHAPTER EIGHTEEN

I pulled myself along as quickly as I could, flashlight in my mouth, elbows digging in, legs dragging behind. All I wanted now was to get out from under the collapsed roof. I was so grateful to see the way out. I turned off my flashlight and was thrown into darkness. There was no light coming from outside any more—the sun had set while I was inside. I quickly turned my light back on and crawled out.

Iris was sitting on the ground. The matron was looking at her leg, and Jonathan, Ryan, and Philippe hovered over her. She looked up at me.

"Michelle?" she asked.

"I found her," I said.

"And . . . and. . . ?"

I shook my head and looked down at the ground. "I'm sorry. There's nothing that can be done."

Iris's head dropped into her hands and she began to

sob. I didn't really know Michelle, hadn't exchanged more than a dozen words with her, but I knew that the two of them had known each other for a long time. Michelle was a lot older, a widow with grown children, but I figured she had been sort of like a mother figure to Iris. It had to be hard. I felt as though I had to say something.

"It would have been fast," I said. "I don't think she would have suffered." At least not much. "How are you doing?"

"Not broken," the matron said. "Bruised . . . but not broken."

"It hurts but it's not too bad. I should help."

She started to get to her feet and I placed a hand on her shoulder, holding her in place. "There are lots of hands to move things."

"But I should be supervising or doing something," she said. "I can't just sit here."

"The matron is giving directions. You need to just sit and take it easy for a bit. Wait until Pastor Dave and my father get back and then talk to them about what you can do."

She nodded her head. "Thank the Lord they won't be too long. I'm sure your father and sister are just fine."

Up until that instant it hadn't even crossed my mind to think that they wouldn't be.

"Safest place to be in an earthquake is in a vehicle," she continued.

"I guess that makes sense."

"Especially at the speed they would have been travelling along those roads."

That was even more reassuring. She was right. Maybe they'd be delayed a little bit, but they'd be here before too long. I was completely sure. Almost completely sure. What if a building fell on their car, or if they drove off the road, or the meeting was late and they were still inside a building when it hit or. . . ? I couldn't let my mind go that way.

"I guess we'd better figure out what we do until they arrive," I said.

Philippe and the matron began talking excitedly in French. I tried to pick out words. They were talking so fast and with so much Creole slang tossed in I could barely understand anything they said.

"Could you please tell me what you're talking about?" I asked.

They stopped and looked up at me.

"The buildings," Philippe said. "Some are still standing but not safe right now . . . could still come down."

"Aftershocks, right?"

The matron nodded her head. "One dormitory, the girls', has shattered windows. The building twisted and broke them. The other, for the *garçons*, has a cracked wall and the beams are sagging. It could come down."

I thought about the beams in the dining hall, how big and heavy they were, and how some of them had just snapped in two and others had crashed down to the floor. I had no desire to go back inside under any roof right now. Better to be outside.

"The dining room is *fini* . . . no more. No kitchen, and the generator is smashed."

"So we don't have any light?"

She shook her head. "Just the flashlights, and we will make a fire for warmth and that will provide some light."

"That means we're going to sleep outside, right?"

"*Oui.*"

"So do we bring the beds outside?" I asked.

"*Oui.* Mattresses, blankets, sheets, and pillows should be brought out," the matron said. "We will sleep under the open sky."

The sun had set but there was still some light bending around the curve of the earth, so it wasn't completely dark yet. I knew how dark it would get soon, and we didn't want to be relying on those little flashlights for everything.

"We'd better move quickly while there's still some light," I said.

"There is one other way for light," Philippe said.

I watched as he ran over to a little, rusty yellow pickup truck that was sitting off to the side. He climbed in. I figured it was just a piece of scrap metal, but then I heard the engine cranking, trying unsuccessfully to catch and start. At last it roared to life and a gigantic belch of black smoke came pouring out of the tailpipe. There was a loud grinding of gears as he put it into motion, backed it up, did a little turn . . . and then I realized what he was doing. He slowly drove the truck over. It had one light that was burned out or missing completely, but the other light, yellow and cloudy, was still bright enough to light the scene—the eerie scene.

Caught in the light were all the kids, huddled together in little groups, sitting on the ground. Their expressions were grim and worried and frightened and stunned. I could understand all of those feelings because my thoughts, my feelings, kept cycling through those same emotions. We had to talk to them, to reassure them, to somehow make them feel more at ease. If my father had been there, he'd have known what to say. So would Pastor Dave, but he wasn't there either.

"We need to talk to them," I said.

"Yes, yes, we will tell them what to do," the matron said.

"Not just that. We need to tell them about Michelle. And we have to tell them that everything is going to be okay . . . that they're going to be safe."

"He's right," Iris said.

I helped Iris to her feet. She hobbled forward, leaning on me.

"We need to talk to all of you," Iris said. "Please, I need everybody to listen." She turned to the matron. "Can you translate what I'm going to say, please?"

"Of course."

"I'm not really sure where to start," she began. "I just wish John . . . Pastor Evans, or Pastor Dave, were here right now—and I know they will be here soon—but until then you have to know that we're all safe right now."

That was a good place to start. Her words were being translated as she talked.

"Because of a risk of aftershocks we're going to be sleeping outside tonight. We'll be bringing all the mattresses and blankets out here. It will be just like a little camp-out. It'll be sort of fun."

"Fun" wasn't the word I would have used.

"I have some news, though, that I have to share with you." Her voice cracked over the last few words, and I could tell she was on the verge of crying. "I just have to tell you . . . tell you . . . " She started to sob.

I put a hand on her shoulder. "It's okay . . . I'll tell them," I said softly, and she nodded her head ever so slightly.

My mind spun around, trying to think of the right way, the right words to tell them. Then I remembered what my father had told me: never use words like "gone," "was lost," or "passed on"—be direct, tell the truth, use the right word.

"Michelle was in the dining hall when it collapsed. She was hit by a beam. She died."

One of the girls started crying. Naomi reached over and put an arm around her, comforting her.

"I'm sorry," I said. "I wish there were something we could have done, but there was nothing."

"It was God's will," Iris said.

I looked over at her in disbelief. Did she really believe that God wanted Michelle dead?

"We need to pray for Michelle's soul," she said, sobbing.

I couldn't believe what she was doing. If she really thought that God had killed Michelle—that it was his will—did it make any sense to pray to the very being that had caused her to die?

"Yes, we need to thank God that the rest of us are safe," she continued. "And give thanks for the life of my dear friend, Michelle, who is now in a better place."

Did she consider trapped under a beam in the collapsed dining hall a "better place"?

"Our Father chose to spare us. He used his power to safeguard our lives," she said.

Maybe he should have used his power to stop the earthquake from happening. That would have been a lot better. If he'd done that, Michelle would still have been here instead of lying underneath a collapsed beam. Besides, if she had gone on to a "better place," maybe we should have been upset that we had to stay here in a worse place.

"Do you want to lead the prayer?" Iris asked me.

I was both shocked and surprised. I shook my head.

"Then I will," she said. "Could we please bow our heads."

Everybody bowed their heads. Everybody except for me and Philippe.

"Our Father, who art in Heaven," she began.

Great, fall back on the Lord's Prayer. Quietly I walked away. Philippe followed behind me. They could go ahead and pray, for all the good it would do them. We had work to do. God wasn't going to be dragging the mattresses outside.

CHAPTER NINETEEN

I sat on one of the blocks that had fallen down when the outer wall of the compound collapsed. In the distance, in the darkness, I could see nothing except for a few little pinpricks of light—fires burning, either for heat or light or both. Or possibly they were fires that had originally been set by people for those purposes but which had been overturned, released, set free, and spread when the earth moved and stoves toppled. Up above, oblivious to what had happened below, the millions of stars twinkled brightly.

What I *couldn't* see was the only thing that I really wanted to see. Down there in the dark was the unseen road, quiet and untravelled. What I wanted—what I needed—was a pair of headlights to come slowly bumping along the road, and behind those headlights, in the vehicle, I wanted it to be my father and sister and Pastor Dave.

I kept playing mental games. Closing my eyes and

opening them expecting to see them coming, or watching the courtyard and then turning back around. Maybe it was time to look at the courtyard again.

I could clearly see the outlines of our makeshift campsite. We had ultimately brought out the metal and wooden beds, the mattresses, blankets, sheets, and pillows of the people who would normally have been sleeping in their dormitories. Right now I kind of missed the dormitory I'd once complained about—in there, at least I'd have been safe from the mosquitoes.

Most of the kids had settled in for the night and were asleep, or at least lying down trying to sleep. Some were so exhausted that sleep came easily. For others, sleep was an escape, a way to get away from the fears and worries that were troubling them. I wished I could be that way. I could never shut my mind down when I needed to think things through. Like now. I knew there was no point in even trying to sleep.

Thank goodness the sky was clear. I was grateful not only for the light but for the fact that it wasn't raining—one less complication. The fire that had been lit in the compound yard made a little patch of light in the middle of the beds. It was still burning but at this point it wasn't providing much light, and probably no heat except for the beds immediately surrounding it.

I quickly turned back to the road and . . . nothing. They should have been back by now. They should have been back three hours ago. But what did I expect? An earthquake would have caused problems along the road. Maybe a part of it had collapsed, or a bridge had gone out . . . I just hoped they weren't on the bridge when it went. Wait, there were no bridges along that whole route. They were fine. It was just that the earthquake had made it harder to get here. Not impossible, just harder. They'd be here soon.

"Do you want some company?"

I spun around, startled. It was Naomi.

"You should be sleeping," I said.

"We *all* should be sleeping, you included."

I laughed. "Not likely."

She sat down on a block beside me. "You must feel like Joshua," she said.

I gave her a questioning look.

"The original Joshua from Jericho, the Old Testament. You're sitting on the wall that came tumbling down," she explained.

"Oh, yeah," I said. "I guess the big difference is that I'm not planning on killing all the people inside."

Now she looked confused.

"After the wall fell, Joshua ordered his men to kill everyone and everything in the city," I explained.

"Really?"

"'Then they utterly destroyed all that was in the city, both man and woman, young and old, ox, sheep, and donkey, with the edge of the sword,'" I quoted.

"It says that?"

"Joshua six, verse twenty-one. According to the Old Testament once the walls had tumbled down, then upon God's orders Joshua had his men kill every living thing in the city."

"That can't be right."

"It isn't right, but it is correct. Never question Bible verses when you're talking to a preacher's kid." I paused. "But don't worry, it's not like it really happened. Archaeological evidence shows that Jericho wasn't even settled at the time it was supposed to have been destroyed. The real miracle would have been how Joshua destroyed a city that had already been deserted."

Even in the faint light I could see her look of confusion and disbelief.

"Look, it's a nice story, but it's like the rest of the Old Testament, a bunch of stories."

"You don't believe it's God's word?" she asked, sounding troubled.

"It's man's word, written by man. Who do you think decided which books to include or exclude from the Bible?"

"I'm not even sure what that last part means," she said.

"The church got together about three hundred years after Jesus and decided which books were inspired and true and which to leave out," I explained. "A whole lot of it is nothing more than a series of stories, parables, and myths designed to get across a message. You can't tell me you actually believe in Noah's ark, Jonah being swallowed by a whale, Adam and Eve, six days of creation, and the whole world being less than ten thousand years old."

"Well . . ."

"Come on, just think about it. What about the theory of evolution . . . which is more than a theory because it has so much proof? What about dinosaurs, fossil evidence, carbon dating? The next thing you're going to tell me is that the sun rotates around the earth."

"Of course it doesn't. We all know that."

"It wasn't that many hundreds of years ago that the Church killed people who believed that, or—" I stopped myself. This wasn't the time or place for that discussion. "You didn't come out here for a debate about religion."

"I just wanted to make sure you were okay," she said.

"I'm fine. I'm good."

"You're worried about your family."

"Shouldn't I be worried?" I asked.

She nodded. "But they'll be okay, I'm sure of that. They're probably just delayed because of the quake. The road might be blocked, and then with nightfall . . . they might not be able to get here until tomorrow. You're not going to sit here all night, are you?"

"Probably not. Listen, I know what you're saying makes sense . . . but still, I think I'll wait a little bit longer. It's not like I'm going to be able to sleep anyway. I just want to know how bad it was," I said. "How big this quake was, how it affected Port-au-Prince. But we have no way of knowing."

"I wish our phones worked," she said.

"They worked down in Port-au-Prince . . . at least before the quake. I don't know if that's changed now. If only we had TV, or even a radio." I pointed down to the dining hall where the radio used to sit. "But even if it wasn't crushed, even if we could get it, we still wouldn't have any electricity because of the generator being smashed."

"It's too bad we don't have a portable radio."

"Yeah, that would be—" Then I remembered who *did* have a radio!

I could hear the radio playing as we approached Louidor's home. We stopped by the door and Philippe knocked on the side of the box. The radio kept playing but there was no answer or response.

I reached over and knocked myself—louder. Still no answer.

"Maybe he's not home," I said.

Actually, that would have made it easier because what I really wanted was the radio, not him.

"He is always with the radio," Philippe said.

He reached down and opened up the little door at the end of the box. The radio instantly became louder, and I could see its blue-green controls glowing in the darkness in the far corner. But where was Louidor? I turned on my flashlight and caught sight of him instantly. He was underneath a thin blanket, face down, stretched along the side of the box. He was asleep . . . or was he . . . was he. . . ? Just then he let out a loud snore.

"He's asleep," I said. "He's just asleep." For a split second I'd thought about Michelle—dead, still there, trapped under the beams of the dining hall.

The loud music was replaced by the screeching voice of the announcer. He was speaking in rapid-fire French, and although I couldn't understand the words I understood the tone—he sounded panicked, desperate.

"What is he saying?" I asked Philippe.

"The quake, he is talking about it," he said.

"What is he saying?"

"Shhhh . . . quiet . . . let me listen."

The announcer continued to talk—no, practically scream—about what had happened. I waited, trying to be patient, for Philippe to translate. Finally he stopped talking and music came back on.

"Very, very, bad," Philippe said. "Very big."

"How big, how bad?" I demanded.

"They said it was a seven . . . I do not know what that means."

"Seven," I mumbled. I tried to remember what I'd learned about earthquakes in geography class. They were measured on something called the Richter scale, and each point on the scale was much bigger than the next . . . was it ten times as big? I wished I'd paid more attention in that class, but who would have ever thought I'd need to know any of that stuff?

"There is damage, much damage in Port-au-Prince," Philippe said. "Buildings collapsed, even the Presidential Palace . . . many people are trapped . . . many more have died."

"How many people?"

He shook his head. "They said many, but they did not say how many . . . they may not know."

Louidor's eyes popped open and he sat up. "Many, many . . . *milliers*."

"Thousands?" I asked.

"Many thousands," Philippe said.

I felt my legs get all weak and shaky. Thousands. Many thousands. And my father and sister were down there someplace.

"There have been fires, and people are looting, robbing, much bad things," Philippe continued. "That is what the radio said."

My legs gave way and I started to slump to the ground. Philippe reached over and grabbed me by the arm, steadying me, keeping me standing.

Louidor started talking, quickly, in a combination of French and Creole, and Philippe answered.

"What is he saying?" I asked, not sure if I wanted to hear anything more.

"He wanted to know about the orphanage . . . about the orphans. I told him that all are well."

Louidor continued to ramble on, his voice getting faster, the pitch higher, and then I picked up a few words that I understood—Port-au-Prince, and Sodom and Gomorrah, and then Babylon. Was this a geography lesson or was he talking about the Bible?

"What is he saying now?" I asked.

"He was just saying that this is God's work," Philippe said. "He is taking care of the wicked, that Port-au-Prince is wicked and God is cleaning away the wickedness."

I wanted to ask if he was crazy, but of course I already knew the answer to that.

"We have to go. *Merci* . . . thank you," I mumbled as I turned and started to walk away.

I'd gone only a few feet when I was stopped in my tracks by the sound of crying, anguish. I spun around, looking for where it was coming from, but in the darkness I couldn't see anything, anybody. The desperate wail was getting louder. Whoever it was, they were coming toward us.

Philippe and Louidor stood beside me. The voice—it was getting louder, closer. It was female, but it was hardly human. There were no words. It sounded more like the anguish of a wounded animal. Then I saw a shadow coming along the road, staggering, stopping and starting, a dark outline against the slightly less dark night. One person, coming up the road. She suddenly stopped and froze in the road. There was a flash of light as I saw the whites of her eyes, reflecting the light of the moon above.

"*Au secour . . . au secour . . . mon bébé,*" she cried out.

"She needs help with—"

"With her baby," I said, cutting off Philippe. "Ask her what's wrong."

"*Qu'est qui est arrivé à ton bébé?*" Philippe asked.

She staggered forward and collapsed into Louidor's arms. She was crying, talking, screaming, and sobbing.

"What is she saying?" I asked. "Where is her baby?"

"Her baby is in *la maison*. She got free, but the *bébé . . . non . . .* still in the *maison*."

My mind flashed back to the dining hall and Michelle. Poor mother. Poor baby. I hoped it had at least happened quickly.

"She says the baby is still alive," Philippe said. "It is still crying. She can hear it. She came for Pastor Dave to help."

Philippe spoke to her. I understood enough to know he told her that Pastor Dave was not here, and she started crying even more loudly.

I stepped forward. "Tell her we'll try to help."

CHAPTER TWENTY

The little truck rumbled down the road. Philippe was at the wheel, and I was beside him. In the back, in the bed of the pickup, sat the woman—her name was Suzette—along with Ryan and Jonathan and Louidor. Louidor had the radio at his side, and the loud music spilled in through the open windows. The one headlight of the truck was the only light, and it was the reason we'd brought it along in the first place. I wanted as much light as possible, and our little flashlights weren't going to be enough for what we might need to do. Assuming there was anything we *could* do.

As we bumped down the road we continually came upon people either on the road or running out to meet us. It was like being part of a bad horror movie. People were caught in the headlight, often in nightgowns, or without shoes, or with one shoe, looks of terror and confusion on their faces. Those that ran out to see us also looked disappointed when they realized it was just us driving in a little beat-up pickup truck. I think they were hoping for somebody or something more official. As far as I could see there was no one official here. It wasn't like the police or fire department were coming out to help.

Most of the people we passed, however, seemed to barely react, hardly bothering to get out of the way of the truck. They just staggered along. It was as if they were so numb or in such shock that they couldn't even acknowledge us. They just drifted by, like ghostly apparitions, eyes open but not really seeing.

A few people had waved and screamed for us to pull over, asking for help—help we really weren't in any position to offer. How awful that people would look to *us* for assistance. It was true that along with the people in the back of the truck we'd brought our tools—a few shovels, the sledge-hammer, some saws and hammers—but really we couldn't do much for anybody. I just hoped we could do something for Suzette. Were we going to help move rubble so that she could find the body of her baby? I'd never seen a dead baby and I was hoping to keep it that way.

Suzette started screaming and I turned around to see her standing, arms flailing, being held by Louidor as she tried to jump out of the moving truck.

"Stop, you'd better stop!" I yelled.

Philippe slowed down and pulled the truck over to the side of the road. Almost instantly Suzette jumped out and started running for a house—or what was left of a house. She rushed up to one of the people standing near it and collapsed into the arms of an older woman.

Philippe turned off the truck and the little engine fell silent. We climbed out, as did the people in the back, grabbing tools, and then walked over. Louidor held the sledgehammer in one hand and in the other his radio, blaring out another loud song.

We all stopped at the edge of the collapsed building. It was hard to say what it had looked like or how big it had been, but now it was nothing more than a pile of rubble—blocks and bricks and beams and sheets of metal—lying in a gigantic heap on the ground. Most of the people were just standing around, silently staring, while a few were moving debris, bricks or blocks, over to the side, making a little hill that they'd separated from the mountain that remained.

"This is a family compound," Philippe said. "These people all live there."

There were children, lots and lots of children, and old people, but the only males were either very old or very young.

"Where are the men?" I asked, fearing for a second that they were all trapped in the building.

"They are down in Port-au-Prince. Most are day labourers. Most of the women would have been working in the field when it hit, thank goodness. But others, like Suzette and her baby, were inside."

I looked from one end to the other. The building had completely collapsed. I know Suzette had said she heard crying, but how could the baby possibly have survived, and what good would it do for us to go in and try to find it? There really wasn't any point in risking anybody's life to recover a body. Somebody would have to just tell her that we couldn't help. But would she even be able to understand me, with her broken English and my broken French?

"Philippe, we have to tell her. There's nothing we can do—"

All of a sudden the woman ran over toward us. She skidded to a stop in front of Louidor and grabbed at his radio, trying to take it away from him. He held on tightly and the two of them wrestled over the radio, both screaming and yelling—she in despair and he in desperation. Neither of them was very big but Louidor was clearly taller and outweighed her. Still, she held on.

Finally he shook her loose and she tumbled to the ground, and he began cursing at her as she started to sob even more loudly. Why did she want the radio? What was she after? Was it that she didn't want to hear about the disaster? Or was she just grief-stricken, or annoyed by the sound, or. . . ?

"Ask him to turn off the radio," I said to Philippe.

Philippe shook his head. "No, not good, not good to do that."

"Then maybe he could walk away. Take him away, walk him away from here so the radio isn't so loud."

Philippe walked over, said a few words to Louidor, and the two of them walked away. At the same time I walked toward the collapsed house. I'd taken no more than a few steps when Suzette jumped to her feet, grabbed me by the hand, and started to drag me forward. She was much smaller than me, but there was iron in her grip, and I was practically pulled off my feet as she dragged me forward and—what was that sound? Was it really a baby crying? I turned my head, trying to capture the sound again, but there was nothing. Had I just imagined it?

She stopped dragging me at the corner of the house. She pointed at the collapsed structure and started screaming again, speaking so quickly that all I could make out was the word "*bébé*." Yes, I knew her baby was there, but there wasn't much I could do about it, any more than I could have helped Michelle. If the house had collapsed on the baby, it was dead.

Then I heard faint crying again. A few brief sounds and then nothing. Was it coming from the house? There was too much background noise between her screaming and the sobbing and crying of the people huddled around the wreckage. I couldn't hear anything.

"Everybody be quiet!" I called out, but nobody seemed to listen or understand what I was saying.

"*Fermez la bouche!*" I yelled—something the French teacher had said to me on more than one occasion—and everybody suddenly stopped everything and turned to face me. I put my finger to my lips, signalling that I wanted silence.

I walked the few steps to the edge of the wreckage and listened. Now I could hear nothing but silence. Whatever sound I thought I'd heard had just been inside my head, wishful thinking. Maybe Louidor wasn't the only person who needed a radio. And then, unbelievably, I heard the crying again. Soft and low, but clear, and coming from the wreckage of the house.

The baby was in there. And it was alive.

CHAPTER TWENTY-ONE

I turned around slightly and passed Philippe a cement block. I half lifted, half pushed it through the dirt. He, in turn, did the same and moved it back to Ryan, who would pass it to Jonathan behind him and a whole little army of people moving it from the narrow path we'd made through the rubble to the outside.

My flashlight caught the scene, light bouncing off the walls of the cave we were creating, excavating. It was now more than twenty feet long. We had broken through an outside wall right where Suzette had told us she thought the baby was, right by where it sounded to me like the crying was the clearest. We'd then started shifting, shoving, and moving the wreckage out of our way. The dirt floors of the house were a blessing. In places where the roof had collapsed almost down to the floor we were able to use our shovels and hands to dig into the floor to find our way.

I placed a hand against the beam that hung precariously above my head. I pushed against it and it held firm. Whatever was holding it up was solid. If there was a cave-in—either from another earthquake or from us disturbing the wreckage—this would be a safe spot. I almost laughed out loud. Safe was outside. Really, safe was thousands of miles away, back in Canada.

Thoughts of home and my father and Sarah flooded my mind. I hadn't even thought of them since we'd started here. I couldn't think about them. I had to focus on what I was doing and what was happening. I couldn't help them, but maybe I could help this baby.

"Everybody be quiet!" I yelled over my shoulder.

The tunnel got quiet but there were still loud voices coming from outside.

"Tell them to all shut up!" I screamed.

Quickly there was silence. Too much silence. No sounds of a baby crying. Was it asleep or. . . ? It was just asleep, that was all. Babies slept most of the time. I just wanted it to keep making noise, keep crying. Not only would it let me know it was still alive, it would reassure me that I was moving in the right direction. I hoped for a sound. I was almost even prepared to pray if that would have helped, but there was nothing.

Directly in front of me the way was blocked by debris. It looked like the remains of a table and some chairs all crushed together in a twisted, wooden roadblock wedged between the collapsed roof and the dirt floor. I pulled up the hammer and gave it a little tap. There was an echoing sound. There was a hollow, an opening on the other side.

I pulled myself up onto my knees, as high as I could get with my head touching the beam, and used my leverage to swing the hammer with all the force I could muster. It smashed against the wood, splintering it, and the baby started crying again! Had it been hit by a piece of flying wood, or had I startled it or simply scared it back awake? No matter what the reason, the crying was now so loud, so clear, and so close that it was obviously coming from the other side of the hole I'd smashed in the piece of wood.

I dropped back to my belly and pressed my flashlight and my eye against the opening and—there it was! Just a few feet away was a little baby—a white diaper, black skin, and white, white eyes, and mouth opened wide and screaming, reflecting back the beam of my flashlight.

"I can see the baby!" I yelled. "I can see it. I can almost reach it!"

There was a cheer from behind me and then a louder echo of cheers from outside as the word was passed along.

I took the claw end of the hammer, put it in the hole, and pulled against the wood, splintering off shards, enlarging the hole until it was big enough that I thought I could get my arm and my head through. I dropped down, crawled forward, and squeezed through, leading with my arm holding the flashlight. Then I twisted and turned so that I could see the space remaining between me and the baby.

It was almost all open space, at least two feet high, a beam, some metal roofing, crushed furniture, and almost nothing in between. All I had to do was get through this one blockage, these few pieces of wood, and I could scoop up the baby and get out of there.

The baby had stopped crying. It was just lying there, eyes wide open like it was studying me as it lay there on a dirty blanket and what looked like the smashed remains of a wooden basket, a crib.

"It's okay, baby," I said softly. What was its name? I didn't even know if it was a girl or a boy . . . but did that matter?

"I've just got to get through this and I can get you," I said, speaking both to the baby and to Philippe behind me.

I used the claw of the hammer to make the hole bigger and bigger. Now there were only a couple of pieces of wood . . . two legs of a chair, jammed, blocking my way. I grabbed one of the legs and started pulling and wiggling and—the beam over my head sagged and the whole building screamed out! I covered my head with my hands and arms as dust and dirt showered down and I prepared for the whole thing to come crashing down on me . . . but it didn't.

I looked up. The ceiling was still above my head, but a few inches lower than it had been.

"Is everybody okay?" I asked.

There were mumbled responses and nodding of heads, but the most visible thing was the look of fear and terror in their expressions and eyes. I knew they were seeing the same thing when they looked at me.

"Did I do that?" I asked.

"Aftershock," Ryan said, his voice barely a whisper echoing down the tunnel. "This . . . this is . . . dangerous."

I nodded. It was dangerous, and there was no need for him to even be here now.

"Back up," I said. "Get out, go back outside."

Jonathan didn't need to be asked twice. He quickly spun around and climbed out from under the wreckage. Ryan hesitated for a split second and then did the same.

Philippe didn't move.

"You too," I said.

He shook his head. "The baby. We cannot leave the baby."

"We're not leaving the baby. I'm not leaving. There's no point in you being in here, it's a one-man job."

He didn't move.

"There's nothing you can do to help. If it collapses it's better that it's just one of us."

He still didn't move.

"Look, if it collapses I want you to be out there so you can dig me out. Okay?"

He gave a slight smile and then nodded in agreement. "Be careful," he said, and then he turned and crawled out. I waited until he was outside and I was alone before turning back to the task.

Then I realized that the baby wasn't crying any more. Had it simply stopped or had something happened? Just because the roof had held on this side didn't mean that it had held there. I threw myself to the ground and aimed the beam of the flashlight through the hole. The baby's eyes were open and it looked calm. I wished I could feel that calm.

My whole body felt warm—no, hot—as though a flush had gone through me. There was sweat pouring down my face, and my legs and arms were shaking. And was there suddenly less air in the space? Had the opening closed down? I turned the flashlight back and saw the opening was still there, leading to the outside. There was air.

The baby was calm because it didn't know any better. Ignorance was bliss. It didn't know about aftershocks or structural integrity or the fact that this whole building could come down, killing us both. This wasn't helping to calm me down at all.

I knew I had to hurry, that the sooner I started the sooner I'd be finished, but I had to slow myself down first. I couldn't let the rush confuse my thoughts. It wasn't just an aftershock that could pull this place down.

I closed my eyes and instinctively started to pray, saying the Lord's Prayer. I said the first few lines and then stopped myself. I hadn't voluntarily said a prayer since my mother had died. Why did I think it would help now when it hadn't helped then?

And then I had the strangest feeling. Somebody was with me. I opened my eyes, embarrassed that I'd been caught praying, and turned around to tell them to get out and . . . there was nobody there. I was still alone, but I didn't feel alone. The shaking seemed to lessen, my breath was coming more easily, and my head seemed less frantic. How stupid. Did I think the spirit of the Lord was with me? The few seconds of prayer had just been like a meditation, and it had slowed down my thoughts enough to become calmer. That was all.

I turned back to what I had to do. I put my hands on the first piece of wood blocking my way. I tried to wiggle it, but it wouldn't budge. It was solidly wedged between the fallen roof and the ground beneath. It was too solid to smash through with a hammer, but that wasn't my only tool.

Behind me, on the ground, was a large handsaw. I took it, turned it sideways, and set the teeth against the wood. I made a short, fast stroke and the saw cut into the wood. I lengthened the stroke, back and forth, back and forth, the teeth eating into the wooden post. The motion of the saw kicked out sawdust but also caused dirt to float down on me from above. I was now more than halfway through. I pressed my free hand against the wood, opening up the cut so the saw could move more freely. It was almost through, and then I stopped. What if this was what was holding the roof in place? What if I finished the cut and the roof caved down on me and the baby, killing us both?

I ran the flashlight up and down the length of the post. I couldn't see where it went; the top was lost in the wreckage. Maybe it was just jammed there but it wasn't holding up the roof. Or *was* it? There was only one way to find out. There was another choice, though. I could just crawl out, tell them I couldn't get to the baby, or have somebody else go back down and finish the job. Why was it up to me, anyway?

I was free to just leave, and that meant I wasn't going to go. It wasn't that I wasn't afraid, because I was. It wasn't because I thought God was going to take care of me, because I'd seen the way he took care of my mother. It was because

I knew I was here and I had to do it because nobody else was here. It was up to me to save the baby.

I spun around so my feet were by the wooden post. I pulled back my legs, ready to slam against it, and then hesitated. Either this was going to work or it wasn't going to work. Either I would slam through or I wouldn't. Either the roof would cave down on me or it wouldn't. There was only one way to find out.

I slammed my feet against the post.

CHAPTER TWENTY-TWO

My legs went right through the post, snapping it cleanly into two pieces. I held my breath. But more importantly, the roof held.

I spun back around and crawled forward, through the opening and toward the baby. As the light from my flashlight hit its eyes the baby turned away, and it looked as though it was going to cry again. I aimed the beam slightly off to the side.

"It's okay little . . ." Was it a girl or a boy? "Little . . . *baby*."

I reached out and placed my hands underneath the baby, gently picking it up. It was so light, so little. I'd never held a baby so small. How old was it, anyway? It couldn't be more than a few weeks, or a month or two at the most.

I pressed it close to my chest, sheltering it in my arms. It was now safe . . . well . . . it would be safe once we got out of here. But how was I going to do that with the baby in my arms? Maybe the way out was backwards.

I continued to hold the baby on my chest with one arm and began shuffling head first, backwards on my bottom and back, toward the outside. I ducked down low, almost lying down, to get through the first opening. I placed my hand overtop of the baby's head, protecting it from being bumped by the low overhang. Past that point there was more space, more height, and I moved, on my bottom, extending my legs and then pulling them up, pushing my butt forward, and repeating that like a caterpillar until I was right at the opening, right there, almost out. I stopped, wanting to take a few more seconds, to catch my breath, and just *be* . . . just the two of us.

"You're okay . . . we're both okay," I whispered in its ear. "All you need now is to be with your mother, to have her hold you in her arms."

Then I was filled with a thought. "You know, baby, that's all I need too."

"Joshua!"

I startled. It was Philippe.

"We're coming out," I said. "The baby is all right!" I called out.

There was silence, and then a cheer went up as he must have passed on my words.

I shuffled the rest of the way and then, as soon as I could, stood up, the baby in my arms. Suzette rushed forward, crying and sobbing, and I handed the baby to her. She took the baby with one arm and then, to my surprise, wrapped her other arm around me, pulling me forward until she and the baby and I were all held together in her grasp. She was crying and shaking so much that it felt as if it were me shaking and crying. And then I realized I *was* shaking, and those tears flowing down my face weren't just coming from her eyes but were also mine.

She let go of me and others, everybody, came down and started hugging us, shaking my hand, offering congratulations. I brushed away the tears, hoping the darkness would hide them.

"What is your baby's name . . . umm . . . *nom de bébé?*" I asked.

"Emmanuel," she said.

I laughed. The Saviour. Maybe I hadn't had anything to fear in there.

"Your name?" she asked hesitantly.

"I'm Josh . . . Joshua."

She came over and handed the baby back to me. She said something to her family and they all cheered and smiled.

"What did she say?" I asked.

Philippe smiled. "She said that her baby, Emmanuel, will now be known as Emmanuel Joshua."

I wanted to tell her it wasn't necessary, that she didn't have to do that. Instead I looked down at little Emmanuel Joshua, and he looked back up at me and smiled.

If there had been any fairness, my father and sister would have been waiting for us when we got back. There wasn't and they weren't. I sat on the edge of the bed, a blanket over

SHAKEN

my shoulders to ward off the cold. Around me I could hear the sounds of sleeping. I was starting to feel tired myself. The rush of adrenalin I'd experienced was giving way to exhaustion. Sleep would be good. I'd close my eyes, and when I opened them it would be morning and they'd be here then for sure. And if they weren't?

My mind started going off in directions I didn't want it to travel. I thought about my father being gone . . . gone . . . what a word to use. I thought about my father being dead. No mother, no father. An orphan at sixteen. How would I care for myself? But more important, how would I care for Sarah? She would be so destroyed that . . . and then I had a terrible thought.

If something had happened, if my father was dead, I hoped that Sarah had died too. She couldn't survive without my father. She was so hurt, so troubled, so scared with the death of our mother that it would be better if she were dead too. Without my father, she wouldn't be able to survive.

If I was going to pray—and I wasn't—I would have prayed that they were both fine. But if they couldn't be fine, I needed them both to be dead. It was good that I didn't believe in Heaven or Hell because thinking like that would have sent me straight to Hell. What sort of person would ever hope that his little sister—his innocent, fragile, delicate little sister—would be dead? No, I didn't want her dead. I just wanted her not to hurt any more.

I looked up at the gap in the wall. Philippe and Louidor were sitting there, half asleep, guarding the opening. There had been more reports on the radio about widespread looting, about violence breaking out across the country. They were there to make sure none of that violence leaked into the compound. It made me feel safe to see them up there. I lay down on the bed, turned over, the springs groaning under my weight, and then pulled up the covers until everything except the tip of my head was protected. I closed my eyes and felt myself drifting off.

CHAPTER TWENTY-THREE

My eyes popped open, and for a split second I didn't know where I was or what those sounds were. I sat up and it all came back in a rush. I was in a little bed, surrounded by other little beds, all of which were empty, in a courtyard in an orphanage in Haiti after an earthquake. Even thinking it through in my mind didn't make it seem any more real.

Around me there were the sounds of people hammering and sawing. I looked over to the source. Ryan and Jonathan were on the roof of the dining hall. What were they doing up there? It wasn't that high off the ground any more, but still, why risk having it collapse further with them on top of it?

I got out of bed. I didn't have to check my shoes for scorpions because they were still on my feet. I looked down at my shirt. I was a mess of dirt and stains, ground in to my clothing as I'd dragged myself through the dirt and around the wreckage rescuing Emmanuel . . . Emmanuel *Joshua*. That was worth more than a ruined shirt.

There were clusters of kids all around the courtyard. Some were playing jump rope, others were running and laughing. It was as if the reality that surrounded them wasn't real, or hadn't happened, or had happened so long ago that they'd forgotten about it and it didn't bother them any more. Or maybe this was their way of trying to deal with it—to pretend it wasn't there.

"Good morning!" Naomi sang out as she came walking over.

"Hey."

"This is for you," she said. She handed me a cup of tea and a piece of bread covered with jam.

"Thank you," I said. I took a sip of the tea—still hot, and sweet, the way I liked it—and then took a big bite of the bread.

"We figured a hero should get the chance to sleep in a little."

"I'm no hero."

"Tell that to the mother of Emmanuel Joshua."

"I just did what anybody else would have done. If it hadn't been me it would have been Philippe or one of the other guys."

"We let you sleep in as long as you could," she said.

I looked at my watch. It wasn't even seven in the morning, so that would hardly constitute sleeping in.

"My father and Sarah . . . are they here?"

"It's still early," she said.

Which of course meant that they weren't here. I didn't even want to think about it. I couldn't think about it.

"Even if they left at first light they wouldn't be here until at least ten o'clock," she said.

That made perfect sense, but it didn't settle my thoughts.

"What are they doing?" I asked, pointing to the guys on the roof.

"I asked them to try to get to the infirmary," Naomi said.

"Are you injured or sick or. . . ?" Then I remembered. "Your insulin, right?"

"I used the last I had with me this morning," she said.

"But the insulin in the infirmary isn't good."

"It wasn't *that* good, but it's better than nothing," she said.

"My father and Pastor Dave will bring back new insulin."

"I know," she said. "I just . . . just wanted to make sure."

What that meant was that she didn't feel entirely confident they *would* be back, and she wanted to have an alternate plan, even if it involved bad insulin, which of course was better than none at all.

I popped the last of the bread into my mouth and then washed it all down with the remaining tea.

"I'll go and help them," I said.

"I'll go too," she added.

We started walking. Louidor, perched up on the wall, his radio still playing, stood up and waved to me.

"Hey, *mon ami!*" he yelled out, flashing me a big smile.

"*Bonjour, comment ça va?*" I called back.

"*Très bien, mon ami!*" he yelled back.

"I thought you didn't speak French," Naomi said.

"A few words."

"He's very friendly," she said.

Then I noticed the wall where he was standing. The gap seemed bigger than I remembered it.

"Strange," I muttered.

"What?"

"The hole in the wall where Louidor is sitting seems longer, bigger, larger."

"It is. More bricks fell this morning when the aftershock hit."

"There was another aftershock?" I exclaimed.

"Pretty big. Not like the first quake, but big. I can't believe you slept through it."

"I guess I was pretty tired. When did it happen?"

"Around six. It sort of rattled me out of bed," she said. "It made the beds shake, and then, of course, there was the crash."

"Yeah, I guess a chunk of the wall falling down must have been pretty loud."

"Not the wall blocks, the girls' dormitory."

I turned to look in the direction of the building. I was shocked to see the roof was tilted to one side and some of the wall had caved in.

"Wow. I guess it was good that nobody was sleeping in there," I said.

We climbed up onto the roof of the dining hall to join Ryan and Jonathan. Suddenly this seemed like less of a smart idea. They'd already pulled some of the metal sheets off the roof and were standing partially inside the wreckage, visible only from the waist up.

"Hey, guys, need any help?" I asked.

"I think we pretty well have it handled," Ryan said. He leaned into the hole where they'd removed some metal sheets. "You okay down there, Philippe?"

"Not good," he answered, his voice echoing out from within the collapsed structure.

I dropped to one knee so I could peer inside. What was not good? Did he want me to go down with him? Before I could even think to do anything he appeared below and started to climb up to where we stood.

"It is not good," he said. "It cannot be gotten to. It is blocked, the refrigerator."

"Can we move whatever it is that's blocking it?" I asked.

"No. Many beams, blocks. If we try to move then the whole thing would . . . would . . . *bang*," he said, moving his hands to show how it would collapse.

"But she needs that insulin," I argued. "Without it she could . . . "

"Could die," Philippe said, finishing the sentence with the words I didn't want to say in front of Naomi.

How stupid was it that I didn't want to say them—as if she didn't know what could happen.

"If we try to move then maybe we will die," Philippe said. "I am sorry."

"Thanks for trying," Naomi said. "I'll be fine until they get back with the new insulin. It shouldn't be that much longer. Until then I'll just be careful with what I eat and try to regulate my levels. I'll be fine . . . honest."

She wasn't really convincing me, but I thought she was trying to convince herself even more than she was us. I'd just keep a close eye on her.

CHAPTER TWENTY-FOUR

I shifted one more time to keep as much of myself as possible in the shade cast by the parts of the wall still standing. I'd been sitting there for close to four hours—it was almost noon. It was mainly me and Louidor. Me watching the road, waiting for my father to return, and Louidor just sitting there, humming and singing to himself along with the radio. I'd been listening for so long I was starting to think maybe I could sing along too, because the songs were all starting to sound familiar—or at least pretty much the same.

No vehicles had come along the road, but there had been a lot of people on foot. Some of them were carrying sacks or suitcases, or pushing wheelbarrows filled with possessions, or riding on little donkey carts loaded down with things. People were fleeing from falling buildings, from collapsed homes, looking for relatives who still had buildings standing so they'd have some place to stay, some shelter.

Occasionally Louidor would call out to them, wave, and exchange a few words.

When Philippe was with us he'd translate some of what was said. We got little snippets of information from the passing survivors. They had terrible tales to tell. We heard that there had been widespread damage throughout the entire country. Survivors said that it wasn't just homes that had been destroyed but schools, hospitals, and even government buildings, and that hundreds of people had been killed in the countryside around us. What they didn't tell us with their words or their walking they shouted out with their eyes and expressions. These people had seen destruction and death.

What were less believable were the radio reports. Jammed in between dance music, and delivered in voices that were practically screams, they just didn't seem real to me. It also didn't help that some of the reports contradicted what they'd said a few minutes before. At least, that's what I understood from the French I could follow, and from the bits that Philippe translated.

There were reports that the capital had been reduced to rubble. That all of the government buildings had fallen, the major hospitals had been destroyed, and that even the Presidential Palace had collapsed. They said that there was no longer any telephone communication in Port-au-Prince because all of the cellphone towers had been knocked down, that the airport was closed because the runway was fractured, that the docks at the port had been destroyed, and that asphalt roads had been split and ruptured.

And then there were the reports of deaths. One of the reports said that more than a hundred thousand people had died. *A hundred thousand.* How could that be true? How could that even be real? It couldn't be. No way. That was just the crazy announcers getting caught up in the panic. How could they even know, if the government was in chaos and the telephones weren't working? They were obviously just making things up. What I did know was that in the absence of information rumour quickly became king. But what was I supposed to believe? If only there'd been a report in English, something that I could understand. How great would it be to turn on CNN . . . wait . . . maybe I couldn't get CNN, but maybe I could at least get some information in English.

I turned to Louidor. "*Excusez-moi,* could I. . . ?" What was the French word for borrow? Wait, he knew more English than I knew French.

"I want to listen to an English station, if there is one," I tried to explain. "*Anglais sur radio?*"

His face brightened and he smiled. "*Ah! Anglais! Oui!* Of course!"

He started fiddling with one of the dials and the music stopped, replaced by static and more static. Was that the only radio station still running? And then there was a voice speaking English! And with an English accent! And he was talking about the earthquake! All I'd had to do was ask.

Louidor started to talk and I hissed him into silence.

"In the time since the original earthquake, which occurred at four fifty-three and registered seven point zero, there have

been more than thirty-five aftershocks with a magnitude of four point two, with twelve of those having a measured magnitude of greater than five. More aftershocks are anticipated and we strongly recommend that all buildings, unless specifically designed to withstand earthquakes, remain unoccupied."

The announcer's voice was calm, and he sounded logical, and the English accent seemed to lend an air of credibility to what he was saying.

"Tens of thousands of people are now sleeping in parks and open spaces spread throughout the capital, while thousands and thousands of others have left the city and are seeking shelter in the countryside."

That would explain all of the people we saw passing by. But if they were coming from the city on foot and had already gotten out here, then why wasn't my father here yet? Probably those people hadn't been in the city when it happened but out toward this area.

"While reports of damage have been filed from around the country, some of the greatest damage has taken place at Port-au-Prince, which is only sixteen miles east of the epicentre of the initial quake. Confirmed reports are that many government and public buildings, including the Palace of Justice, the National Assembly, the Supreme Court, and Presidential Palace, have all been severely damaged and are no longer functional. Further, most of Port-au-Prince's municipal buildings have been destroyed, including City Hall, which has been described by a reporter with The Washington Post *as 'a skeletal hulk of concrete and stucco, sagging grotesquely to the left.'"*

This was even worse than I'd allowed myself to believe,

and what made it scarier was that somewhere down there were my father and sister. That is, unless they were on their way back. They had to be on their way back.

"Included in the buildings that are severely damaged are the three medical facilities in Port-au-Prince, including one that has completely collapsed, along with the hospital in Pétionville and the St. Michel District Hospital in the southern town of Jacmel, which was the largest facility in the southeast of the country."

But if the hospitals were destroyed, how were they going to treat all the people who were injured?

"Communications have been severely disrupted throughout the country. Most of the radio stations have been knocked off the air. The telecommunications system has been damaged, and telephone and Internet service is severely disrupted or nonexistent throughout the country. The control tower at Toussaint Louverture International Airport has been severely damaged, as was the Port-au-Prince seaport, rendering both unusable for immediate rescue or relief operations. The Gonaïves seaport remains operational, although the road system is in chaos. Roads are blocked by surface disruption or are severely blocked by debris, making internal transportation as problematic as attempts to bring in aid from outside."

That was it, right there. That was why they weren't back. The roads were all blocked. I was sure they were trying to come here, probably pushing their way through obstacles, but it wasn't going to happen fast. It could take all day, or maybe days. That road hadn't been in very good shape *before* the earthquake.

"And while we must caution that, given the absence of functioning government, the issues of communication, and the destruction of infrastructure, there are limitations in our ability to provide a completely reliable account, it is credible to state that more than one million people have been left homeless, more than two hundred thousand have been injured, and the confirmed death toll is something in excess of one hundred and fifty thousand people."

Those numbers rolled around my head. How could I even imagine that many people being dead? I couldn't. And on some level I didn't care about them. I just cared about two people.

"We will continue to file reports as they become available. This is Nigel Carruthers reporting for the BBC from Port-au-Prince, Haiti."

I slowly got up and started to walk away, and then stopped and turned back around. "Thank you, Louidor . . . *merci beaucoup.*"

He smiled and nodded.

Now I knew how bad it really was. It was reassuring and disturbing all at once. Reassuring because at least I knew. Disturbing because of *what* I knew.

I could continue to sit there and wait for my father and sister and Pastor Dave to get back. They might arrive today, or tomorrow, or maybe not for days and days to come. Maybe not at all. I couldn't let that thought occupy my mind. But then I realized, while I could wait for them to return, one person couldn't.

What about Naomi?

CHAPTER TWENTY-FIVE

I called over the matron, Iris, Naomi, and Philippe and explained that I needed to talk to them all. Iris was hobbling, her leg sore and painful but at least functional. It could have been so much worse. She could have died.

I knew what needed to happen next and I had a pretty good idea what I was going to say to them. Now I just needed them to agree, or at least not *disagree* so much that they would try to stop me.

Philippe stood, while the matron and Iris took seats on the wooden chairs and Naomi sat on the grass beside Iris. I studied Naomi. She looked a bit pale, but her eyes were bright. She had a little smile on her face and she seemed okay.

"You wanted to tell us something?" Iris said.

"I wanted to tell you what I want to do." That wasn't strong enough. "What I need to do." Still not enough. "What I'm *going* to do."

Iris looked questioning, Naomi worried, the matron concerned, and Philippe looked suspicious.

"Look, I've been listening to the radio, and the roads are really not good. Many roads are blocked by buildings or walls that have collapsed, or the surface has been smashed, broken, and movement is difficult."

"That's why your father isn't here yet," Iris said. "I know he's fine."

I wish I could have been that certain. "It could be days and days before he gets here. Gets here with the insulin that Naomi needs."

Now I had everybody's attention.

"But Naomi can't wait a few days. She needs that insulin soon. Today."

"I should be fine until tomorrow," she said.

"Really?"

"Probably . . . if I'm careful with what I eat."

"Have you eaten anything today?" I asked.

"A little bit. I can't eat much. If I don't eat I don't produce blood sugars, or at least I keep them lower so I don't need the insulin . . . well, not as soon."

"What if my father can't get here until the day after tomorrow, or two days from now? Would you still be okay?"

She didn't answer, which was, of course, an answer.

"Then we need him to arrive sooner," Iris said. "We need to pray for his early and safe arrival."

"Pray? You think if we pray he'll get here sooner?"

"If prayer can move mountains, then it can move some

debris from the road to let them pass," Iris said. "It's in the Bible . . . Mark, I think."

"Luke and Matthew," I said.

"I meant Matthew," she replied, sounding embarrassed. "Like a grain of mustard seed, you can say to this mountain, move here to yonder place, and it will move, and nothing will be impossible to you.'"

"That's it!" Iris exclaimed. "We'll pray to move the debris so they can get here sooner."

"So you think that if we pray, just sit and pray, then it will all work out?" I asked, incredulous.

"If we pray with good faith . . . is that Matthew, too?" she asked.

"The best quote is from James. 'Only it must be in faith that he asks with no wavering. For the one who is wavering is tossed by the wind.'"

"Exactly. God can move mountains as long as we pray and have faith in our prayers."

"Just because I can quote it doesn't make it right," I said. "I don't want faith. I want the pickup truck. *That* pickup truck," I said, pointing at the beat-up old truck. "We don't have to move the mountain if we can move toward it," I said. "We have to go down to Port-au-Prince."

"But if they can't get up here, why do you think you can get down there?" Iris asked.

That was a good question, but I had an answer. "We don't have to get all the way down there. We could meet them on the road."

"What if you miss them?" she asked.

"We can't miss them. There's only one road, one way to get here, right, Philippe?"

He nodded. "Until just before Port-au-Prince."

"Then we can't miss them. It's a narrow road," I argued.

"Unless you miss them right in Port-au-Prince."

"If we get all the way to Port-au-Prince and we haven't met them, then we have to go to the embassy. They'll have insulin; that's where my father was going to get it in the first place. Besides, they'll know . . . they'll know about my father and sister. If . . . if . . . they are . . ."

I let the sentence trail off. I couldn't say the words, but there was no need. Everybody knew what I was thinking because they were thinking the same thing.

"But you don't know the way to Port-au-Prince," Iris argued. "And why do you think you could even find the embassy if you were able to get down there?"

"I can't. I need help." I turned to Philippe. "Would you come down with me . . . with us?" I said, gesturing to Naomi.

He nodded his head. That was good.

Naomi looked a little bit surprised and a lot worried. Somehow I didn't think she'd realized that she had to go with me—there was no point in getting the insulin unless she was there to take it.

"But that truck," Iris said. "Could it take you all the way to Port-au-Prince? It looks about ready to break down."

"I'm sure it will be all right," I said, looking to shut down any objection she might make.

"The truck is . . . is," Philippe shook his head and

grimaced, "not so good."

"Then that settles it," Iris said, sounding satisfied.

"No, it doesn't. If it gets us partway that's better than no way."

"But what if it breaks down only a mile or two from here?" she asked.

"Then we'll have a shorter distance to walk back instead of going to the city, but at least we will have tried."

I had to end this discussion. She couldn't really stop me if I decided to go—but somehow I did want her permission.

"'Pray as though everything depended on God. Work as though everything depended on you,'" I said. "St. Augustine."

When in doubt, draw on a religious passage. I think I could have found one to justify almost any action or inaction.

"God does not want us to simply pray and wait, but to take action. Pray while you work," I said, although my plan was to work without prayer.

Iris looked more convinced. She was teetering on the edge of agreement. I had one more card to play to push her over.

"Iris, it's my father and my sister. I have to go to them, to try to find them. You understand."

That wasn't just manipulation. Those words weren't just coming from my mouth or my head but from my heart and my soul. I *did* need to go. I *did* need to find them. I couldn't just sit and wait. Wait and hope that they were fine. I had to go down there, try to find them, and help them if they needed my help. Sitting and praying and waiting hadn't saved my mother. It was time to try something different.

CHAPTER TWENTY-SIX

We stood in a big circle, holding hands, as Iris led us in a prayer for our safe journey. I had Naomi on one side of me, and I knew without looking that she had her eyes tightly closed and she was praying in good faith.

Philippe, across the circle, had his eyes open as wide as mine, although his head was slightly down. Was that respect or simply that he didn't want to be too obvious? I knew a little bit about putting on a veneer of respect. It was hard to be in a church service with your father leading the congregation when you didn't believe much that he was saying. Did that make me a complete hypocrite? Maybe it just made me a pragmatic hypocrite.

Every minute standing here was another minute that we weren't heading down the road. We still had six hours before sunset, which was much more than we'd need to get to the city under normal circumstances, but this was as far from normal as we could ever get.

It was still possible that we'd meet my father and sister coming up the road before we got too far. I had a premonition and quickly turned toward the gate, but there was no one driving into the compound—just the open gate and Louidor standing beside it. It was good to have him there, watching, guarding. The things—the people—that necessitated there being a wall with broken glass at the top surrounding the compound were still out there. The earthquake hadn't changed that. In fact, if the reports of looting in the capital were correct there was even more need for a strong wall.

While we were gone, Ryan and Jonathan had promised to lead the kids in efforts to rebuild the wall, mixing cement and either reusing the blocks or replacing the broken ones with the blocks that were earmarked for the new dormitory. Interestingly, the new dormitory walls had stood strong. I felt proud—and angry. Why hadn't the people who had made the other buildings made them better, or stronger?

The prayer went on and on. I wasn't surprised. I'd found that the more worried people were, the longer they prayed. Although in many cases it sounded like begging instead of praying. More like little children making a wish list for Santa. And we all knew there wasn't any Santa Claus. For me this was nothing but a waste of time, but I knew it was important for some people, Naomi among them. I knew she found this sort of thing comforting, the same way some people had lucky charms or stepped over sidewalk cracks or wished on stars. They all made about the same amount of sense. Did anybody think that God was up there listening, waiting to "fill their order" like some sort of warehouse drone?

Then I remembered something my mother had said to me when I was about ten. I'd been praying every night to make the soccer team, and still I hadn't made the cut. She told me then that just because you didn't get what you prayed for didn't mean that God hadn't listened—just that he'd said no. I hadn't thought about that for years. I guess, being here, where nobody got anything they prayed for, the memory had naturally come to the surface.

I was starting to pray for this prayer to end, but Iris continued to drone on and on. She really wasn't very good at this, but I had to give her credit for sincerity, even if the Bible passages were stale, common, and in one case just plain wrong. People often got confused between Matthew and Mark. It was very common to mistake one disciple starting with the letter M for another disciple starting with the letter M. Maybe there shouldn't have been two disciple names starting with the same initial. After all, Jesus *had* renamed people. He'd changed Simon's name to Peter, because in Greek *petros* meant rock, and he said "on this rock I will build my Church." Maybe he would have been better to have renamed either Mark or Matthew. Then the books of the New Testament could have been "Matthew, Buddy, Luke, and John." Oh well, hindsight's twenty-twenty.

"Amen!" Iris called out at last, and everybody echoed.

I chuckled to myself. At least one of my prayers had been answered.

Naomi gave my hand a little squeeze before she released it. I knew she was scared—scared to come with us and scared to stay behind, in case they never arrived with the insulin. Coming with us was probably the lesser of two evils, and she trusted me. I couldn't help but think that trust might have been misplaced.

Everybody moved along with us as we walked toward the truck. There was an almost festival feeling to it with the kids—the orphans—all smiling and happy and skipping. I don't think they had a real sense of how serious all of this was, not just for us, but for them. What would happen to them if something had happened to Pastor Dave? I guess their innocence was their armour. I didn't have any armour.

"Do you have everything?" Iris asked.

"I think so," I said.

"Lots of food and water," Naomi said.

We had enough supplies to last for a week. Not because anybody expected us to be out there that long. At least, I didn't think that's what it meant.

"And extra *essence*," Philippe said, referring to the gasoline, two canisters, strapped into the back of the truck.

Again, it was much more gas than we were going to need, but too much was better than too little. There were no gas stations along the whole first section of the road, and who knew what we'd find when we got closer to the city.

Philippe and the matron exchanged a few words and then he turned to the children and barked out what sounded like orders. They all nodded their heads obediently in agreement.

I tapped my hand against my moneybelt, tucked under my shirt. Inside were my passport and some American currency. I also had more money tucked inside my left sock. Actually, more of my money was in my sock than in the moneybelt.

"Do you have your passport?" I asked Naomi.

"I've got it."

I reasoned that we might need our passports for ID if we ran into soldiers, or if we had to prove to the embassy staff that we were Canadian citizens before they'd help.

Thoughts of my sister and father kept crowding into my head and I kept pushing them out again. Maybe I didn't believe that praying would lead to positive things, but I did think you had to keep your mind aimed in a positive direction. It wasn't that bad thoughts would lead to bad things, but that they could cloud your thinking. I couldn't afford cloudy thinking.

I opened the door for Naomi and she climbed in. I wanted her in the middle. I climbed in beside her and closed the door. It sealed with a tinny sound. The cab was small and I was pressed right against her.

Philippe climbed in and started the truck . . . or at least *tried* to start the truck. The starter growled and the engine whined and whined as it rolled over but didn't catch. He pumped the gas pedal and I could smell the *essence*—was he going to flood the engine? What if we'd gone to all of this trouble, and nothing was going to happen? No, that wasn't how this would play out. If I had to take a backpack and start walking toward the city I was going to—

The engine roared and a belch of black smoke poured out of the tailpipe, filling the air with acidic, caustic fumes. The kids started cheering. I felt like cheering as well.

Philippe put the truck into gear—fought the stick to get it into first—and the truck shook forward as he released the clutch. The kids gave another big cheer as we crept across the compound and stopped again at the gate, where Louidor stood guard. Louidor stooped down so he could look in the driver's window. He and Philippe spoke, although Louidor was doing most of the talking and Philippe was nodding his head and saying "*Oui*" a lot.

"Joshua," he said then, and I looked over. "Mon ami."

He reached over and offered his hand. We shook.

"This is . . . this is . . . *pour vous.*"

Out of his jacket he withdrew a machete! He leaned into the car and instinctively I pulled away and—he wasn't threatening me, he was offering it to me.

I drew back my hands. "No, um, *non, merci* . . . I'll be okay."

"No, you take it," Philippe said as he reached over, took the machete from Louidor, and tried to hand it to me. I still hesitated.

"I should not be the only one with a knife," Philippe said. He pulled up his shirt to reveal a large knife, in a sheath, tucked down the side of his pants.

"I'm sure we won't need those," Naomi said.

Philippe shrugged. "I am not so sure, but I know I'd rather 'ave it and not use it than need it and not 'ave it."

That made more sense than I would have liked. I took

223

it. It was heavier than I'd thought it was going to be. "Thanks, Louidor . . . *merci beaucoup*." I put the machete down on the floor by my feet.

Philippe put the car back into gear and we started out through the gate. I looked out the back window and watched as Louidor swung it closed. We turned and he was lost from sight, but I could still see the high wall and then, as we turned again, I could see the hole in the wall. Dozens of kids—both orphans and mission kids—were standing there on the blocks, waving and smiling and calling out to us. I gave them a little wave back.

"I guess we're on our way," I said absently.

"I guess we are," Naomi replied, although with her there was a real questioning tone, doubt in her voice.

"There really isn't much of a choice," I said.

"I know," she agreed.

We also both knew that even though a bad choice was better than a really bad choice, it still didn't make it a good choice.

CHAPTER TWENTY-SEVEN

There was a steady stream of refugees moving along the road, all of them moving away from the capital. We were like fish swimming upstream, and we had to slow continually to negotiate our way around donkey carts or groups of weary, worn-out people. They walked, almost trance-like, with their eyes either on the ground or staring ahead but not really seeing. It was almost like watching actors in a cheap zombie movie. Except zombies didn't carry bags or push wheelbarrows loaded with possessions.

On numerous occasions Philippe had to honk his horn to break the trance and get their attention so they'd move off the path and let us pass. Only the smallest children seemed to take notice of us. Well, at least they were the only ones who waved. For everybody else it was as if it felt wrong to do that, like laughing at a funeral.

We had just about the only vehicle on the road. It had

been almost an hour and we had only come across three buses, all heading away from the capital, and all with people practically spilling out of the windows, their roofs piled high with parcels and even passengers. Each time, Philippe had pulled our little truck over to the side to let them pass. The only rule of the road in Haiti seemed to be that bigger had the right of way. I wished we were in something bigger, like a Hummer or a tank. That would have made me feel less exposed. There was something grimly unnerving about being out here that was making me feel more and more anxious as we drove.

I figured that somebody had to be going the same direction as us, it was just that we hadn't overtaken them yet, or they hadn't overtaken us. We couldn't be the only ones heading toward the capital.

The road wasn't nearly as bad as I'd feared, and we seemed to be making slow but steady progress. Slower than I'd have liked, but that couldn't be helped.

"We're doing okay," I said to Philippe, wanting him to confirm what I thought was true.

He nodded his head. Not as enthusiastic as I would have liked, but still agreement.

"The damage around here isn't that bad," I added. "At least, it's no worse than it was for us."

That was true. There were buildings, homes, sheds, and barns with collapsed roofs and tumbled-down walls, but it was no worse than at the compound. There were even people out working the fields, carrying water, tending to their livestock. I guess life had to go on. Crops needed to be worked and animals needed to be cared for, and people had to eat. I was suddenly grateful for the extra food we'd brought along. I took a swig from my water bottle.

The truck slowed down and then came to a stop. I wanted to ask why, but I soon saw the answer. The road in front was blocked with bricks from a house that had collapsed and partially tumbled onto the road.

"Can you go around it?" I asked.

Philippe said nothing. He was looking around for the answer. I looked too. Hopefully he saw something that I didn't see, because it looked as though the slope on one side was too steep and the debris from the house blocked the other.

"There is only one way," Philippe said. "We must go along the road."

"You can't get over it, can you?" I asked, knowing the answer before I asked.

"Too big . . . the big buses could get over, or a big truck. We cannot do it. We have to clear the road."

He climbed out of the truck, and Naomi and I followed. He left the truck running.

"Shouldn't you turn it off?" I asked.

"*Non.* We have enough *essence.* If I turn it off it might not start again."

That made sense. This was not a good place for the truck to quit on us. We were way too far from the city to think we could walk that far, and it would be a long walk back to the compound, and we would have come all this way for nothing.

I picked up some bricks and heaved them out of the way. Philippe did the same. Naomi bent down to grab some.

"Should you be doing that?" I asked. "Maybe you should sit in the truck."

"I have diabetes, I'm not an invalid."

"But what about the insulin?" I asked.

"My last testing showed that my sugars were a little high. It's better for me to do something physical to burn up the sugar in my blood."

"In that case, maybe I should sit in the truck and you can move everything," I joked.

"I don't think I need that much exercise."

Naomi joined in, grabbing a brick and tossing it off to the side of the road. It rolled down the slope, gaining speed until it hit the bottom.

"I was wondering, can you really control your diabetes with exercise and not eating?" I asked.

"It's not so much not eating as *what* I'm eating. Diet and exercise are part of it. Some diabetics don't even need insulin at all," she explained.

"But not you?"

"I still need insulin, but if I'm careful I can go longer without needing to use it."

"Then you need to be careful."

"Now you sound like my mother," she said.

"I'm not your mother."

"Okay, then you sound like my boyfriend."

That surprised me. "I . . . I didn't know you had a boyfriend."

"Well, I don't. Not right now. We broke up a few weeks ago."

"Sorry," I said.

"Sorry that I'm unattached right now?" she asked. "That certainly makes a girl feel wanted and attractive."

"No! I'm just sorry that you had to go through that. It must have hurt," I said.

"It wasn't fun, but it wasn't the worst thing in the world." She paused. "We all know what it's like to lose somebody we love."

I didn't want to even think about my mother. Especially not now, not with my father and sister still out there. I prayed . . . I *hoped* that they were still out there, okay.

"When you think about what happened here, thousands of people killed, hundreds of thousands hurt, and maybe millions without homes, it makes me realize how insignificant my little breakup was," she said.

Or the death of one person . . . no, it still hurt. The hard part was thinking that each of those people who had died in the earthquake had people who cared for them, people they'd left behind, people who would have to go on without them.

Little by little we took down the pile, clearing a path until it looked as though it was almost low enough and wide enough to let the truck through. As we worked we were passed by more than two dozen people—a family with two small children, individuals, or groups that were probably related in one way or another. Philippe exchanged a few words with most, and Naomi and I threw in a few "*Bonjour*"s and "*Comment ça va?*"s. Philippe's goal was to try to get some information about the road ahead.

As one couple approached, Philippe greeted them loudly in French, and they looked up and slowed down to speak to him. Philippe was asking questions, and they answered—well, the man answered. His responses were short and quiet and flat, like even talking was almost more effort than he could muster.

I heard Philippe mention Port-au-Prince, and the woman suddenly jumped into the conversation. Her voice was loud and sharp and emotional—a direct contrast with that of her husband. She was shaking her head and her eyes were wide and she looked scared. She went on until finally the man reached out and put his arm around her, calming and silencing her.

Philippe thanked them, and as they started to walk he trailed after them. I watched as he pulled out one of the bags containing our food. He took out two sandwiches and handed them to the couple. They nodded enthusiastically and thanked him emphatically and then went on their way. They had gone no more than a few steps when they unwrapped them and began to eat.

"What did they say?" I asked.

"He said the road was broken in many places. That it is much more worse the more we travel. Very, very bad damages."

"But we can travel along the road?"

"He thinks," Philippe said, shaking his head, "but he does not really know if a truck can get through."

That was good and not good. If a vehicle could get through then we could reach the capital. But if a vehicle could get through, why hadn't my father and Pastor Dave come back?

"What did the woman say?" Naomi asked.

"She did not think that we should go to Port-au-Prince."

"Why not?" she asked.

Philippe hesitated. "She said that it is . . . bad in the city."

"Bad damage?"

"Yes, the damages are very bad. But there is more."

"What more?" Naomi asked.

Philippe looked at me as though he was asking permission to tell her. I nodded my head. I wanted to know too.

He took a deep breath. "There are troubles. There is not enough food or water or places to sleep. There has been looting, robbing. There is violence. Much violence."

"Is it safe for us to go there?" Naomi asked.

"We're going to meet my father long before we get to the city," I said, before Philippe could answer.

Naomi reached out and took my hand. "We'll keep going."

CHAPTER TWENTY-EIGHT

With each mile there seemed to be more—more people, more destroyed buildings, and more breaks in the road. Some were minor enough that Philippe was able to drive and thump and bump the truck over them, rocks scraping against the bottom of the vehicle. Other times he was able to pull off the road and drive around them, although once we got so stuck in a field that I didn't think we'd ever be able to get free. Philippe was able to talk some people into helping push. There never was a lack of people around, all of them moving away from the capital.

I caught a glimpse of another vehicle ahead, bright rays of sun reflecting off a windshield. I held my breath, hoping that it was them. It wasn't. It was another one of those crazy little buses. Of course that didn't mean they weren't inside it. After we'd passed the first few buses, I'd realized it was possible that Pastor Dave's bus had broken down or been damaged and they couldn't use it. In that case, the bus would probably be their only way to get back.

We slowed down, as did the bus, as we approached each other. It was overflowing with people stuffed in so tightly they were pressed against the windows, and there were five or six people sitting on the roof among the parcels and luggage tied on top. They bounced up and down as the bus bumped along the rutted little road. It was probably good that there were packages for them to hold onto—or maybe they were anchoring the packages in place.

I craned my neck to look. I was sure they weren't on the roof, and I didn't see any white faces inside, but then I couldn't see all of the faces.

Philippe tooted on the horn to get the attention of the people inside and we all strained to look as it passed. We didn't see any familiar faces.

He put the truck back into gear and we jumped forward. At least we hadn't wasted any more time. Twice we'd met these buses at places where the road was too narrow for us to pass, and we'd had to back up until there was room to get off the road.

"How far do we still have to go?" I asked Philippe.

"Far. We have travelled less than half the way."

I'd just glanced at my watch a few minutes before and knew this wasn't good. It was after four, and at this pace we weren't going to get to Port-au-Prince before nightfall. If we turned around now we might, just might, get back to the compound before dark. But how would that help Naomi?

No, there was only one way, and that was forward, regardless of what was ahead of us.

"I will try to move a little faster," Philippe said.

He shifted gears, the gearbox grinding as the little vehicle shook and shuddered and then picked up speed. He wasn't going to be able to pick up enough speed for long enough to get us there in time. I knew that, but I was glad he was trying. The more distance we put between us and the compound the less likely we'd even think about turning around.

Dim had become dark almost an hour ago and our pace had become even slower, even though the roadblocks had been cleared in many places to allow vehicles to pass.

The world around us was basically lost, so all we could see was the road ahead of us, or at least the little bit illuminated by the truck's one weak yellow headlight. That was almost reassuring in a strange way. I could almost pretend that what was out there *wasn't* out there. At least until we passed right by a collapsed building or through a crowd of people moving along the road or sitting at the side. More zombies with blank, shocked expressions. I tried not to look at them.

I did find myself wishing that the door could lock or I could at least afford to roll up the window, but we needed it open to allow air to flow in. Instead I became more aware of the machete at my feet. I didn't want to pick it up because I didn't want to get Naomi upset or scared. At least more scared than I suspected she was already feeling.

"How are you doing?" I asked her.

"About the same as I was ten minutes ago when you asked me."

"Just making sure."

"I appreciate you making sure, but I'm fine. Really."

Philippe brought the truck to a stop at a little intersection where our dirt road met another dirt road.

"Here, they could come from either way," Philippe said.

"Which way do you think they would come?" I asked.

He shook his head. "Either, but neither."

"What does that mean?"

"They won't travel now. We should not travel now."

"How far are we from the embassy?" I asked.

"Ten, maybe twelve miles."

"We're close. Too close to the city to stop now," I said.

"No, no. We are too close to the city to *not* stop now."

I thought I finally understood what he meant. "Do you think it's too risky . . . too dangerous?"

"Where the embassy is it is a not good area."

I thought about my sister's backpack being stolen in broad daylight on a main street—before the earthquake, before the whole city had been thrown into chaos.

"So what do you think we should do?"

"We wait until light."

I looked at Naomi. "Can you wait? Are you okay until morning?"

"I think I'm okay."

"Could you check your blood . . . please?"

I pulled out the flashlight and turned it on as she went

into her bag and removed her testing kit. She pricked her finger and a little trace of blood dripped out.

"Well?"

"It's high, but not too high," she said. "I'll be okay until tomorrow."

"Then we'll stop here. We'll wait until first light."

Philippe put the truck into gear.

"I thought we were going to stop," I questioned.

"Yes, but not here in the road."

He drove the truck off the track and into the flat field off to the side. There was a little building—maybe it had been a house once, before the walls had collapsed and the roof caved in. It was dark and appeared deserted. He pulled the truck around to the side of the house so that the collapsed walls stood between it and the road, providing some protection.

He turned the truck off, but instead of simply stopping, the engine kept chortling and shaking, and then there was a gasp and the motor stopped and we were engulfed by the silence of the night.

"So we'll sleep in the truck, right?" Naomi said.

"Not luxury but the best we can come up with. It'll be a little tight in here but there's room for three."

"Not three . . . two," Philippe said.

"We can all fit in here," I said.

"Someone must watch. I will watch first. You sleep first."

He climbed out of the truck and closed the door behind him. He slumped down against what remained of the wall of the little house, his back against it, his eyes looking forward.

"Are you going to be able to sleep?" Naomi asked me.

"Not right away, but you should close your eyes and try."

"I will. But first I'd better say my prayers."

She put her hands together, closed her eyes, and brought her hands up to her face. I watched, and listened. I could hear her quietly "talking" but couldn't hear what she was saying . . . praying. It was a long prayer. I guess there were lots of things she wanted to ask for. There were a few things I could have suggested.

"Amen," she said loudly. She opened her eyes and looked right at me and smiled. "*Now* I can go to sleep. Until I say my prayers it just doesn't seem right. It's part of my routine."

Routine, rut, ritual, superstition, stupid . . . choose a word.

"Maybe now even more than usual I feel as though I need God's grace, to have him watching over me," she said. Her eyes were closed, her voice already sleepy, and she was turned away from me. "I just want us all to be safe . . . especially your father and sister . . . I said an extra prayer for them."

I knew what I was supposed to say. Something like, *Thanks, that means so much to me*, or, *God will protect them*. "Go to sleep," I said softly.

She nodded her head ever so slightly and then turned over so she was now facing away from me with her head resting against her hands.

I was pretty sure sleep was not going to come easily for me. This was the perfect storm: not being able to sleep normally, sitting up all crowded and cramped on the uncomfortable seat, exposed, and worried—not just about what was happening and what could happen just outside our vehicle, but because I was concerned about Naomi and her blood levels. I'd have to keep an eye on her and make sure that she was just sleeping . . . how could I do that without actually waking her up? I'd have to think about that. Maybe I'd just watch and listen. It would be great if she snored.

On top of that, I knew that I'd have to spend part of the night on watch, so I'd be thinking the whole time about having to get up anyway. Of course, in some ways, that was even more reason why I *should* try to catch some sleep now while I could.

Naomi had mentioned routine. There had been a routine in my house. Stories, followed by my mother singing a lullaby, and ending with a prayer. I still read at night, and I often used to listen in while my mother read to my sister . . . I still listened to my father reading to her, although he wasn't nearly as good at it.

Reading was one of the things that helped me get to sleep. If I'd had a book—and enough light to read by—that would have helped. No book. No mother. Not even my father. The only thing I could do was pray. As if that was going to help . . . but it wouldn't hurt, would it? If God didn't listen to prayers it didn't matter, but it could help to settle my thoughts, maybe help make me a little bit more sleepy. I needed to sleep.

I looked over at Naomi. Her eyes were closed. She wasn't even facing my direction. I looked around for Philippe. He was nowhere to be—no, there he was, still sitting on the ground, leaning against the wall. He wouldn't be looking at me, and even if he did he wouldn't be able to see what I was doing. I certainly wouldn't be able to tell if *he* started to pray. But no, this was stupid and just plain useless. What was the point? Even if God was listening, and I was sure he had a few other things to occupy him right now, that didn't mean he was going to listen to me. Why should he? It wasn't like I was praying in "good faith." But then again, even if he didn't listen, all I'd done was waste a few minutes. It wasn't like I had someplace else to go right now or something else to do.

I took one more fast look around. Naomi was sleeping. Philippe was too far away to see.

Slowly, carefully, I brought my hands up to my face and interlaced the fingers. I closed my eyes. It felt familiar. It felt good.

Dear God, I said in my head. *It's been a while. I know that. I know you know that too because you're supposed to be all-knowing.*

I tried to gather my thoughts for what I was going to say next. My mind did feel more clear, more calm.

I figure you have a lot of things you're dealing with now. There must be millions of people praying, asking for somebody to be alive. I'm doing the same. Please, just this once, could you please spare my sister and my father? Could you bring them to me, or me to them? If you do that, I'll never ask for anything again. I'll start believing again . . . at least believing more. I'm not asking for anything for myself and I won't bother you any more. Okay, thanks for listening.

Was there anything else? Nothing else that mattered.

Amen, I said silently.

I lowered my hands and opened my eyes. Somehow I did feel better.

"They're going to be okay."

I startled at the sound of Naomi's voice.

"I prayed for them too," she said. "Try to go to sleep." She closed her eyes and then turned back around, away from me.

I guess I should have felt embarrassed. Instead I felt calm, reassured, and maybe even a little comforted.

CHAPTER TWENTY-NINE

I shifted my weight slightly so that the rough edges of the wall dug into another part of my back. It was uncomfortable, but there was a reason for it—I'd drifted off a bit but never gone completely to sleep. On the horizon there was a faint but certain line of light beginning to form. The sun was just starting to come up. I was so grateful, so relieved to see light again. With the morning came new hope—and new challenges.

While the night had given us the illusion of being invisible, it had also hidden everything else and made it impossible to see what was around us. Other than one vehicle—a big truck of some kind—the road had been empty all night. I'd heard what I thought were people moving past but hadn't actually seen anybody. Of course, more than once I'd heard sounds in the distance—a man calling out, a baby crying, dogs barking. And now, as the sun was starting to come up, I heard a chorus of roosters crowing, welcoming the new day. It was time to get going.

I got to my feet. My back was sore and I stretched to try to work the kinks out. I took a few steps, then stopped, bent down, and retrieved the machete from the ground. It had been my companion for the past few hours, since I'd relieved Philippe at around three in the morning. It now had to be close to six.

I started to walk toward the truck when my attention was caught by movement on the road. It was a person— one person—quickly coming our way. Instinctively I tightened my grip on the machete. This person could be a threat, or—wait . . . was that. . . ? I recognized the shirt first, and then the person wearing it. It was Philippe! I rushed to meet him.

"Where were you?" I asked. "I thought you were sleeping!"

"Looking at the road ahead."

"And?"

"That way is impossible," he said pointing back the way he'd come. "Collapsed buildings and the road has . . . has . . . gone."

"What do you mean 'gone'?"

"Down the hill."

He made a gesture with his hand and I understood— there had been a landslide.

"So that means we go that way," I said, pointing down the other road.

"We try."

We walked back to the truck, and at first I was a little thrown by not seeing Naomi through the window. I looked in and there she was. She was stretched out—as much as she could be—on the seat. Her neck was awkwardly kinked to the side, her head resting against the door, her eyes closed, her mouth open, and a little bit of drool was running down her chin. I also noticed that her chest was slowly rising and falling and she made a little whistling sound as she breathed. It was a reassuring sound. She was fine.

"Naomi," I called out softly. "It's time to get up."

She didn't answer, move, or respond. I was no longer reassured.

"Naomi!" I practically yelled.

She jolted awake, her eyes popping wide open, and she practically sprang into a sitting position. She looked frightened.

"Sorry," I said. "I didn't mean to startle you. It's time to get up. We have to get going."

"Yes . . . of course . . . okay," she stammered, still half asleep and half disturbed. "I just have to use . . . have to find . . . a washroom . . . a place to relieve myself."

I opened up the door for her. "Just around the corner of the house is a spot."

"Thanks."

She got out of the truck. I watched her stand up and walk. She seemed steady on her feet as she disappeared around the side of the house.

"There's not much chance that we're going to run into them now, is there?" I said to Philippe.

"So many ways to come," he said. "Probably not."

"Then we have to get to the embassy. You know the way, right?"

He nodded his head.

"How long do you think it will take us to get there?"

This time he shook his head and shrugged, and of course I knew that was a stupid question to ask. He had no way of answering because he had no way of knowing what was between us and the embassy.

I thought of a question that he could answer. "You hungry?"

"Very."

I opened up the pack and pulled out three sandwiches. I handed one to Philippe, who unwrapped it and began eating. I did the same. The bread was now a little bit stale but it still tasted wonderful. My mother always said food tasted best when you were hungry, and I was starving.

Naomi turned the corner and started back toward us. I studied her. She was walking normally, no stumbling, at a good pace, and her expression seemed right. She was even smiling a little bit. I walked over to meet her.

"Breakfast is served," I said as I bowed slightly from the waist and offered her the third sandwich.

"Thanks for the offer," she said, "but I'm going to pass."

"You're not hungry?" I asked, astonished that that could be the case.

"I'm hungry. I just shouldn't."

"But if you're hungry then you should . . . this is about your blood levels, right?"

"If I don't eat I don't accumulate as much sugar in my blood," she explained.

"So if you don't eat they don't go up?" I asked.

"They don't go up as fast. Before they discovered insulin, one of the methods of treatment for diabetics was to severely limit food intake. Some people called it the starvation method."

"And that worked?"

"It worked for a while. Eventually they all died, but it took longer," she said.

That sent a shiver down my spine.

"Don't worry," she said, "I'm not going to die by not eating for a day."

"Okay, good . . . that's good," I stammered. "You should check your levels now. Maybe they're not too high."

"I already checked."

"And?"

"They're high. Not too high, but higher than I'd like. I'll be okay. I'll just keep drinking a lot of water. This will be a twenty-four-hour fast, like a special diet plan. I could afford to lose a pound or two."

"Well I wouldn't say that. We'll just make sure it isn't twenty-four hours. We'd better get going."

"I'm ready," she said. "I'm just not sure the truck is ready."

"The truck?" I turned around. The hood of the truck was up and Philippe was half hidden, leaning in, looking at the engine. "He's probably just checking something. You know, adding water or something."

Even as I said that I had a terrible fear that that wasn't what he was up to. We rushed over to join him.

"What are you doing? Adding water to the radiator?" I asked, hopefully.

"It would not start," he answered.

"Are you sure?" I asked before I realized how dumb that sounded. I was full of bright questions this morning.

"It would not even make a sound. I will try again. You listen."

He climbed off the bumper, leaving the hood open, and went into the cab of the truck.

"Okay, go ahead and try!" I yelled out.

"I *am* trying!" he called back.

There was nothing. Not a groaning, grinding, pinging, or clicking. The engine just wasn't responding.

I circled around to his open window. "Any idea what could be the problem?" I asked.

"I know nothing about trucks. Do you?"

"I know enough to know this isn't good. It could be the starter or the generator or even the battery. Can we get somebody to help?"

"I will ask people in the 'ouses around, but no . . . I do not think so."

Naomi and I sat, backs against the wall, in the shade, watching as the two men fiddled around with the truck, while Philippe stood by, looking helpless. The men lived in one of the hundreds of houses that lined the road in the direction of the city. I didn't know if either of them knew much more than we did about engines, but they were trying. So far, trying wasn't succeeding, but they weren't giving up.

I took a big swig of water and passed the bottle on to Naomi.

"I just hope they can get it to run," I said.

"I've said a little prayer for that, too," she said. "But I guess it's in God's hands."

"Those hands might be a little full right now."

"They're big hands," she replied. "I was just thinking that maybe it's his will that we just sit here and wait, and your father will come right down that road, and that's why God didn't let the truck start this morning."

"I'm not sure God had much to do with the truck not starting. I think that has more to do with it being twenty-five years old, worn out, and pushed harder than it should have been pushed . . . but I was fantasizing about them coming along the road, too."

"You know they're fine. For all we know they're probably back at the compound now, wondering where we are," she said.

"That would be terrible!" I exclaimed. "Not that they're safe, but, I mean, because I brought you out here, and if you'd just stayed at the compound you'd be okay. I feel so bad making you come along."

"*You* didn't make me do anything. I made the decision. I'm just so grateful that you were so concerned about me that you decided to do this. You didn't have to. You're not the one who needs insulin. I don't know if I've thanked you enough for what you've done."

ERIC WALTERS

"So far I haven't done anything except get us stuck in the middle of nowhere," I said.

I startled at the sound of the hood of the truck being slammed shut. I looked over and Philippe started toward us. Both Naomi and I got to our feet.

"Well?"

"Do you have money?" he asked.

"Sure, of course. How much do you need?"

"Twenty dollars."

I pulled out my wallet, took out a bill, and handed it to him. "Is this for the men for fixing the truck?"

"They could not fix it. It needs parts."

"Is the money for the parts?" I questioned.

"The parts cannot be gotten."

"Then what's the money for?"

"For the men. For trying to 'elp, and so that they will watch the truck and make sure it is not stolen until we return."

"Return from. . . ?"

He shrugged. "You must decide. Either we walk forward to the embassy or back to the orphanage," Philippe said.

"It would take *days* to walk back to the orphanage," I said.

"At least two. Maybe we could get a ride partway on a bus going that way," he suggested.

"That would cut down the time . . . assuming we could get a ride."

"Maybe yes. Maybe no. They are very crowded and they might not stop, and probably they are not going to where we are going."

"And the embassy?"

"We could start now and walk. We could be there by dark."

I turned to Naomi. Really, it was her decision to make.

"I don't think we can go back," she said. "It's too many days, and if they're not there and there's no insulin, then . . . " She let the sentence trail off. "We need to go forward. We need to go to the embassy."

"I agree," I said.

Philippe didn't look happy.

"Do you agree?" I asked. "Is that what you think we should do?"

"I will do what you want. But the men, they said it is very bad ahead. Very dangerous. They said that they think that we should go back."

"I don't think we have much choice," I said.

"Then we need to 'urry. We need to get there before dark." He paused. "When darkness comes it will be . . . it will be . . . much worse."

CHAPTER THIRTY

The sun was now high enough in the sky that there was virtually no shade, except the little that was cast by the houses clinging to the side of the road. The road, the hills, everywhere there were little houses . . . although calling these hovels "houses" was very generous.

They were mostly little huts, brick and mud and metal thrown together in a haphazard way that seemed to lack plan or order or organization of any sort. The irony was that the simplest places seemed to have withstood the quake the best. Bricks and blocks and timbers had twisted and broken and crumbled and tumbled, while those made up of metal sheeting and pieces of scrap wood somehow remained standing. Or maybe it was just that they were so dilapidated to begin with that there wasn't much to damage. On the drive up—before the earthquake—I'd noticed that many of them already looked to be on the verge of tumbling over.

As the sun had risen higher in the sky more people had started to appear. Some had already started to rebuild their homes. Men and women and children were shifting rubble, moving bricks and blocks, clearing spots, and even hammering together shelters out of scraps of wood and sheet metal that they'd scavenged from the remains.

We passed many people who hardly even noticed our passage. Others noticed, but only offered stunned, shocked, numb nods. I wondered what they had seen or what or who they'd lost. Others smiled or waved and called out greetings. In some ways those people—friendly and nice—were almost more disturbing to me. It was as if they hadn't noticed there had been an earthquake.

A man yelled out to us from a field. We all turned. He was walking toward us, cutting across the ground to intercept our path. What did he want? And then I noticed he wasn't alone. There were two, no, three other men trailing behind him. They were all young—maybe in their early twenties. He kept yelling out at us and waving his hands in the air. There was something about his tone, his posture, that made me feel anxious.

"What does he want?" I asked Philippe.

"I do not know."

They came onto the road directly in front of us and stood there in a line, blocking the way. We stopped directly in front of them, and the biggest—who seemed to be the leader—started talking to Philippe. He was smiling, but there was something about his smile that wasn't friendly. He pointed directly at me and Naomi, said something, and the other three loudly laughed, but there was no joy in the laughter. My bad feeling got worse.

Philippe answered back in quick Creole French, and I couldn't understand what he said or the next few bursts of conversation between them. I was getting more uncomfortable by the minute. I thought about the pack on my back—or more specifically about the machete in the pack on my back. If I put down the bag and undid the clasps and did it all casually so they wouldn't get alarmed, I was sure I could get out the machete.

Philippe said something and they all burst into laughter, but this time it sounded like real laughter. Then they all stepped aside.

Philippe thanked them, and we started walking again, right between them, two on each side. I reached out and took Naomi's hand and guided her in front of me. I wanted her where I could see her. Single file we walked past them. I tried to watch in both directions out of the corners of my eyes without being too obvious. As we moved ahead I listened intently for the sound of shoes against stones, in case they came after us. Nothing. And then I heard something and spun around, just in time to see them head back into the field.

"Philippe, what did they want?" I asked.

"They wanted to know why I was walking with two rich white kids."

"And what did you tell them?"

"I told them you were white, but you were not rich. I said to them if we had money, did they think we would be walking?"

"And that's when they laughed?" I asked.

"Not then. I told them I was walking you to someplace where you could get some money, and then *I* was going to rob you."

"Were they going to rob us?" Naomi asked.

"They were thinking about it, but I told them you did not 'ave enough to make it worth their while. They believed me."

Naomi stumbled, and I reached and grabbed her by the arm.

"Are you all right?" I asked.

"Fine, just tripped on a brick."

The road was still littered with debris from the houses that had collapsed.

"Do you want something to drink?" I asked.

"That would be nice."

I started to stop to pull off the pack and Philippe grabbed me by the arm. "Not now. We will keep moving, just in case they change their minds. We go a little bit further."

I wasn't going to argue.

I felt a little bit of a surge in speed as we hurried along, trying to distance ourselves from the four men. I kept sneaking little glances over my shoulder, just to be sure we weren't being followed. With each step, and no sign of pursuit, I was feeling more confident that we had left them behind. But just because we'd left them behind didn't mean there weren't more like them in front of us.

I swung the pack off my back so it hung on one shoulder and undid the buckle holding it closed. Still walking,

I reached in and felt around for the machete. I shuffled it around so that it was free of everything else. Free in case I needed to pull it out quickly.

The road dipped and we rounded a curve. There were dozens and dozens of houses and little storefront shops and stalls. As usual, every single one of them was destroyed and deserted. The only difference now was that there was less open space between the clusters. We were getting to the point where the houses—or the remains of houses—occupied all the land. And now, everywhere we turned, everywhere we looked, there were people. Many of the people were on the move—again, always moving away from the city—but others were just sitting beside the rubble, what remained of their homes, and more and more people were digging, trying to reclaim something from the nothing. It seemed like an impossible task.

"Are we in the city now?" I asked. "Is this Port-au-Prince?"

"Yes . . . no . . . it is difficult to say where the city starts."

"But we are getting closer," I said.

"Each step is one step closer."

"What time is it?" Naomi asked.

I looked at my watch. "Just before one in the afternoon."

We'd been walking for almost six hours. I didn't think I'd ever walked for six hours straight in my life.

"Philippe, how about if we take a short break?" I suggested.

In answer he turned off the road and found a little piece of shade cast by the remaining wall of a destroyed house. We joined him as he sat with his back against the wall. I could feel the coolness of the brick through my shirt. It felt good. It felt good just to be out of the sun. In the shade of the wall it was much cooler . . . but I wasn't sure how I felt about standing this close to a wall that could easily come tumbling down like the other walls of the house. I guessed we wouldn't be staying there long, and the shade did feel good.

I pulled out one of the water bottles in the pack and handed it to Naomi. She took a big, long drink and then handed it back to me.

"How are you feeling?" I asked.

"Tired. And really, really hungry."

"Maybe you could just eat some bread."

"A little. I'm feeling a bit light-headed, but that has more to do with the walk and the heat and not eating and less to do with my blood sugar. At least I hope."

I pulled out three of the six remaining sandwiches. It was beginning to look as though we hadn't packed enough food. I handed one to Philippe and the second to Naomi. She carefully took it from me, as if she thought it might bite her. And then I realized that in some ways it could—how the conversion of food to sugar *could* harm her.

"I'll just eat a little bit of the bread and avoid the peanut butter as much as I . . . " She stopped talking and a strange, curious look came to her face. "Hello . . . how are you?"

I turned and looked where she was staring. Two little girls were sitting in the shade of a tree by the corner of the house. They were so little and still that I hadn't even noticed them. The bigger of the two couldn't have been any more than eight or nine, and the other was tiny, young, maybe four or five—although I'd learned that kids here were often older than they looked, so maybe they were both older.

"Don't be afraid," Naomi said.

They did look frightened.

"Tell them not to be afraid, that we're friends," Naomi said to Philippe.

He relayed the message. They didn't look convinced or any less scared.

"Are you hungry?" Naomi asked as she held out her sandwich toward them.

Again Philippe asked them. The older girl said something that I could barely hear but couldn't understand.

"She said they have not eaten since the quake," Philippe told us.

"But that was almost two days ago!" Naomi exclaimed.

She stood up and walked toward them. The bigger girl slipped an arm around the little one protectively. Naomi ripped the sandwich into two pieces and offered them to the girls. I thought they'd hesitate but they didn't. They started wolfing the food down hungrily until it was gone.

"Get another sandwich for them," Naomi said.

I got up and Philippe followed behind. We walked over and stood overtop of the two of them—actually three, because Naomi had sat down right beside the girls. Their hands and faces and clothing were dirty. I handed Naomi another sandwich and she divided it, giving it to them.

"Are they sisters?" Naomi asked. "How old are they?"

Philippe asked and the older girl answered.

"Yes, they are sisters. The older girl, she is called Annabelle, and she is ten. Her sister, who is five, she is named Juliette."

"Those are pretty names. Ask them where their parents are."

Again Philippe spoke to them. I picked out a word or two—*mère* and *père*, mother and father—and the older girl didn't stop eating but she answered and then pointed to the ruins of the house. Were their parents on the other side of the house? They were probably trying to salvage some things from the wreckage.

"What did she say?" Naomi asked.

Philippe looked as though he wasn't sure what to say. I knew that he'd understood her, so that couldn't be it. I had a terrible feeling.

"Well?" Naomi persisted.

"She said her father is . . . they don't know . . . he was in the city . . . they hope he will come back soon."

"And their mother?"

"She is there," Philippe said, pointing at the wall of the house.

"She's on the other side of the wall?" Naomi asked.

Philippe shook his head slowly, slightly, and sadly. "No. She is still in the house . . . under all the bricks."

"You mean she's trapped!" Naomi exclaimed.

"Not trapped. She is not alive."

Naomi looked shocked. "No," she said. "Maybe she's okay . . . she could be okay . . . right?"

"I don't know," I said. "I . . . I . . . I could check." Why had I said that?

"Could you?"

"Yes. Of course." I turned to Philippe. "Can you come with me?"

CHAPTER THIRTY-ONE

Three walls of the house had collapsed inward and the roof was piled on top of that. Anybody who was in there would have been killed . . . but baby Emmanuel had survived, so maybe their mother could have survived. This was no worse than that house . . . well, not that much worse. But where did I even hope to start? Where did I begin?

I looked up. Philippe was already poking around in the rubble. He walked around the side, looking, tilting his head to one side and then the other. Was he listening? Did he hear something, the way I had been able to hear Emmanuel crying? I went over to his side.

"Do you hear something?" I asked.

"I am listening with . . . with . . . my nose."

"You're smelling? What are you trying to . . . " I let the sentence trail off as I realized the answer.

"Do you smell?" he asked.

As soon as he mentioned it I did smell something. Something bad.

He climbed out onto the wreckage, his footfalls noisy against the corrugated metal roofing that was now almost at ground level. He touched his nose with one finger and then pointed down. I knew what he meant.

The metal sheeting was littered with bricks that had tumbled down on top of it when part of the wall fell inward. He bent down and started to pick up bricks, tossing them off. I hesitated for an instant—I didn't want to climb on the wreckage, or on what could be beneath the wreckage. Slowly, carefully, I climbed up and onto the roof, and moved over until I was beside him. I took a deep breath in through my nose. I did smell something, but not really much, and I didn't know what it was. Regardless, if he thought this was the place . . . I bent down and picked up a brick and tossed it to the side.

"Finish the bricks," Philippe said.

Before I could think to answer he'd jumped off the roof and disappeared around the corner of the one remaining wall.

I felt very uneasy, alone, on top of a collapsed building standing on top of . . . on top of a body. There wasn't time to think about it. Quickly, brick by brick, I cleared the sheet of roofing and then removed the few bricks from the one beside it. The two sheets were attached with little rivets but many of them had popped off and there was a crease between them. I bent down and inserted my fingers and tried to pull them apart, but they wouldn't separate.

"'ere," Philippe said. "I will do."

He was carrying a pick that had been in the back of the truck. He inserted the end in the gap between the two pieces of sheeting and then pressed his weight against it. The separation got bigger and then there was a *pop* and he almost fell over as a number of the rivets snapped all at once and a valley opened up between the two sheets. He dropped the pick and then dropped to his knees; taking the metal in his hands, he started to peel it back. I stepped out of the way and looked into the gap and into the remains of the house. Instantly I saw the bodies.

Not one but *two* women—girls, really, hardly older than me. One was wearing a brightly coloured dress, covered with cheerful flowers. She was partially buried under an avalanche of bricks, her head smashed open, her face down, looking away from me. The second, even younger than the first, was lying beneath timbers and bricks. Her body was twisted into awkward, impossible angles and her dress was stained with large, dark-red patches—blood. Her face was turned upward, toward me, her eyes open and empty, and there were flies, hundreds of flies, all over her face.

I felt a rush of heat; my stomach churned as I quickly turned away and stumbled off the sheeting. I jumped down onto the ground and at the same time my lunch resurfaced. I bent over and vomited. I doubled over and vomited again. This time it was more like dry heaves, more noise than volume.

I needed a drink of water to wash out my mouth and settle my stomach. I stumbled around the corner of the building and I looked up. Naomi and the two little girls were staring at me. Naomi's look was so questioning, so hopeful.

I shook my head. "I'm sorry . . . there was nothing we could do."

Naomi bent down and wrapped one arm around Annabelle and the other around Juliette. She held on. I waited for her to let go but she didn't.

She looked up at me. "Are you sure this is what we should do?"

"They're going to be all right," I said. I now turned to Philippe. "Right?"

"They will be cared for," he answered. Philippe had gone to neighbours and asked them to look after the girls. "They will stay with them until their father returns."

Naomi turned around so that she was facing toward us and away from the girls. "But there have been so many deaths. What if their father. . . ?" She let the sentence trail off. There was no need for her to say anything more.

"When we return from Port-au-Prince, Pastor Dave and me, we will stop here . . . to see . . . to check," Philippe replied.

"And if their father hasn't returned?" she asked.

"Pastor Dave, he will try to find family."

"And if he can't find any family?" she pressed.

"They will be cared for. The pastor says he can always find room."

Naomi smiled. She seemed reassured. I wasn't. With the buildings at the orphanage destroyed, how was he going to care for the children already living there? And what about all of the orphans across the entire country? If so many people had died, there were going to be so many more orphans. What if Pastor Dave wasn't even alive?

I looked down at the two little girls. Maybe we had more in common that any of us knew. Maybe we were all orphans. At least they had each other. I might be all alone.

"Are you sure there isn't another way?" Naomi asked.

"No other way," I said. "They can't come with us, and we can't wait here."

"Is there anything else we can do for them?" she asked.

"We've done what we can do," I answered.

We'd given the neighbours thirty dollars to buy food for the girls and for themselves. That would feed them all for many days to come.

"And their mother and their auntie?"

Annabelle had told us that the second woman we found was their aunt, their mother's sister.

"Naomi, honestly, there's nothing more we can do."

I looked at my watch again. The seconds were ticking off. It was close to two-thirty. I didn't even want to ask Philippe about our chances of getting to the embassy before dark because I knew I wouldn't like the answer.

"We have to go," I said.

Naomi didn't move.

"Now," I said.

I offered her my hand. Reluctantly she took it, and I helped her to her feet. She gave the girls another hug. Philippe said something to the girls and then to the neighbours. I nodded my head as though I understood and agreed with what he was saying. Naomi gave the girls one more hug and then we turned and started to walk.

CHAPTER THIRTY-TWO

The pavement was the surest sign that we were finally, really in the city. Like the long road we'd been on, the city streets were clogged with rubble and debris. At the bigger intersections small campsites had sprung up. Colourful bedsheets and tarps had become primitive tents. City-dwellers whose buildings had been destroyed, or who simply wouldn't go back inside for fear of the next aftershock, were camped out in any space large enough, far enough from buildings, to put up a shelter. In a city this crowded, with buildings almost on top of each other, the intersections were the closest you were going to get to open space.

There was a film of smoke in the air that you could see, smell, even taste. The air was acidic and awful, and even gulping water didn't clear the burn from my tongue. All around us plumes of smoke were rising into the air. We'd passed more than a few fires already. Smouldering and burning piles of garbage and debris seemed to be everywhere. I wasn't sure if they had been set for warmth and light at night, or just to try to clear away the refuse, or simply as an act of frustration or vengeance or anger. What I did know was that they were everywhere. The fires, and people.

We'd seen so many people flooding out as we'd walked in that I'd thought the city would be emptier. Instead it seemed to be as overcrowded as ever. That might have just been because everybody was out and on the streets. People weren't risking staying inside.

There were, however, almost no vehicles on the streets. Except for those parked at the side of the road, demolished, destroyed, buried under bricks and blocks and timber, or completely crushed as buildings toppled onto them. It made sense—the roads were almost impassable. We weren't moving very quickly, but on foot was probably the only way to move.

There was one other way to get around. We heard a helicopter pass over, high in the sky. I waved at it before I realized just how dumb that was. Desperation creates dumb. It was too high, moving too fast, and we were just three little needles—two of them white—in a gigantic, burning haystack. There was no way they'd notice us.

Occasionally, however, somebody on the ground would do more than notice us. They'd come up and ask for food or water, or money, or for our help—ask if we could do anything. Philippe explained that because we were white they thought we could do something. And there was no shortage of people needing help. Everybody needed help, including us.

Philippe skidded to a stop. I was going to ask him why when I saw the answer. On the street dozens and dozens of men were crawling out of and running away from the wreck-age of a destroyed building. Each man was loaded down, his arms filled. One was carrying a case of water, while another had a gigantic package of toilet paper.

"Looters," Philippe said. "We have to turn around . . . we have to get away."

"We'll just walk around where they are—"

"No!" Philippe exclaimed. "It is dangerous."

"But they're just stealing groceries."

"If they steal from a store, they might steal from *you*. People see white skin, they think you have money. Other people have asked. Some might just take. They could have knives, machetes, even guns. We must leave."

I didn't need to be told again. We spun around and started to backtrack down the street. I hated to move in the wrong direction, but it was better than not being able to move in any direction.

"How much danger is there?" Naomi asked.

Philippe shrugged. "We will be careful. Not so much . . . it is still light."

The implication was that at dark it was going to be worse. I just hoped Naomi hadn't picked that up.

"Will we be at the embassy before dark?" she asked.

Obviously she had understood. I looked at my watch. It was less than two hours until nightfall.

Philippe didn't answer. The delays at the beginning, the difficulty moving, the obstacles, and the distance we'd had to travel from the place the truck had failed us had all conspired against us.

"We will move fastly," he said.

"But first we need to take a break," I suggested. "Just a minute."

Nobody argued.

I aimed us toward a patch of shade created by the remaining wall of a building. My need for shade was greater than my fear that it might fall. We stopped and I pulled the pack off my back. I pulled out one of the remaining bottles of water and handed it to Naomi.

"How about if you test your levels again?" I suggested.

She nodded her head. She pulled out her testing kit as I pulled out the last two sandwiches from the pack, handing one to Philippe.

Slowly, casually, I took Philippe by the hand and led him slightly away and then turned my back to Naomi so she wouldn't be able to hear me.

"Do you think we can get to the embassy before dark?"

"No, it is not possible."

"How dangerous is it going to be?" I asked.

"Very. I would never go 'ere after dark before."

"So what do you think we should do?"

"Maybe wait, find a place to 'ide and rest until morning. Better to be 'idden than out in the open."

I nodded my head, thinking through what he was saying. If he thought we should do that, it made sense. But that decision wasn't going to be made by him or me. Even though she didn't know it, that question was being answered by Naomi . . . or at least by her blood sugar level. We might not have any choice but to push on. I hated that out-of-control feeling.

"Are you sure it's still dangerous at night? Maybe things are different now," I suggested.

"Different, yes. Better, no."

"What exactly happens at night?"

"People come out. Bad people . . . gangs, because there are no soldiers out at night."

"But there are no soldiers or police out now in the *day*," I pointed out.

We hadn't seen anybody who was official or government either patrolling or attempting to rescue anybody.

"Nobody is bothering us during the day," I continued.

"Not yet. Night is different. In the dark people think nobody can see what they do, even God."

"I'm not sure God is watching anything here."

"He is watching," Philippe said.

His answer surprised me.

"Like he's watching you pray with your eyes open?" I suggested.

"He watches. I do not think he cares if my eyes are open or closed, as long as my 'eart is open."

That answer surprised me even more. I didn't know what to say. I turned away and walked back toward Naomi.

"What are the results?" I asked her.

"Higher."

"How much higher?"

"I need insulin soon."

"Then you'll get it. The embassy isn't that far. Are you good to walk?"

"Unless you're going to carry me, I think I'll have to be fine."

The fire in the middle of the street seemed to span the entire width of the road. The smoke was thick and black and overwhelming of all my senses. The only good thing was that the flames were so bright and lit up such a large area, it was as if night was being temporarily suspended.

"We can get around it," I said, although it was more a question than a statement.

"We can try," Philippe said.

We had to try. From what Philippe had told us, the embassy was not too much farther away and straight ahead of us. We couldn't afford it to be much farther or longer. At least Naomi couldn't. I now knew the signs well enough to know that her blood levels were getting dangerously high. She was stumbling and tripping more easily and her words were slurred and her eyes glassy.

"You good?" I asked her.

"Good. Great," she said.

That wasn't how she sounded.

I angled to the far side of the road, where there was a bigger gap between the fire and the remains of the building. As we got closer I could feel the heat being thrown out—it was tremendously hot. We fell into single file to get as far away from the flames as possible. Philippe took the lead. I fell in behind him, and I reached back and took Naomi's hand to guide her. I didn't want her to stumble into the fire.

I turned my head slightly away from the flames to get some protection from the searing heat, but I noticed that Philippe was looking straight into the flames as we passed. Why would he do that? I turned my head slightly and out of the corner of my eye I looked into the fire. It was pretty amazing. I'd never seen a fire that big, that bright, that powerful. What was in there that was making so much smoke, such hot flames?

There were wooden beams, burning brightly, piles of garbage, tires, and . . . I did a double take. I could see a body, on fire, the flesh bubbling and burning and melting off the bones! And then I saw a second body and part of a third, and another, and—I stumbled.

"Don't trip!" Naomi said.

I looked back. She gave me a smile. She hadn't seen what I had seen.

"Are you all right?" she asked. Her smile faded to a look of concern.

"I'm good."

I pulled her forward so that she was beside me, and I used my body to shield her from the fire and what was in it. She didn't need to see that. I just wished *I* hadn't.

We made it past the fire and then Philippe stopped. His expression was shocked. "In the fire . . . there was—"

"Many things," I said, cutting him off. There was no question now that he'd seen the bodies. It just wasn't necessary to share that knowledge with Naomi. "And there is no need to talk about it. Let's just get—"

My words were cut off by a piercing scream—it was Naomi. There was a look of complete horror on her face and she was pointing—but pointing away from the fire.

I turned and instantly saw what she had seen. Just a few feet away were the still smouldering, charred remains of a human body tied to a telephone pole.

CHAPTER THIRTY-THREE

"Just take another sip of water," I said softly.

Naomi kept sobbing. We were sitting off to the side of the road, just down from the fire, in among the crumbled remains of a building, using the still-standing wall to shield us from the body. The only way I could get Naomi to stop staring and pointing and screaming had been to get something between us and it. The light from the fire still spilled over the wall and provided enough light to disguise the night.

Gently I placed a hand under her chin and lifted up her head so that she was looking straight into my eyes.

"Take another drink of water," I said.

She nodded her head and then tipped back the bottle, draining the last little bit—the last water we had.

"Why?" she asked. "Why?"

"I don't know why." I turned to Philippe, but he just shook his head.

"I just know that we have to get going. Now. Before it gets any later. You need to get some insulin."

I didn't give her a chance to say yes or no. I stood up, took her by the hand, and pulled her to her feet. She didn't resist.

"How much farther?" I asked Philippe.

"Not far . . . straight . . . maybe ten or twelve blocks."

"Good. Naomi, you keep your eyes on me. I don't want you to look back. Do you understand?"

She absently nodded her head. Her eyes were becoming so glassy I didn't think she fully understood, and I wasn't sure whether she'd be able to see even if she did look back. Her whole condition had plunged in the thirty minutes it had taken to calm her down. Thirty minutes we didn't have to waste.

We took a few steps and then we froze. Cries and screams came rolling down the street. Philippe dropped to his knees, taking shelter behind the debris, and I did the same, pulling Naomi down beside me. At first I couldn't see anything, and then people came into view—men and women and children—running as if their lives were at stake. And then behind them came more men, chasing after them with clubs and sticks and machetes. They surged forward, overtaking the last of the people they were chasing.

A man was knocked to the ground and four of the men swarmed him, striking out with the sticks, beating him. He screamed out in pain, his arms flailing, trying to ward off the blows, and then he went limp, not even reacting as the blows continued to rain down on him.

The four men, barely breaking stride, turned away

from the body and raced off down the street in pursuit of other targets.

I looked over at Naomi. Her expression was blank. Either she hadn't seen . . . or she was getting farther into a hyperglycemic state.

"They're gone," I said.

"They could come back," Philippe said.

"Then we'd better move right now before they do."

I started to get up but Philippe grabbed me by the arm.

"Because they are gone does not mean there are no others," he said.

"But we have to get to the embassy. We have no choice."

"We could wait until morning. It would be safe . . . safer."

"Naomi can't wait. I have to take her."

I thought harder about what I was about to say because I really didn't want to say it. But I had to.

"You don't have to go. You can stay."

To be out there with Philippe was terrifying. To be out there without him was beyond that. But what difference was he going to make if a mob attacked us? They'd just kill three of us instead of two.

He let go of my arm and then got to his feet. He offered me a hand and pulled me up.

"Pastor Dave would go," he said. "Jesus would not let you go alone."

"You're not Pastor Dave or Jesus."

"I still try to be. Come, quickly."

I took Naomi by the hand and helped her to her feet.

274

Together we stumbled out of the wreckage and onto the street. It was deserted except for the man's body. I looked back toward where they had run, toward the fire. There was nobody. I just wished the fire weren't burning so brightly because it made us so visible, so exposed.

"Come, quickly!" Philippe said.

We started walking, almost running. I towed Naomi along with me, her feet shuffling along the uneven pavement. If she tripped I could keep her from hitting her head but I couldn't stop her from falling. Anxiously I looked back. She smiled. I looked past her, almost afraid to see what I might see. There was still nobody on the street.

We slowed to a walk as a mound of bricks partially buried the road. Carefully, watching the path that Philippe was navigating, I followed behind, holding Naomi even more tightly by the hand. We scaled the heap and started down the other side. The road behind was now out of sight. Out of sight somehow made it safer in my head.

Up ahead the road was clear and empty. The gang had scattered whatever people had been in the street. They were probably taking refuge, shelter, hiding. That's where we would have been if we'd had any choice. We were the only people on the road. And then up ahead, out of the darkness, a man appeared, and then another, and another and another, until they practically filled the road. And each of them carried something in his hands—a stick, a machete, an axe, a shovel.

Slowly they walked toward us. I had to fight the urge to turn and run, but Naomi couldn't run, and really, I couldn't escape them either.

"We'll just . . . we'll just give them all of our money," I stammered.

"Robbers kill so there are no witnesses," Philippe replied. "Stand behind me."

"No," I said. "You stand *beside* me."

I stepped forward so we were shoulder to shoulder. Naomi was right behind us. I swung the pack off my back and put my hand in so it rested on the machete. I saw that Philippe had his hand tucked down the waistband of his pants to where I knew his knife was hidden.

The men came forward, the first few stopping directly in front of us while the rest surged past to surround us on all sides.

The man started to say something in French.

"Speak in English!" I demanded.

He stopped speaking. He was obviously as surprised by what I'd said as I was for saying it. If I was going to die, I at least needed to understand what was being said.

"Why are you out here?" he asked. His English was good.

"We need to get help for our friend," I said. "She's sick."

"Lots of people are sick. There is no help."

"If we can get to our embassy we hope they can help," I explained.

"You are Americans?"

"Canadians."

"Ah . . . your embassy is close."

"That's where we're going. It's just up ahead," I said, pointing in the direction they'd come from.

He shook his head.

"It's not that way?"

"That way is blocked."

"Look . . . my friend . . . she's very sick. She needs help. If you could just let us go on our—"

"You cannot go."

"We don't have much money, but you can have whatever we've got," I pleaded.

"We don't want your money."

He turned to the man beside him and said something in rapid-fire French. The man nodded, and then he and more than half of the men walked away, down the road. Why had he done that? Then I realized that he didn't need all of those men to take care of us. Now there'd be fewer people to split the money and fewer people to witness what he was about to do.

I pulled the machete out of the bag, and at the same time Philippe pulled out his knife and brandished it in front of him.

The man took a slight step back and then—to my surprise—smiled. And the men around him smiled, and a couple chuckled. I guess it was pathetically funny to think that we might somehow fight off all of them—even half of them were so many more than us.

"You are brave boys," he said.

I didn't feel very brave.

"Put away your weapons," he said.

"You put away yours!" I ordered.

His smile got bigger. I didn't blame him.

"We mean you no harm," he said. His voice was calm and gentle, but his eyes were fierce, and there was a look of pain, anguish, visible even in the limited light.

"If you don't want to harm us, just leave us alone!" I screamed, my voice cracking over the last few words as I tried to sound brave but only sounded scared.

"We cannot do that."

"Then you'll have to fight us."

"Maybe 'brave' was the wrong word. Foolish is what you must be."

That did feel more like it.

"We will not fight you, but we will not leave you. If we leave, you will be killed. There are many bad men out tonight."

I knew that—I was standing there with a dozen of them right in front of me.

"You come with us," he said.

"We're not going anywhere with you!" This time my voice held.

He turned to the man beside him and handed him the axe he was holding. He held his hands up, palms toward me. "You must come with us. We are going to take you to your embassy."

CHAPTER THIRTY-FOUR

We made our way through the streets, surrounded by the twelve men. I had my arm around Naomi, not just to shelter her but to help keep her on her feet. She was now so stunned that she wasn't even reacting to what was happening around her. It was as if she wasn't even aware there was anything that could go wrong.

The men turned to the left, down a side street, not in the direction of the embassy.

"Why are we going this way?" I asked.

"The other way is blocked. Many buildings fell," our guide replied. "Don't be afraid. If we wanted to harm you we would not need to take you someplace to do that."

His blunt statement made sense. Perfect, awful, scary sense. If they had wanted to harm us then or there, there was nothing we could do to stop them. I could do nothing except believe him—although I still didn't understand why he was there. I wanted to know.

"I was wondering, if you don't mind me asking, why are you all out here?"

"There are many bad people out. Stealing, harming, looting, even killing. You have seen such things, yes?"

"Yes. Looting, and then there were these men and they had sticks, and they beat a man to death."

"There have been many deaths. Much violence. The man who was beaten, was he a good man or a bad man?"

"What?"

"Was the man looting or harming others? If we found a man doing those things we would serve justice as well," he explained. "We are here to protect, and that might mean using force. There are gangs with guns."

"What would you do if you met one of those gangs?" I asked.

He lifted up his shirt slightly to reveal a pistol tucked into his pants. "We would shoot them." He let his shirt fall down to cover the gun again.

He'd said it so calmly, in such a matter-of-fact way, that I had no doubt he was telling the truth, that he would do it.

"Without police, without soldiers, there is only us to protect . . . the way we are protecting you."

"Thank you . . . thank you for doing that."

He shrugged. "We had no choice."

"Your English is very good," I said.

"So is yours."

I started to say something when he began to laugh. It was a warm laugh, which made it seem even stranger being out here surrounded by . . . by . . . hell.

"This boy with you," he said, pointing to Philippe, "is he your servant?"

"I am no servant to anyone!" Philippe snapped angrily.

Getting them angry did not seem like a great idea. Even if they did say they were here to help us. "He's our friend," I said.

"And where did you meet this *friend*?" he asked me.

"He's from the children's home where we're staying," I said.

"An orphanage? Why were you at an orphanage?"

"We're here as part of a mission trip, with our church."

He nodded his head. "That is why most whites come. Either to save our souls or steal the few resources we have left."

"I'm not here to do either," I said, suddenly realizing that my tone wasn't much friendlier than Philippe's. "We were just here to help."

"And who was to help *you*? Who is it that runs such a program that lets you go out onto the streets at night alone?" he questioned.

"My father is running the trip."

"And he let you go out by yourselves?" he demanded.

"No, of course not!" I paused. "He doesn't know. It's just . . . just that he's here in the city . . . somewhere. He wasn't with us when the quake hit."

The man suddenly stopped walking and turned to face me. "And you do not know where he is?"

I shook my head. "I don't know about him or my sister."

The expression on his face suddenly matched the expression in his eyes. "It is hard not to know. At least I know where my family is."

There was something about his words, his expression, the way his whole body slumped that made me realize there was more—something terrible.

"Your family . . . where is your family?"

"Gone," he said. "My wife, my father, my sons, and my daughter. All gone. All taken from me in the quake."

I felt my whole body shudder. "I'm so sorry." I didn't know what else to say. He'd lost his whole family . . . had I lost my whole family?

He turned to me. "I will pray for your father and sister to be found. You must stay strong. You must have faith."

"Faith?" I questioned. "After all that's happened to you, how can you still have faith?"

"Faith is all I have left. I know God is still watching over us."

"Watching and seeing?"

"Watching and seeing and listening. Remember, even when your prayers are not answered that does not mean God is not listening. Just that—"

"He said no," I said, completing his sentence—completing my *mother's* sentence.

"You know that saying?"

"My mother always used to say that to me."

He smiled. "So did mine." His smile faded. "*Used* to say. Has your mother passed?"

"This year . . . six months ago."

"I am so sorry. There is something else my mother used to say to me. Faith is only faith when there is nothing else. Have faith."

"I wish it were that easy. I just need for Naomi to get help."

"Your friend, she is diabetic," the man said.

"Yes, she is. She needs insulin, soon," I said.

"She does look hyperglycemic."

"Are you a doctor?"

He laughed and shook his head. "My daughter had diabetes. There were times when we could not get insulin, so I have seen the signs. I'm sure she will get it at the embassy."

"She needs it soon."

"As it will be. There is the embassy."

Up ahead I could see the high stone walls and the big metal gate. Behind the walls was the building—they had lights! They must have had their own generator.

"That's a beautiful sight," I said. "We're going to be okay."

We walked forward and I noticed there were people—hundreds and hundreds of people—standing or leaning against the wall or sitting on the pavement in front of the gate.

"Why are there so many people here?"

"They know that aid will come, and most people trust the Canadians. They know if there is food to be given that it will be given out by them," he said.

The crowd was large, but subdued, almost eerily quiet. As we came toward them they moved aside to allow us a space to get to the gate. It was closed. I placed a hand on the metal and felt a rush of relief. We were here. Inside that gate was a small piece of Canada, people who could help us—who could help Naomi.

They'd also be able to tell me about my father and sister. Suddenly all the sense of relief washed away. With some things it was better not to know, so at least you had hope. Even if you didn't have faith, you could still have hope.

"Hello!" the man yelled through the bars of the gate. "We need to talk to somebody!"

Two soldiers appeared out of the shadows. They were both carrying machine guns and they were dressed in green fatigues with little Canadian flags on the shoulders. The flag made me feel so happy. We were here. They'd open the gates and—

"The embassy is closed for the night, sir," he barked. "Come back in the morning."

"We can't wait until the morning," I said as I stepped forward.

The expressions of the two soldiers suddenly changed. They looked shocked to see a white kid outside their gate.

"I'm Canadian." I pulled Naomi forward. "We're *both* Canadian."

I turned to Naomi. "I need your passport," I said.

She fumbled around in her pocket, found it, and handed it to me. I pulled out mine and passed them through the bars to one of the soldiers. He turned on a flashlight he'd been holding and shone it on our passports.

The soldier holding our passports turned to the other. "Get the C.O. and embassy staff. Get the chargé d'affaires."

"What if he's asleep?"

"Nobody is sleeping, but if he is, wake him up. Tell him we have two more of the missing Canadians."

The soldier rushed off.

"How many Canadians are missing?" I asked, although I was only interested in two of them.

"There are more than 2,000 Canadians in Haiti. We still have more than 850 unaccounted for."

"Unaccounted . . . does that mean . . . some are . . . some are. . . ?"

"Some are dead. We have confirmed deaths."

My heart sank. I knew there were deaths, tens of thousands of deaths, but somehow I just thought it wouldn't happen to us.

"But for most it just means we don't know where they are yet. Communication is a mess and transportation almost impossible. We think we know where most of them are, but we don't have the manpower to go out and get them or make sure they're fine. We just don't know. It would be easier if they all just walked up to the gate like you two. . . On second thought, though, no . . . that would be worse. You two shouldn't have done that. You could have been . . . well, something really bad could have happened."

"We had help." I looked first at Philippe and then at the man—I didn't even know his name.

"You two really should have stayed where you were," the soldier said. "Even we don't go out there unless we're in large groups, especially at night."

"We had no choice. We had to get help for Naomi. She needs insulin. And I need to find out about my father and sister. They weren't with us when the quake hit. Would somebody here know about them?"

"Somebody might. If they've reported in or were confirmed as . . . I'm sure they're just fine."

I knew what he'd been about to say—confirmed as dead. I'd made it all this way, through all of this, possibly to be told that they were dead. So much for prayers, so much for faith. But at least I knew Naomi would be fine.

"The reports, can you tell us how many people have died?" I asked.

"Latest estimate puts the death toll at over 250,000."

"That can't be right." How could you even imagine that many people and then think of them as dead?

"It's right. A quarter of a million fatalities, another 300,000 with significant injuries, and more than one million people homeless."

There was movement behind him now and a man, followed by the original soldier and two others, rushed forward. He wasn't what I'd been expecting. He was a little man in mismatched clothing and he was wearing flip-flops. Maybe they had woken him up.

Barely glancing at us, he grabbed our passports and looked at them, studying them. Then he looked up, first at Naomi and then at one of the passports—hers, I assumed—then at the other and at me. His look was serious, suspicious, and a little confused.

"Open the gate," he ordered at last.

I almost burst out laughing.

One of the soldiers quickly started to unlatch the gate. In response, the crowd around us suddenly became animated. People who had been sitting stood up, while those standing started crowding toward us, toward the gate.

The gate opened just slightly and six soldiers came out of the shadows and passed through. They pushed against the crowd, forcing them back, yelling out orders in French for the people to move back. We were trapped between the two sides, pushed in both directions. I wrapped my arm around Naomi and then propelled her forward, between two of the soldiers through the open gate.

I reached back and grabbed Philippe and tried to push him forward but one of the soldiers stepped in front of him, blocking his way.

"He's with us," I said. I looked past the soldier to the little man—the man in charge. "This is Philippe, he's with us."

"Is he a Canadian citizen?" the man asked.

"No, he's from here, he's Haitian."

"Then he can't come inside the grounds."

"What?" I exclaimed.

"Only Canadian citizens. We can't let everybody in."

"Not everybody. Him. He's with us!" I had to raise my voice to be heard over the crowd, which was getting more agitated and louder. "If *he* doesn't come in then *I* don't come in."

"What?" the man demanded.

"You heard me. Either he comes with us or I don't go inside."

"That's ridiculous!" the man snapped.

"Yeah, it probably is. Take care of Naomi. Get her some insulin, quickly. I'm staying out here."

"That's insane. Do you know how dangerous it is for you to be out there?"

"Then let me in. Let us *both* in."

"If you stay outside the gates you could be killed. Are you willing to take that risk?" he demanded.

"Are *you* willing to take that risk? Are *you* willing to be the one who turned away a Canadian citizen?"

He opened his mouth to say something but didn't. He looked angrily at me and then turned to the guards.

"Let them both in," he said.

The soldier stepped aside and I propelled Philippe through the opening and then stopped. I hadn't thanked that man. I spun back around.

"What are you doing?" the little man asked.

"I have to do something."

"Nobody else will come in! Do you understand?"

I ignored him. I reached out my hand to the man.

"I need to thank you," I said as we shook hands.

"No need."

"If you hadn't been there, I don't know what would have happened to us."

"You were in God's hands. He placed me where he needed me to be."

"You have to get inside, immediately!" the man bellowed from behind the bars.

I ignored him. "I wish I could believe that. I wish I could have faith like that."

"This quake, it destroyed buildings, brought down a city, but don't let it destroy something even stronger. When the earth on which you stand has been shaken, maybe all that is left is the faith from above. You need to go inside. Now."

I started to turn around and then stopped. "I don't even know your name."

He smiled. "I am Gabriel."

"Like the angel."

His smile grew. "Go inside now, and may God be with you always."

He turned and walked away.

I quickly turned around and slipped between the soldiers and through the small opening in the gate. The soldiers followed after me as the crowd surged forward, pressing against the gate as it closed once again.

"That was pretty stupid," the man said.

"Maybe, but it worked. Naomi needs to get insulin as soon as—"

"She's already been taken to the infirmary. While you were out there causing me unnecessary grief I was taking care of business inside. Now, first things first, Mr. Joshua Evans, I imagine you'd like to see your father."

"My father is here!" I exclaimed.

"Your father *and* your sister."

I burst into tears, and the little man—the little angry man—reached out and put an arm around me.

"You're fine. They're fine. It's all going to be okay," he said quietly.

"I'm just so . . . so grateful." I'd almost said "blessed,"
but stopped myself. Now I just had to stop the tears.

"Believe me, we're *all* grateful," he said. "Your father has
spent the last day screaming at us that we have to go up to the
country to rescue all of you. We had to tell him that we didn't
have the men or the capacity. Now that you're here, you can
tell him that everybody is fine . . . they are fine, right?"

"They're all good." Then I remembered Michelle.
"Except for one person. There was a death. She was in the
dining hall when it collapsed."

"Was it one of the children?"

"No, it was Michelle. One of the women from the
church."

"I'm sorry, but . . . well, nobody wants a child to die.
Tell me about it after you've seen your father. He's going to
be so glad . . . heck, we're all going to be glad. There were
times I thought we were going to have to tie him into bed."

"Bed . . . is he hurt?"

"My apologies. I should have told you. He has a compound fracture of his right leg."

"And my sister?"

"Not a scratch, not a bruise. The whole building collapsed, fell down around them but not directly on them. More
than a dozen people were killed." He paused. "We haven't
been able to recover all the bodies from the wreckage."

"There was another man with them. His name is—"

"Pastor Dave? He's alive and kicking and complaining.
Demanding to be released so he can return to the orphanage. It's been all we've been able to do to stop the two of

them from hobbling out of their beds and commandeering a truck!"

"But he's fine too?"

"He was hit in the head by falling debris. He has a pretty good gash on the side of his head, a concussion, some fractured ribs, and a broken collarbone."

I let out a deep sigh. I hadn't even realized it, but it was as if I'd been holding my breath forever.

"It's a miracle that they didn't die," the man said.

A miracle . . . or an answer to a prayer.

"Your father will still require surgery. He's got to be evacuated back to Canada on the first flight." He smiled. "Now that you're here and safe, I'm guessing we'll be able to convince him to go. The infirmary is right here."

He went to open a door.

"Could I just have a second?" I asked. "I just want to be strong . . . for my sister."

"Of course."

"And could I be alone? Please?"

"Certainly." He looked confused, but he left, leaving me alone in the corridor.

I rubbed my face with my hands, trying to remove traces of tears. I brushed off my clothes and then patted down my hair. And I had one more thing to do. I dropped to my knees and brought my hands to my face. I needed to say thank you.

CHAPTER THIRTY-FIVE

I pushed through the door and started to look around when I was practically tackled by my sister, who threw her arms around me and began to sob.

"It's okay," I said, reassuringly. "I'm fine. At least now that I know *you're* fine, too."

I didn't need to ask her about my father. I saw him, in a little bed among dozens in the corner of the room. His leg was encased in plaster and held in place, suspended by a piece of white rope from the ceiling.

"I can't believe you're here!" he called out, his voice breaking as he spoke. "I'm just so . . . so . . . relieved . . . so happy."

Carefully I sat down beside him and he wrapped an arm around me.

"I was just so shocked when I saw Naomi and Philippe . . . and then when I didn't see you . . . I thought maybe you were . . . " He burst into tears.

In the rush of everything I'd forgotten that they'd gone before me—of course they would have brought Naomi here.

"I'm fine. We're all fine," I said. I tried my best to sound calm, to be strong. "They said they have to fly you out as soon as possible."

"They told me they have a spot for me and Sarah on the evacuation flight tomorrow. I told them that I couldn't go, not knowing whether everybody was safe."

"Now you can go. We *are* safe. We're here."

"Not just you and Sarah. Everybody. I have a responsibility for everybody, all of the children, and Iris and Michelle."

For a brief second I thought about telling him about Michelle, but there was no point. Not right now, at least.

"They're going to be fine. The embassy will get them out. Besides, what do you think you could do?" I asked.

"I don't know. Maybe I'm not thinking straight. Pastor Dave is going to be released tomorrow. He's going back. I was going to try to go back with him and—"

"You can't go back," I said, cutting him off. "You have to be realistic. You have to leave, and you need to take Sarah with you."

"Sarah and you." The embassy official had come into the room now, and my father turned to him. "Will there be space for my son on the flight if I agree to go tomorrow?"

"I'm not sure, but I think it's doubtful. The age of your daughter and what she came through, well, she needs to go back with you. But your son? We really need those flights to evacuate the injured."

"If he's not going, then I'm not going!" my father exclaimed.

"Yes you are!" I said. "You *are* going. First flight, and you're taking Sarah with you. I'll be fine here for a few days. Besides, I have things I have to do."

He looked confused and concerned.

"If Pastor Dave is going back, I'll go back with him and Philippe up to the compound."

"You can't do that," my father said.

"Yes I can. Somebody has to go back to help care for everybody and I'm the only one available," I said. "What do you think you could do with that broken leg?"

"But . . . but . . . but . . . " he stammered.

"You need to get home and have the surgery. Not just for your sake but for Sarah's. She needs to get home."

I turned to the embassy official. "How long before you can send somebody up to evacuate the people from the mission trip?"

"We can't make any promises, but it will be at least a week. We'll let their families know they're okay right away, but it might be ten days till we can get them on a flight, tops."

"Then I'll be home in a week or ten days," I said to my father.

My father looked as though he was going to object, but then he stopped himself.

"Sarah, could you please go and get me a drink of water?" he asked. "And bring one for your brother?"

She hesitated.

"Please, Sarah, I really need a drink of water," he said.

Reluctantly she headed off.

"Could you please leave us alone to talk?" he said to the embassy man, who quickly retreated.

My father reached out and took my hand. "I know you didn't even want to come here to begin with."

"I didn't."

"And you don't have to stay here now. You can go back with us. I'm sure I can convince them to let you on the flight."

"That would only take away a seat from somebody who really needs it . . . somebody like Naomi. Besides, if we were needed here before, we're needed here even more now. I'll go up with them and help. Maybe we can even finish the dormitory. That building is even *more* important now."

My father hesitated. I couldn't quite read his expression, but I knew nothing he said was going to change my mind. What he did say, finally, was, "I want you to come home with us, but I understand. And I'm proud of you. I know you don't necessarily believe right now. But you're following the teachings."

"I'm just trying to do the right thing."

"I know none of this has been easy for you," he said.

"It hasn't been easy for anybody in the whole country."

"I don't just mean this. I mean your mother's death. It's shaken your faith," he said.

"Hasn't it shaken yours?" I asked.

"I had to give you and Sarah something to believe in. I had to be strong, even when it caused me to question everything I believed in, everything I've devoted my life to. When your mother died, you must have questioned whether there even was a God . . . I know I did."

"You?" That was a real shock to me.

"She was such a good woman, and we all prayed so hard, and I thought that if there was a God he would have listened . . . I even wondered if he was punishing me for not believing or not having enough faith or . . . " His words trailed off and he began to cry.

I reached out and took his other hand. "Dad, God didn't take her or not take her. I don't know why she died and some people live. I just don't know . . . nobody knows. And I couldn't help but have my doubts about everything."

"And all of this, all that's happened here, must have made those doubts even stronger," he said.

"It did." I paused. "And then it made my *belief* even stronger." I paused again. "I don't know how to say this, because it doesn't make sense. I don't know about prayers or the Bible or what's right and what's wrong, or what's just a lot of garbage . . . but . . . but . . . "

My words were failing me. I was too tired and relieved and scared and confused and hungry for anything to make any sense whatsoever.

"It's okay to doubt. It's okay to have questions," he said. "We all have lots of questions and very few answers. At least not answers we can confirm. You just have to believe. You have to have faith."

"I'd like to believe there's a God . . . but I don't know."

"Nobody can know," he said.

"What I do know is that we need to act like there is a God. That no matter what, we have to try to do the right thing. And the right thing is for me to go back with Pastor Dave and with Philippe."

"I'm going to be so worried. To leave without you . . . I just don't know."

"I do. I'll be fine. I'll be taken care of." I stopped, and a smile came to me. "I just finished walking through hell. And even in hell, there was still an angel walking along with me."